THE HOUS

When Fergus Oliver journeyed reluctantly to the Scottish border to take over his unexpected inheritance, he took with him memories of Oliver's Keep, which he had done his best to forget. But there in the old tower, the past mingled with the present to overshadow the future. There, also, came Helen Oliver, widow of the cousin whose heir he had become through the sadness of war. It is Helen—straight from a Japanese internment camp—who helps him appreciate belonging to a family and the debt he owes to a house which, but for her husband's sacrifice for his country, might have been her home. Helen teaches him to disregard pride and find the fulfilment of love, and, through her devotion to another man's child, eventually finds her own.

Novels by Jean S. MacLeod

TWO PATHS
THE SILENT VALLEY
THIS MUCH TO GIVE
BRIEF FULFILMENT
THE BRIDGE OF YEARS
ONE LOVE
THE TRANQUIL HAVEN
SOWN IN THE WIND
AND WE IN DREAMS
THE HOUSE OF OLIVER
RAVENSCRAG
TOMORROW'S BARGAIN
THE CHALET IN THE SUN
ABOVE THE LATTICE
KATHERINE
THE VALLEY OF PALMS
ROADWAY TO THE PAST
ONCE TO EVERY HEART
CAMERON OF GARE
MUSIC AT MIDNIGHT
THE STRANGER IN THEIR MIDST
THE MAN IN AUTHORITY
DEAR DOCTOR EVERETT
MASTER OF GLENKEITH
AFTER LONG JOURNEYING
THE WAY IN THE DARK
MY HEART'S IN THE HIGHLANDS
JOURNEY IN THE SUN
HEATHERBLOOM
SILENT BONDAGE
THE PRISONER OF LOVE
THE ROWAN TREE
AIR AMBULANCE
THE GATED ROAD
THE LITTLE DOCTOR
THE WHITE COCKADE
THE SILVER DRAGON
THE DARK FORTUNE
SLAVE OF THE WIND
THE BLACK CAMERON
SUGAR ISLAND
CRANE CASTLE
THE WOLF OF HEIMRA
THE TENDER GLORY
THE DRUMMER OF CORRAE
LAMENT FOR A LOVER
THE BRIDE OF MINGALAY
THE MASTER OF KEILLS
THE MOONFLOWER
DANGEROUS OBSESSION
MIST ACROSS THE HILLS
LAMOT OF ARDGOYNE
UNSEEN TOMORROW
THE CIRCLE OF DOUBT
FLOWER O' THE BROOM
BLEAK HERITAGE
RELUCTANT FOLLY
BLIND JOURNEY
PENALTY FOR LIVING
THE RECKLESS PILGRIM
FORBIDDEN RAPTURE
THE SHADOW OF A VOW
ONE WAY OUT
THE WHIM OF FATE
THE LONELY FURROW
THE RAINBOW ISLE
RUN AWAY FROM LOVE
SUMMER RAIN
SEQUEL TO YOUTH
HUMAN SYMPHONY
LIFE FOR TWO
SUMMER ISLAND
RETURN TO SPRING
MOMENT OF DECISION
THE JOSHUA TREE
THE LIGHT IN THE TOWER
THE WAY THROUGH THE VALLEY
THE SCENT OF JUNIPER
ADAM'S WIFE
THE RAINBOW DAYS
OVER THE CASTLE WALL
TIME SUSPENDED
THE PHANTOM PIPES
JOURNEY INTO SPRING
VIKING SONG
ISLAND STRANGER
SEARCH FOR YESTERDAY
THE RUAIG INHERITANCE
MEETING IN MADRID
BRIEF ENCHANTMENT
BLACK SAND, WHITE SAND
CRUEL DECEPTION
MORETON'S KINGDOM
ZAMORA
A DISTANT PARADISE
BEYOND THE REEF
VALLEY OF THE SNOWS
THE OLIVE GROVE

THE HOUSE OF OLIVER

BY

JEAN S. MACLEOD

MILLS & BOON LIMITED
15–16 BROOK'S MEWS
LONDON W1A 1DR

First published in Great Britain 1947
by Mills & Boon Limited

This edition published in 1985 by
Mills & Boon Limited, 15–16 Brook's Mews,
London W1A 1DR

ISBN 0 263 75448 0

MADE AND PRINTED IN GREAT BRITAIN BY
COX & WYMAN LIMITED, READING

CHAPTER ONE

'PULL up, Syd Willing, we're in Scotland!'

The voice held a ring of laughter which brought the small, battered saloon to a halt on the brow of the hill as quickly as the request had done. It was good to hear the Commander laugh again, thought Syd, good to know that those dark moods from which he suffered at times might be passing. Not that the Commander had ever let them affect other people—maybe it would have been better if he had done and let off steam a bit. Perhaps a fellow might have helped then, if it was a thing where a bit of help would do any good, but just to be sort of groping around in the dark trying to guess what was the matter wasn't a lot of use. If a fellow could have *done* something—anything, but the Commander had never been one to talk much about himself. Syd thought that he knew as much about ex-Wing-Commander Fergus Oliver as anyone, but sometimes he wondered if half the man wasn't hidden too deep for any human being ever to reach. He thought it now, with a kind of baffled irritation, as he pushed his chauffeur's cap to the back of his head and scratched the bald patch in front reflectively. When they had left Solum Lacey he had been quite sure that the Commander hadn't wanted to come to Scotland very much, but now there was that ring of laughter in his voice and he looked as if he were enjoying it. It beat Syd, it did. When you had seen six years of war in the air with a man, when you had been one of his crew from the time he was just a flying-officer and a beginner and had come through with him until he was a Wing-Co. and were finally demobbed together, you thought you knew all about the man you worked for. You knew he meant it when he had said you'd stick together, that there might be plenty more 'blood and sweat and tears' but that you'd make out together in the long run, but often he wondered if he knew the man deep inside.

That was how it had been when they had donned their first suits of civvies together and set out for the farm the Wing-Co. had bought in Sussex. Syd hadn't thought much of the idea of a farm at first, but it had been near enough London and Syd was a Cockney born and bred. The farm, too, had not been prepossessing and it had certainly called for the 'sweat' and almost reduced Syd to the 'tears,' but he had stuck it because to be with the Wing-Co. was worth a whole truck-load of luxuries, and in the end Solum Lacey had done something to him.

What it was Syd was not quite sure, but when the Wing-Co. had told him they were going to be uprooted it *had* felt like pulling something up that had gone deep into the soil.

There had been no question of his being forced to come north; he had been given a free choice, and Syd knew that he hadn't hesitated more than the second it took to cast a longing glance along the road that led to London.

And all this was in the nature of a windfall for the Commander. Syd looked about him dubiously.

'Well, Syd, what do you think of it?'

'There's an awful lot of hills and grass, sir—'

'And not much else? Well, Syd, I suppose you've said it, but here we are and here we'll have to stay for a bit.'

'Here, sir?'

'Well, not exactly right on top of Carter Bar, but down in the dale yonder, as far as you can see along that winding road—and maybe a bit farther!'

'Yes, sir.'

It was the old formula by which Syd Willing had accepted this man's rulings for over six years—unquestioningly—although often his expressive face spoke volumes.

Fergus Oliver chuckled.

'Syd! I believe you'd go anywhere short of the North Pole as long as you were driving this blessed old car!'

'I'd go anywhere you wanted me to, sir.'

'Willing by name and willing by nature!'

'That's me, sir!'

Fergus Oliver's eyes roved across the landscape spread out at their feet, across the near slopes and the green dales between them to sweep up again to Cauldcleuch and Wisp Hill and the broad shoulders of Ettrick Pen. They had drawn up where the narrow white roads went down into Scotland, winding ribbons losing themselves among the undulating green to spring into being again far away, following the course of a silver stream.

Although it was six years since he had last seen it, he knew the land before him as he had known every acre around Solum Lacey, and it was here that his heart lay.

How, then, had he come back to it reluctantly?

His eyes darkened as the car moved on, gathering speed as it slipped down the narrow road. They were bound for Oliver's Keep and a host of memories, some happy, others impregnated by that sadness which comes of loss. He had never dreamed that he would visit the Keep again for the reason he was going back now. In earliest youth and in the first few months of the war he had thought to return gladly, but now he was going back reluctantly to claim an inheritance which should never have been his.

He thought of Kenneth Oliver, the cousin he had so greatly admired, who now lay buried in some nameless grave in the Malayan jungle, and he thought of the girl Ken had married out there two months before the catastrophe, whom they had never met.

They! He smiled bitterly at his use of the word. He was thinking of the family, his four remaining cousins, whom Syd called whimsically 'the real Olivers,' meaning, he supposed, that they had really far more right to be at Oliver's Keep than he had.

Well, heaven knew that was true enough, and he had been only too eager to relinquish any claim to the old place which he had known so intimately in childhood and early manhood, but all the attempts he had made to come to some sort of amicable settlement with the Misses Oliver had been in vain. He had been informed coldly and firmly through their solicitors in Edinburgh that, as next in entail, he could not fail to accept the property and that the Misses Oliver were vacating the Keep from that day week. That meant Jean and Hattie and Isobel. Margaret had been away from the Keep in these days . . .

'How far now, sir?'

'About another five or six miles, Syd. We're almost on Oliver territory now and you'll be able to see the Keep itself when we get to the top of the next rise.'

Syd gave him a quick glance. All along he had sensed that the Commander wasn't too happy about his return to the Keep, that, apart from this unwished-for inheritance, there was another—more personal—reason, the reason that brought the old shadow back into his eyes and had kept him almost morosely silent for miles of the way, although he had made an effort to bestir himself from time to time to offer scraps of interesting information about the countryside through which they had passed. It was a long time since Syd had learned about the Percys of Northumberland and the Black Douglases and Border forays across the Tweed, and a kid brought up in London's Whitechapel had had plenty of opportunity to forget about history books, heaven knew, but it kind of made you think hearing the Commander talk of all those scraps so long ago. There had been wars in those far off days, too, waged between men who had been mortal enemies and who had now become brothers. He had a great admiration for the Scottish race, had Syd! He had served under a Scottish sergeant at the beginning of the war and, after all, the Commander was a Scot, even although he had lived most of his life in the south. He had heard it said—humorously—that Scots abroad always suffered a terrible longing to come home but never did, and he was anxious to see this Scotland.

What he could see of it now amounted to a mass of rolling hills with a white road winding among them, on and on, seemingly endlessly, sometimes lost among dense woodland and then seen again, far ahead, dipping steeply or climbing high to the brow of a hill. And when you reached that hill there was always another on the horizon. A bit like life, mused Syd, the philosopher.

As they breasted the next rise Fergus Oliver sat foward in his seat, a tenseness about his long, slim body suggesting both eagerness and reluctance as his eyes followed the curves of the road down into the next valley and across it to where a river had cleft its way through a low ridge in the hills. And here, in the gap, standing four-square to every wind that blew and built as a bastion against marauding onslaughts from the south, stood Oliver's Keep, his new home and old sanctuary.

Fergus Oliver had come to it often as a boy from school in the long vacations when his uncle had taken the place of parents in India, and he had come even more frequently as a youth when those parents had died together battling against an epidemic of cholera and Walter Oliver had been his only near relation.

He had thought of Oliver's Keep in those days as the home of all romance, justifying its original purpose as a place of safety for all who used it, a haven of peace set there among the quiet hills, yet grimly capable of resisting all onslaughts from without, conscious of its strength, steeped in years of glorious tradition, a proud old castle guarding the pass between the dales.

Now he saw it standing strangely aloof, no welcoming smoke rising from its hidden chimneys, standing silhouetted against the grey sky, resentful of intrusion. Fantastic imaginings, perhaps, but that was how he felt returning this way—the intruder, although the Misses Oliver had advised him coldly and correctly that he was only accepting his own.

Did Margaret think of him in that way, also?

There were no gates into Oliver's Keep. A side road swept suddenly and unexpectedly away to climb across a hog-backed bridge and along a rough track winding up to a narrow gorge which had once been a moat but was now spanned by the grass-grown road. Here, rugged and grey, the Keep sprang up from the virgin rock, its grey walls rising sheer from the moat as if it had been hewn from the rock itself.

A formidable old place, thought Syd Willing, and as far as the eye could see, miles from anywhere. The blinkin' edge o' beyond, in fact! If it wasn't for the Commander . . .

'Well, Syd, that's it!' said Fergus Oliver, coming out of his reverie. 'Think you'll be able to stick it?'

'One place is as good as another to me, sir. I've knocked

about a bit in my time. Funny thing, though, I've never been to Scotland before.'

'Once you've been,' his companion said strangely, 'you'll always want to return. It does that to you, Syd.'

'Well,' said Syd, 'do we just park here, or is there a garage?'

'There are stables—or there used to be. Through that arch there and turn to your right.'

The younger man had given the instructions automatically as he got out of the car. He knew every detail of the enclosure and every inch of the land that lay out there beyond the river, stretching between it and the hills; knew each well-kept farm and shepherd's cottage and the grey village hidden down yonder among the trees. Margaret and he had explored every foot of it . . .

He looked up again at the old, crow-stepped fortress as if asking some question of it and thought that it seemed to frown down at him. Then the heavy, nail-studded door swung back, and a small, stout woman in a tweed costume and black hat stood looking down at him without a smile.

'Ye'll be Mister Oliver?' she asked, knowing that he could be no one else.

'And you must be Mrs Michie,' Fergus said, extending a hand, but she either did not see it or refused to take it, turning abruptly back into the vast hall behind her.

Fergus Oliver followed her slowly, memories crowding thick and fast about him. He saw the art and love and patience which had modernised the old house without sacrificing any of its original grim beauty, the concessions to comfort so cunningly concealed, the clever reproductions among the hangings which he knew were comparatively new and the old armour gleaming against it like shadowy ghosts of the past, saw, also, that much of the original furniture had been left in the hall, which was a proud gesture on the part of his cousins—on Miss Jean's part, probably. These things belonged there, part of Oliver's Keep down through the centuries, and they were destined to pass out of her family's care as inevitably as the Keep itself.

He noticed his own humble possessions, sent on in

advance, huddled in a corner, as if ashamed of their presence there among the more worthy relics of a glorious past, good quality stuff of another age picked up here and there to furnish Solum Lacey, but without the timelessness and solidity of the older furniture.

'They came up by the carrier,' Bessie Michie informed him without interest. 'I didn't know where you would want them put, so I thought they'd be just as well in the hall till ye had time to look about ye.'

He thought to tell her that he knew every room in the Keep, had a memory of the view from every window, had seen youth dancing till daybreak in that vast hall long before she had ever appeared to caretake it, and then he thought better of the impulse, feeling that she would not be interested. He had been informed through his solicitors that a caretaker had been found in the village to look after the Keep and that no doubt he would be making his own domestic arrangements when he arrived, and now, having made no arrangements, he was regarding Bessie Michie's broad back speculatively, although he did not put his thoughts immediately into words.

'It shouldn't take me long to settle in,' he remarked hopefully. 'I've been farming in the south and I hope to turn my hand to it here.'

'Hae ye a staff wi' you, then?'

She turned at the end of the hall to look at him.

'My man's gone round to the stables to park the car. He's all the staff I have.'

Her black eyes regarded him incredulously.

'Ye'll never manage a place like this wi' one man,' she informed him bluntly.

Fergus Oliver smiled.

'Mrs Michie,' he said, 'can you cook?'

A swift flush crossed her face and her chest puffed out like an indignant pigeon's.

'I see that you can,' he grinned before she had drawn breath to defend herself. 'We're absolutely famished. Do you think you could get us a meal of some sort?'

Their eyes met, and for a moment of indecision the dark ones searched the man's face. He was an Oliver. Ay, he was one o' them! When she spoke again Bessie Michie's voice was not quite so forbidding and some of the stern look had gone from about her firmly compressed lips.

'Ye'll never manage without a woman about the place,' she said brusquely. 'I had ma doots about ye when I heard ye were no' married.'

His jaw hardened momentarily, but laughter broke in his eyes when he said,

'You can remedy that if you will, Mrs Michie. No! not the bachelor state, but the terrible handicap of setting out to manage Oliver's Keep without a woman about the house. Will you stay on?' He glanced round the great room they had entered with its massive refectory table and tall, carved chairs standing in a formidable row against the stone wall. 'You appear to have been a very efficient caretaker so I'm sure I should find you an excellent housekeeper.'

She softened visibly under the flattery, yet she would not let herself be won over immediately.

'I'd have to think about it,' she warned him. 'I'm a widow, but my daughter's wantin' me awa' to England with her to help wi' the bairns.'

He could see that the prospect did not entirely please her.

'Don't you think you'd be as much help here—looking after two bachelors? You like Oliver's Keep, don't you?'

'Aye. It sort of—gets round a body.'

'Then—you'll stay?'

'Maybe. But I'd have tae see.'

'All right. Take your time, Mrs Michie. Syd and I will muddle through till you come along to look after us.'

'Syd'll be your man, I suppose?'

'Yes.' He had turned to look out of the window set deep in the wall which had been enlarged from an old arrow-slit and still remained faithful to its original shape. 'I hope he hasn't lost his way and landed in the moat!'

'Maybe he's come in by the back, Mrs Michie hesitated. 'Perhaps you'd like to tak' a bite o' something to eat in my room,' she suggested. 'There's a bit of a fire on in the hall, but I didn't light one in here, not knowin' exactly when you would be arrivin'. The family took their meals in the round room.'

'Did you serve—my cousins?' Fergus asked, trying to subdue his interest.

'For three years—right up to the day they left. Miss Jean wanted me to go with them, but I had ties in the village. Another o' my girls married the 'smith's son.'

'Bob Christie? Of course, I remember him. But you're not a native of Burndean, are you, Mrs Michie? I don't seem to remember—'

'I'm no', but my man was. John Michie o' the Shaws was his father, but Willie went to Angus to work when he was very young an' we've lived there most o' our time, wi' an occasional visit back just to keep us in mind. Then, when he died in '42, I came to the Keep.'

A dull colour rose under Fergus Oliver's tan, the colour of intense excitement instinctively subdued.

'Then—you'll know where the family have gone?' he asked, trying to sound casual.

But Mrs Michie shook her head, her lips slightly pursed.

'Nobody knows, unless it might be the doctor's wife, who was a great friend o' Miss Jean's. They just went away, takin' their sorrow wi' them quietly, like a' things that go deep.'

The man standing by the window did not speak for a moment. Bessie Michie's words had hit him like a rebuff, but surely she knew that there was nothing he could do about it—nothing he had left undone. He had offered to return the Keep to his cousins, but it had been like trying to scale some gigantic wall to get anywhere near them. They had withdrawn behind their barrier of implacable silence and he could do nothing, for all contact had been a coldly legal affair, made through their respective solicitors.

He followed Mrs Michie out of the dining-room along a stone passage to a small room in the rear of the building where bright chintz and polished brass struck the welcoming note which he had found absent in the great entrance hall. Syd had already made his way in by the back door and was standing rather sheepishly at the end of the passage twirling his cap in his hands.

'I thought I smelt baking,' he explained his obvious intrusion into the kitchen premises. 'An' lumme, I could just about eat a horse!'

Mrs Michie produced cold lamb and scones and tea, accompanied by a square slab of home-made butter, and they ate without regard to possession.

'I'm trying to persuade Mrs Michie to stay with us,' Fergus explained to Syd when they had finished their meal, 'and after this sample of her cooking, I think it's imperative that she should!'

'We could manage,' said Syd, jealous of his own talent in the kitchen which had served them both well enough at Solum Lacey.

But this was evidently not Solum Lacey, as his master reminded him.

'This is a big place to keep up, Syd, and I'll need you outside. We must have a woman about the house.'

Mrs Michie rose to clear the table.

'The fire's on in the hall,' she hinted.

'We'll have a look round,' Fergus suggested. 'Don't trouble to come with us, Mrs Michie. I know my way around.' He turned to Syd as they moved towards the door. 'Best to get your bearings right away,' he explained. 'It's the sort of house that confuses one at first. It isn't too big, but there are all sorts of unexpected passages that can be like a maze if you hit them in the dark.'

'No gas laid on?' asked Syd, appalled.

'No, but we have something which I hope will prove much better. It's electrically lit by our own plant. That's something you can look after if you've a mind to. There's a petrol motor in the basement and it was always very efficient when properly handled.'

'Remember the one we rigged up in Italy?' Syd grinned. 'Cor sufferin' sparrows, it was a daisy! More like a Heath Robinson cartoon than anything else that one was! Still, it lit the old camp up till Jerry spotted us that night!'

Those were the days! said the nostalgic note in Syd's voice as he looked with casual interest at the magnificent mounted antlers hung high among the rafters and the crossed rapiers from battles long ago suspended above the beautiful Adam fireplace installed by an Oliver of that time. The big, open fire threw out a comforting heat before which they sat for an hour yarning while they drew at their pipes, Fergus Oliver listening mostly and now and then letting his thoughts wander from the conversation and Italy down into the past.

At last he jumped to his feet and stretched lazily.

'Like to see the rest of the house?'

'Sure,' responded Syd. 'May as well know my way about in the morning. It might make an impression on the old dame to have the fires cleaned out by the time she sounds reveille!'

'You could try it!'

They left the hall by another passage, a broad, short tunnel leading surprisingly to a flight of stairs running up to the floor above, where a long, stone gallery surrounded the hall on three sides with narrow openings looking down upon it between massive stone pillars which rose to support the roof. The walls of the gallery were hung with rich tapestries and gilt-framed paintings, portraits mostly, and before the first of them Fergus Oliver halted, standing in silent contemplation of the pictured face.

It was a strong face, long, with the high-bridged Oliver nose and deeply penetrating eyes, as if the young soldier possessed the uncanny power of seeing into the future. Had he known? Fergus Oliver wondered, searching his cousin's face as if he might find some sign there, but he already knew that Kenneth Oliver, whose heir he had become so unexpectedly, would hold him no grudge on that score. His thoughts turned naturally to the girl who had married his cousin on the far side of the world and he wondered what had become of her. He knew she would be provided for under his cousin's will, but she was a link with Ken which he thought should have been kept on the family chain. Then, abruptly, he laughed. That part of the chain had nothing to do with him and he had no right to think strongly about it at all. Jean Oliver had let him see that quite plainly!

He passed on down the line of portraits with Syd following at his heels, making a remark here and there which proclaimed nothing more than a token interest. The portraits were all Olivers and each bore some strong family resemblance—the high-bridged nose in the men and the small, pointed chin of the women which in youth made their faces look so delicately moulded, yet more than one Oliver woman had defied an invading host alone in the stern old Keep in the past, holding it as a battlement of honour against her lord's return.

Fergus Oliver's pleasant mouth moved in a slow smile. They had been grand women, these, cut from the same pattern as the Miss Jean and Miss Isobel of today, the kind of women who would uphold the family honour against all odds. Hattie was softer and more kind—more like Margaret . . .

The smile faded out of his eyes and he passed on down the line of portraits, back down through the years. There had been Olivers at Prestonpans, the Olivers of the march of the Forty-five; an Oliver martyred for the Covenant, and a red-coated warrior who had fallen at Sebastapol. The fighting strain ran strongly through the old farming stock, and probably that was why his father had become a soldier. He thought that roots went deeper when a man stuck to the land, but he remembered, too, his own burning desire to fly in the first months of the war just past. It had appealed to him as a crusade, and he had gone out on it with high hopes.

Almost at the end of the line of portraits he came to a standstill once more, and Syd, glancing at him, thought that his face had gone suddenly grey in the wan light. What light there was streamed in at high, slit-like windows far up in the thick wall, striking down obliquely on to the dim canvases in their heavy, ornate frames, and Syd looked at the portrait which had arrested his master's attention and saw a girl of between seventeen and twenty dressed in a wide crinoline with her small, delicate hands clasped loosely in her lap and bunches of dark curls looped up with stiff ribbon bows on either side of her piquant little face. There was no typical Oliver resemblance here; the eyes were wide and far apart and of a clear, soft grey, the nose short and straight between high cheek-bones, the mouth slightly rebellious yet generous in its soft curves, and the tilted chin conveying a strong hint of character that gave strength to the whole portrait, animating it even in that dull corner of the dim gallery.

Syd stood very still, staring at the girl's face. There was something about it—something he should remember. He was grappling with a memory which still eluded him and Syd's brain had never worked quickly. But, cor blimey! of course he remembered! It was the photo the Commander had always carried about with him, the picture that had stood in the leather frame on his locker and had gone with him on every sortie across 'the drink.' It was the girl he had looked at every night before he turned in and first thing every morning!

But was it the same girl? Syd looked again. Well, the hair was different—done in a different way, like, but you never knew what girls were going to do to their hair these days!—but the face was the same, the eyes sort of smiling and not smiling, and the mouth just ready to speak.

'Was she an Oliver, too?' he asked, pointing to the picture with the stem of his pipe, which had now gone out.

It seemed that the Commander had to recall his thoughts from a great distance to reply.

'She was the wife of an Oliver and great-grandmother of the present line.'

'She'd be your great-grandmother, too, then?' Syd was not quite sure how the relationship went.

'No, the—present Misses Oliver and I are not first cousins. It's not quite so direct as that, but it—never used to make such a lot of difference.'

Fergus Oliver's eyes still rested on the pictured face of the girl before them, fixed there with a great longing in their depths, as if he would will the subject of that old painting to come to life and step down into the corridor beside him. Yet, Syd reasoned, this couldn't be the girl whose photograph he had carried round with him all during the war. A guy wouldn't be quite so mad as to cart round a picture of someone else's great-grandmother—even as a mascot, although Syd admitted inwardly that he had seen some funny mascots during his six years of flying, and they had all been treasured for some particular reason. He decided, therefore, that he must give it up, but he was to remember for a very long time afterwards the look which had come into the Commander's eyes when he had first stopped before the painting and be troubled by it until he discovered its true significance.

CHAPTER TWO

It was five weeks since Fergus Oliver had come to the Keep, weeks in which he and Syd had grappled jointly with each problem as it arose and overcome them one by one. During the first few days there had been many, both indoors and without, but after a spell of indecision in which the claims of her family had been weighed carefully against their obvious need of her services, Bessie Michie had agreed to stay with them as housekeeper. The sound of the word pleased Bessie; it was important and although she had very little experience of managing a house of that size, she suited Fergus's simple tastes and told herself that she could learn by experience. She had worked for the Misses Oliver as cook, but women were more exacting than men. In a way, Bessie was loath to admit such a thing, because she had been bound to the old Oliver household by strong ties of liking and respect and still considered the new owner something of an impostor, but she also enjoyed the free hand she was allowed in the bachelor establishment and was glad that she had not been so thrawn as the majority of the villagers who had simply refused to like the new heir in a grim sort of allegiance to the old.

Fergus Oliver had early recognised this attitude among the village people and the estate workers, but he had set out with a quiet determination to conquer it and win their esteem, and already he had made substantial progress. He was settling down at the Keep and almost beginning to like the life there. At least, he was accepting it, realising that there was really only one snag to future progress. He had always had a vague idea that the estate took a great deal of money to maintain it in the way his uncle had done and now he was beginning to realise the facts. Walter Oliver had early interested himself in rubber and had invested strongly in that commodity, deriving considerable profit from his ventures into the world of finance, and most of this income had gone back into the estate in one way or another, making it a model one of splendid farms and well-cared-for land. But the family money had all passed to the Oliver girls and, he believed, to Kenneth Oliver's young widow, as he agreed it should have done by right. There was nothing in him which denied them that, out of what he considered had been a hard bargain from their point of view. He knew what losing the Keep must have meant to Jean Oliver and to Isobel—even to Hattie and Margaret—and he knew, also, that no amount of money would ever be able to compensate them for their loss, but he wondered wryly if Jean obtained any satisfaction from the thought that he had little money to carry on where her father had left off. Yet, on second thought, he knew that her mind would be above such pettiness. She would have wished him to have money for the sake of Oliver's Keep. Maybe that was another reason why she resented him so much—that allied to the old, personal reason!

The days had passed in a round of work, with Syd tramping home beside him of an evening to sink into one of the big leather chairs before the fire in the kitchen while he attacked the books in the business-room leading out of the hall. They had early decided that it would be impracticable to use the whole house and had made themselves reasonably comfortable in a small portion of it, consigning the long table and massive chairs of the dining-room to dust-sheets and closed doors and sleeping in two small bedrooms above the kitchen, where some of its cosy warmth penetrated, rather than in the larger, barn-like 'family' rooms on the other side of the house.

Then, one day, a letter came which looked as if it might change all that. It arrived by the afternoon post and it stood on the sitting-room mantelpiece until they came in at seven o'clock, and more than once in the interval Bessie Michie had wondered about the Southampton post-mark it bore and the address written in a woman's hand.

Fergus Oliver took it down and stood looking at it, frowning in the way he had when he was concentrating on something rather important. He did not seem to recognise the hand-writing, and when he slit open the envelope and took out the single sheet of notepaper it contained he turned quickly to the signature at the end. When he had read it he drew in a swift breath, indicating his surprise, and Bessie watched his eyes travelling quickly over the page to rest again on the signature and knew that there was pleasure behind his surprise now.

'This is from Mrs Oliver,' he said at last, 'Mrs Kenneth Oliver, my cousin's widow. She has apparently just arrived in England from the Far East.'

'My!' exclaimed Bessie, 'Miss Jean will be glad to hear that. Will she know, do you think?'

The embarrassed colour which he could never quite control at the mention of Jean Oliver's name rose under his skin in a swift flush.

'I'm not sure,' he said awkwardly. 'Mrs Oliver has written directly here, thinking, no doubt, that all the family will still be living at Oliver's Keep.'

'Does she mean to come?' asked Bessie bluntly.

'That is why she has written. She says she would like to meet the family and see the Keep, which is only natural. Ken must have told her so much about it.'

Maybe she'd be better to bide away, poor lass, thought Bessie, who had a compassionate heart hidden under her rather brusque exterior, but she kept the thought to herself, fearing that it might hurt the new master, who had a winning way of his own in spite of being the wrong Oliver.

'She'll be staying for a while, of course?'

'Of course.' He looked at her and his eyes were suddenly perplexed. 'Can you do something about it, Mrs Michie? We're a bachelor establishment and we're living rough, but maybe you could make things look—well, right for her—how they used to be, or as near it as possible.'

She thought that he would never consider anything could be the same as it had been while he remained the master of the Keep, and that was a bad thing. The war years had stopped the entertaining and maybe he hadn't the money to entertain in the old Oliver style, but he was living too much alone. He ought to keep a bit of company now and then, Bessie considered, and young Mrs Oliver coming like this would be good for him. He had got into a rut—eating and working and sleeping—and that way of living wasn't good for a man, young or old! She began to think of ways and means of making their guest feel welcomed.

'I'll do out the room in the west turret,' she suggested. 'It gets the best o' the sun and has the bonniest views.'

'It was Ken's room,' he said.

'Would it vex her, do you think—knowing that?'

'I don't think so. She sounds very sensible by her letter.'

'And we'll open up the dining-room—or would you think she'd rather have her meals in the hall?'

'For such a small family party,' he answered, smiling wryly, 'I think the hall would be friendlier.'

'When did she say she was coming?'

'She didn't, but I'll write to her to-night, inviting her at once. After all, she has a right to be here.'

She left him to the mood of semi-dejection which always followed upon thoughts of himself as the usurper, hurrying away to see what could be done about the room in the west turret. It was a big, airy room with faded chintz hangings and fine oak panelling enclosing the cold grey stone of the outer walls, giving it a warmer look than the two larger bedrooms flanking it. The single, deeply-recessed window looked out over the crow-stepped roof to a wide vista of hills and winding river and to the grey spire of the village church rising up from among the trees and the distant valley beyond. From here the road looked like a narrow white ribbon twisting endlessly until it disappeared from sight, and high clouds sailed by near at hand; from here stars shone brightly in a pale sky at eventide seen before they must have been visible from the ground, and here the winds came and whispered, or roared defiantly—and passed by.

It wasn't the room Kenneth Oliver's young wife should have come home to by right, but Bessie thought it would have been a cruel thing to give her the bride's room. She'd be more comfortable here, anyway, and the wee dressing-room that led off it and looked down over the moat would do to hold her luggage. Maybe she wouldn't have such a lot of luggage, though, when she had been all these years in a Japanese prison-camp.

Bessie stood appalled before the thought, wondering if there was anything extra in the way of food she might be able to beg or borrow for 'the young master's wife' as most of the people on the estate still thought of the girl Kenneth Oliver had married on the other side of the world, the girl who should have come home as a bride to Oliver's Keep.

While Bessie thought thus, Fergus Oliver's own thoughts about his cousin's young wife remained confused. He could not see that she would view him in any friendly light and he supposed she would expect to meet the entire Oliver family when she came to the Keep. She had probably heard all about them from Ken, although she had never met them. The Olivers had always been like that, staunch to family ties and closely knit together by their intense love for and pride in Oliver's Keep. But pride can take various forms, and he knew that in Jean Oliver it had become a fierce, resentful thing, up in arms at the slightest suggestion of insult, real or imaginary, and in many ways it had made her hard and embittered. Isobel, strong supporter of her elder sister in all she said and did, gloried in her pride, nursing it like some beloved child, and at heart secretly envious of Jean's position as the new head of the family. The third sister, Hattie, felt pride in a gentle way, conscious of what they owed to their position, yet never daring to cross her elder sisters in word or deed. Colourless, some people had called Hattie Oliver, but she had attained an inner peace that many more striking personalities would never achieve. She had been happy at Oliver's Keep because she had loved it with a selfless love, and Fergus realised that she must now be feeling cut adrift from a sheet-anchor.

And Margaret? He knew about Margaret! Margaret's pride was young and carefree, taken for granted, yet deep-rooted for all that, but to think of Margaret Oliver was opening an old sore and he had determined to put such thoughts from him if he could.

The day came when Kenneth Oliver's young widow was due to arrive at the Keep and Mrs Michie's final preparations were completed.

'You'll meet both trains,' Syd was told, 'in case she

decides to come with the earlier one. It will all depend on her connection from the south.'

Syd was beginning to know his way about Burndean, and in his light-hearted Cockney manner he had already made friends both in the village and about the various farms. One of his latest conquests was the stationmaster at Burndean Junction, and he was not averse to paying a visit in that direction at any time nor irritated by the thought of lingering a while. Syd particularly fancied himself in his chauffeur's uniform and decided that he had worn it too infrequently of late. In other words, it suited Syd much better to be driving the car into Burndean than to be tramping for miles over the estate in the Commander's wake doing a good many jobs that he had no real interest in. Not that he couldn't turn his hand to most jobs! 'Willing to give anything a trial once, that's me' was his motto, and he stuck to it. He'd even farm gladly to remain with the Commander, and it looked as if by 'farm' Oliver's Keep meant hard work morning, noon and night. Hard work never killed anyone, Syd had heard tell, and maybe his trouble was just the loneliness up here in this great tract of land on the wrong side of the Border, but he would stick it and get used to it in time. It would never be said of Syd Willing that he had let the Commander down!

He reached the station ten minutes before the first train of the afternoon was due. Tom Marshall was hoeing in the garden of the station house, but he looked up from his task at the sound of the engine and left his rose border to lean over the gate as Syd pulled up on the cinder approach.

'Meetin' the two-forty—or is it goods?'

'The carrier brought that last lot up for us. No, I'm meetin' the train.' Syd rubbed his hands together. He dearly loved a bit of gossip when it was the kind that did no harm to anybody. 'We're expectin' company up at the Keep.'

Tom's blue eyes opened wider and he removed the pipe from between his lips.

'That's news you're giving me,' he declared. 'Some friends o' Mister Oliver's frae the south, maybe?'

'More than friends.' Syd had been conscious for some

time that his master was far from happy in his relationship with the former owners of the Keep and that he deeply regretted the fact. 'We're expecting Mrs Oliver. She's home from abroad.'

If he had dropped a bombshell in the midst of the quiet garden Tom Marshall's expression could scarcely have registered greater surprise.

'Not the young master's widow!' His pleasant, wrinkled old face broke into a smile. 'Man! but that's grand news,' he declared, adding accusingly: 'How long have ye known an' never let on?'

'We've only had the letter a week,' Syd replied with some dignity. 'Mrs Oliver's not been very long in England, but I reckon as how she wanted to come right here as soon as ever she could.'

'Ay, poor lassie!' Tom murmured, casting his mind back along the years, 'she would that. She's come through a lot since she married the young master, and now she's comin' back without him. It's a strange world. Ay, it's a strange, sad world for some!'

'She's certainly had a rough experience,' agreed Syd, 'and she's been winding up her husband's affairs out there before she came home. He was in the rubber business.'

'Ay, I ken that. The Olivers' money was made in rubber, but they spent it well on the estate.'

As if anyone could tell Tom Marshall anything about the folk at Oliver's Keep! Maybe no' the folk that were there now, but the folk that *belonged* there!

'Here's the train,' he remarked. 'Do you think she'll be on this one?'

'I hope so, but I'll wait for the three-ten if she's not.'

Syd followed the stationmaster on to the platform and stood scanning the carriage windows as they moved past for any sign of an alighting passenger. When the train came to a halt three people got down: the local doctor, hurrying away after a brief word and looking as if he could ill spare the time for a train journey to Edinburgh; a stout matron hung round with a capacious shopping bag and numerous parcels, and a tall, thin girl in tweeds leading a small boy by the hand.

The woman with the parcels hurried after the doctor, but the girl stood on the platform, her two rather shabby suitcases at her feet, hesitating and bending to say something to the child.

'It doesn't look as if Mrs Oliver's come by that train,' Syd observed, glancing to the end of the platform. 'That can't be her—not with a boy.'

Tom Marshall's eyes were fixed on the couple now advancing towards them and a keen light of interest burned in their depths which quickly turned to suppressed excitement.

'Were ye thinkin' no?' he said. 'Well, let me tell ye that's just who it is! It's Mistress Oliver. I'd know the Oliver walk anywhere, an' that boy walks just like his father did before him. Ay, he's an Oliver all right. The young master's son! My! my! Would ye be kennin' the like o' this!'

Syd took an uncertain step in the girl's direction, touching his cap respectfully.

'I'm from Oliver's Keep,' he remarked tentatively.

'And I'm Mrs Oliver.' Her dark, rather sombre eyes were suddenly lightened by a swift smile. 'I'm so glad there's someone to meet us. Is it far to the Keep?'

'About three miles,' returned Syd, instantly enslaved by the appeal of someone who looked very tired and rather lonely while still maintaining that appearance of capability which he so much admired. 'Is this all your luggage, ma'am?'

'Yes, there isn't much.' She bent to pick up her case in the manner of one used to doing everything for herself, but the stationmaster had forestalled her. 'Oh—thank you,' she said gratefully.

Tom cleared his throat.

'I'd just like to say that we're all anxious to welcome ye, ma'am,' he got out as Syd helped her into the car. 'An' we were all sore put about when we heard tell o' the young master's death.'

Her smile was something that seemed to come from a great distance, struggling with tears long unshed.

'Thank you,' she murmured again. 'It is—very kind of you.'

Tom stood back, hat in hand, and the car slid away down the cinder approach and on to the main road. He watched it until it had turned the bend and then he made his way swiftly through his own gate and round the gable-end of the station house to the back door.

'Tib,' he called, 'are ye there?'

'Ay, what is't?' came the answer from the kitchen where Tibbie Marshall was busy with the week's ironing.

'I've some news for ye. There's going to be changes in Burndean—up at the Keep. We'll be having all the Olivers back soon!'

Tibbie's grey eyes lit up and a great joy spread over her comely face.

'Are ye tryin' tae tell me the young master's been found—that he wasna killed by they Jap monkeys after a'?'

Tom shook his head sadly.

'No, I canna tell ye that, but I can tell ye young Mistress Oliver is home frae the East—with her son!'

It was a full minute before Tibbie spoke, but her delight was unquestionable.

'I jist canna believe it's true!' she exclaimed at last. 'What a grand thing, an' how pleased Miss Jean Oliver will be that there's a direct heir after a'!'

Tom lit his pipe and drew on it reflectively for a moment before he answered.

'I'm wonderin' what'll happen to the laddie that's up there now,' he said. 'It'll mean that he'll have to go, for there's been no love lost between him an' his cousins.'

'Can ye wonder,' countered Tibbie. 'It was a sore blow to they lassies to lose their home to a stranger.'

'He wisna a stranger, Tib. Ye ken fine he was here often enough as a laddie, close cousin to them a' up at the Keep, an' I could never understand them fetchin' like this.'

'Ye'd quarrel yoursel' wi' the man that came an' took the roof that was over your head,' Tibbie reminded him tartly. 'But sometimes I think there was maybe another reason for Miss Jean going off as suddenly as she did without a hint to anybody where they were going tae live in the future. It was just as if they had all decided to disappear, leavin' no trace.'

'They wouldna *a*' decide,' Tom remarked dryly. 'It would be Miss Jean's decision, backed up by that besom, Isobel. I never liked Miss Isobel Oliver. Jean had her faults, but there was something about her ye just had to admire. There was nothing to admire about Miss Isobel, as she liked folks tae call her! No, she was a fly one yon—always ay an' no an' smilin' an' noddin', but behind it watchin' a' the time tae see if she could mak' trouble for anybody. The old man kept a tight rein on her, for he knew her, I expect, but even Jean Oliver won't be a match for Isobel. She's too straight an' above board.'

'Ye're havering, man!' Tibbie told him, testing her iron on a wet finger. 'Awa' ye go an' look after your trains!'

'Maybe I'm right an' maybe I'm no',' observed Tom from the doorway, 'but I ken a sly fox when I see one, an' some women are fiends for no reason at a'.'

To this remark his wife made no reply, for although she agreed with him she considered it was not always politic to let a man believe he had stumbled upon a profound truth.

Meanwhile the car from Oliver's Keep ran smoothly along the winding road with the girl in the back seat looking about her with deeply interested eyes, the small boy's hand clasped firmly in hers, and Syd reacting slowly from the surprise he had received on the station platform. He could not understand why the Commander had failed to tell him that there would be a child, nor could he quite believe that his master had changed his mind about the whole Oliver set-up and now wanted to remain in possession of his inheritance in spite of all he had said to the contrary in the past few weeks. He had said more than once, in moments of bitterness or frustration, that he would like to throw it all up and go back south to Solum Lacey or some other place in the sun, and that, Syd had agreed inwardly, would suit him down to the ground. He missed London and the cold up here chilled you to the marrow, but he would stick anything for the Commander's sake and if he wanted to stay here, well, Syd Willing would stay, too!

'The nipper won't have been to Scotland before, ma'am?' he asked, leaning back to address the girl in the rear seat while keeping a keen eye on the road. 'You'll both be findin' it cold after the East.'

That was one thing they would have in common, Syd's tone suggested.

'It can be cold in the East when you're undernourished and without your creature comforts,' she returned pleasantly and without any hint of complaint. 'I'm quite sure I shall like Scotland.'

She was prepared to like it, Syd mused, and maybe that was half the battle. Maybe she had never had a true home out there on the edge of the Malayan jungle in the heat—Syd still thought longingly of the heat!—and she may have looked forward to coming to Scotland to her husband's home. Funny, he thought, one minute you were thinking of the place as the Commander's and trying to resign yourself to a lifetime in it, and the next you knew it belonged to someone else, to the people the villagers called 'the rightful owners' —and all because of a kid!

Syd did not even try to suppress the warmly grateful feeling which rose within him at the thought of the boy sitting in the back of the car looking out with alert blue eyes to the rolling hills stretching away to the horizon with clouds resting almost on their summits and the suggestion of unlimited space that even his child's mind must be conscious of after years of captivity.

The girl seated beside him was also conscious of it, seeing it all through the eyes of the man she had married before these years of captivity had descended upon her, ageing her mentally far beyond her twenty-seven years. She had been twenty-two when the long rearguard action down the Malayan peninsula had begun, a nurse in a military hospital in Singapore rushed to a forward area when there was yet hope that the yellow tide could be effectively stemmed, and two months before that she had married Kenneth Oliver, rubber planter turned soldier, who had taken her on a brief and perfect honeymoon which had been cut short by the news of the sinking of the *Repulse* and the *Prince of Wales*. To the English colony the presence of these two great battleships in Asiatic waters was a complete safeguard to act as a deterrent upon the war lords of Japan, and utter confusion had reigned at the news of their swift loss. The whole meaning of warfare seemed to have changed with this deadly attack from the air, and the thinking few were suddenly aware of their nation's peril. Kenneth Oliver had been among these few, and they had started back for their battle stations together. She had seen him once again after that December morning when they had parted in Singapore, cherishing the popular myth that the island, at least, was impregnable, and these last twenty-four hours together in a small hotel in the city's sprawling suburbs had been the memory with which she had sustained her courage throughout the bitterness of the years that followed.

Now, seeing the land of her husband's birth for the first time, the land he had loved with all the intensity of his ardent spirit, she looked at it through his eyes, seeing it as something dearly familiar because he had described it to her so often and so well.

She had known what she must do as soon as she landed in England. She must go to Oliver's Keep and try to stem this craving for a sight of something which had belonged to him—the home he had loved so well, but it had not been without a certain amount of hesitation that she had penned her letter of introduction to the new heir. He was her cousin by marriage, but she had no idea what he would be like or how he would receive her, and she wondered what her own reactions to the meeting would be.

At this stage, however, she would not think ahead. She could not visualise her first encounter with the man who had stepped into her husband's inheritance, but she hoped passionately that he would not resent her coming. His letter had not suggested resentment. On the contrary, it had been most cordial and welcoming, and it had made her feel almost as if she were coming home.

But to be coming home alone—! The sharp anguish of the thought was like some physical pain cutting across her heart and she could not turn her mind away from the memory of a man's lonely grave on the edge of the Malayan jungle.

For many months, when the definite news of his death had first been established, she had found it hard to believe that she would never see Ken again. He had gone from her so strong, so tall and confident, in the flower of his manhood, and he had been so sure that everything would come right for England. They had the base at Singapore, an impregnable island fortress; they would fight back from there! Once or twice she had thought, if he had to die, she was glad that he had never known about the fall of Singapore and the bickerings and recriminations which had followed it. She, herself, had scarcely realised what they meant, because those six days had been a nightmare to her and to all who had shared her knowledge of the actual conflict. She found herself looking down at the tawny head of the child by her side and wondering what these years in a Japanese internment camp had done to him, trying to take comfort from the fact that he seemed to have been little affected by the hardships they had endured. In common with all the other mothers in the camp, she had given him any little luxuries she could, denying herself, and, on the whole, they had not been badly treated by their captors. The loss of liberty, however, had been a grinding thing, and he had never known the utter joy of complete freedom until recently. He had taken it soberly, and she was glad of the fact, seeing it as an indication of character.

'Have we far to go now?' she asked the man at the wheel.

'Not more than a couple of miles.' He nodded down the winding road ahead. 'After we've passed that bend yonder, you'll see the Keep.'

Syd was remembering his first view of it, its stark aspect standing in the gap between the two valleys, and he wondered what she would think of it. The Commander had said she'd never been there before— been married out East, she had—and she'd be bound to be thinking this was a strange way to come back. But maybe she was thinking it was a grand thing that it all belonged to the boy. Syd pushed back his cap and scratched the thinning patch on top of his head. It beat him, it did, and he wasn't quite sure what to think.

'Oh, Mummy, is that it? Is that the Keep?'

They had rounded the bend in the road and there, ahead

of them, guarding the pass between the hills, stood a castellated building of grey stone, tall and rugged and unpretentious, yet revealing a dignity in its very austerity that the girl in the car recognised and loved on sight.

'Yes,' she said, 'that is Oliver's Keep.'

There could be no doubt about it. It had been described to her in minutest detail on the other side of the world by a man who had loved it intensely, and now that she was seeing it for the first time she felt that her dead husband stood very near. The sudden constriction in her throat was intensified as each well-remembered detail was spread out before her, fitting in, piece by piece, to make the perfect whole. There were the hills, shouldering each other to the skyline, here the gorge where the brown river went down among its trees—larch and thorn and rowan—and there the great rock upon which the Keep had been built so that it looked in its greyness a very part of the rock itself.

The car left the road, crossing a hog-backed bridge over the turbulent river where the sunlight fell dappled through the new leaves, and began to climb the rough track leading direct to the front entrance of the Keep. She had seen old snapshots taken on the stone ledge which formed a sort of natural terrace round one side of the gaunt old building and recognised from other snapshots the sunken garden and the old, dried-up moat which made Anthony exclaim as they crossed it,

'Oh, Mummy, is the Keep really a castle?'

'Almost,' she said, smiling. 'Originally it was built for the same purpose as most castles—to guard the lands round about, and you see how cunningly this one has been placed so that it faces every way from which danger might have come.'

'Did bad men come and attack it?'

'Quite often. They came from the south mostly in those days,' she added with one of her rare smiles. 'From over the Border.'

'And do they ever come now?'

'No. All that is in the past.'

She spoke as if she were preoccupied with the past, but it was a more recent past than that of Border forays and battles long ago. Would there always be wars, she wondered, and blighted hopes and sorrow and death? Her chin went up as she shook the defeatist thought from her. How long ago had she determined to put it all behind her, for the boy's sake and her own? Somewhere, some day, she must set about building a new life and this visit to her husband's old home was the half-way mark, the division between past and future, the now of memories. Afterwards she must put her memories behind her and look only to the future. Financially she was well-enough provided for, Kenneth's share of the Oliver money having come to her as his widow, but where sorrow and loss dwell deep in the heart money is a poor compensation. She was too wise to disregard it altogether, however, realising that at least it represented security for herself and the child.

The car was slowing up on the incline, circling round in the limited space to draw up at the front door, and her heart began to hammer madly in her breast as she saw that the door was open and a man stood on the topmost step. Grey steps they were, hollowed by the feet of Olivers down through the centuries, and the man who had fallen heir to his cousin's heritage stood waiting to receive her at the head of them. She knew that she had been nervous at the thought of this meeting, that she had wondered apprehensively what the new heir would be like, but as he came down the steps to open the car door for her she knew she was going to like him.

Relying too strongly upon first impressions had never been her way, and she had grown to distrust them in the artificial years before the war had swept over the Far East, recognising slowly and at some cost to herself that the most outwardly charming people were often the most hollow, but there was a look in Commander Oliver's eyes which she recognised, a look of sincerity and a willingness to trust which Ken had often declared was her own greatest weakness. He was younger than she had expected, tall and loosely knit, with the long Oliver nose which appeared to be a family hallmark, especially in the men. The snapshots which Ken had carried about with him had all shown it as a characteristic feature, but the rather stern eyes that went with it were not this young man's. His were blue and clear and eagerly welcoming as he said,

'Welcome to Oliver's Keep.'

He looked as if he had meant to say a great deal more, as if he had prepared an adequate speech for her reception, but suddenly they were just looking at each other and smiling and any awkwardness that might have attended their meeting was swept away, and she felt more than welcome.

'You must have had a rotten journey,' he said, and then his eyes went to the child behind her and swiftly back to hers again.

There had been no mention of a child in her letter and the possibility of what this child might mean came to him slowly after the first shock of surprise.

'Mummy,' the boy asked, 'are we getting out?'

'Yes, darling.' She accepted Fergus Oliver's hand and turned back towards the boy. 'This is Commander Oliver, and, Commander Oliver—this is Anthony.'

The boy extended a gloved hand, smiling gravely.

'Do you really own all this lovely castle?' he asked, his eyes sweeping up over the ancient crow-stepped roof to the turrets set four-square to every wind that blew.

'Yes.'

Fergus Oliver's answer had been abrupt because, suddenly, it was uncertain. Did he really own Oliver's Keep? His cousin's wife had come home with a son . . .

He stared down at her, seeing her standing uncertainly on the steps of her husband's home and although there was nothing frail or appealing about this girl with the clear eyes and strong, determined chin who crushed back her own emotions valiantly so that the child might not be affected by their sorrow, he felt a rush of kindly pity filling his heart and hastened to tell her that he was glad she had come. He lifted the boy down from the running-board of the car and carried him up the few steps to the front door, thinking suddenly and irrelevantly how Olivers had carried their brides over that same threshold for generations, carrying happiness into their homes.

Helen Oliver followed behind them, glad that his attention had been taken up with the child because her heart was far too full for the conventional words of a first meeting and, sensing that, he had instantly abandoned them. He set Anthony down in the great, raftered hall where the late afternoon sunshine came streaming down in shafts of mellowed light between the stone pillars supporting the hidden gallery, and the boy looked round him, wide-eyed, at the trophies hanging on the stone walls and the great antlers and crossed rapiers above the fireplace.

The fire of logs had been stacked high and a table spread with a white cloth had been drawn up near its warmth, for the spring day was still cold. Helen went towards it gratefully as a small, stout woman appeared out of the shadows behind a pillar with the tea tray.

'This is Mrs Michie, my housekeeper,' Fergus Oliver explained. 'She will show you to your room later, but we thought you'd like to have tea first.'

Anthony said, 'I'm hungry,' and Helen, as she laughed, noticed that Mrs Michie was looking at him with the same surprise which her master had shown when they had first met on the steps outside.

She had been stupid about that, of course, not telling them about Tony in her letter, but she had been nervous about this first meeting and had taken their knowledge of Tony for granted. Of course, she should have explained . . .

Fergus Oliver was walking towards the shadows with the housekeeper, giving an order in a low voice, and she saw Mrs Michie glance back in Tony's direction, and knew it was going to be all right for the child at Oliver's Keep.

Ever since her arrival in England she had been thinking in terms of Tony; the boy had become precious to her, although she was determined not to spoil him nor make him a 'woman's child.' The way in which Fergus Oliver had shown his instant attraction to him, therefore, pleased her and she smiled as she watched Tony expand during the next hour, telling Commander Oliver of his many new experiences aboard ship which had mercifully seemed to wipe out the earlier experiences in the internment camp. She found herself envying the resilience of childhood and its short memory, and then remembered that there were memories she held which she did not wish to fade.

Soon it was six o'clock and the child's bedtime, and Mrs. Michie came in to announce that she had put a 'pig' in the bed.

Tony surveyed her with round, alarmed eyes until it was explained to him that the 'pig' was made of stone and held hot water to warm a newly made-up bed in the wee dressing-room adjoining his mother's bedroom.

'We might have known he was comin',' Bessie said. 'He'll be near you there for the first night or two while he's strange an' then, maybe ye'll be makin' other arrangements.'

The presence of the child had made a great difference, Bessie acknowledged. It would mean, wouldn't it, that the young master's wife would be back in the Keep for good —its new mistress, bringing up her son there, as he should be brought up, even though his father lay in some lonely grave on the other side o' the world. It was good news, certainly, but in a way Bessie was perturbed by it, for in the two months in which she had served Fergus Oliver she had grown to like and respect him, and the 'Commander's' word had become law to her as firmly as it had to Syd Willing. All the same, justice was justice, and here was the real heir returned to Oliver's Keep, so that they were likely to have the whole Oliver family back under its old, raftered roof before long and a happy understanding reached all round.

Bessie hoped that the Commander would share in the ultimate understanding which she felt so sure about, but in the meantime she would do her best to make young Mrs. Oliver feel that she had truly come home. She stood by as Tony was put to bed, proud to have taken even a small part in settling the heir comfortably on his first night in his new home, and then, as the little boy knelt at the foot of the bed and the slender girl bent over him to listen to his prayer, Bessie stole out of the dressing-room with tears in her eyes.

'God bless the wee bairn!' she murmured as she made her way down the back staircase.

Helen Oliver stood for several minutes in the darkening room after she had wished Tony goodnight, her thoughts of far-off things that came hauntingly near so that she could not bring herself to go down immediately to join the man who was waiting for her in the hall below.

Instead, she turned along the shadowed corridor where a line of portraits hung against the wall—soldiers in gay uniforms, ladies in crinolines with soft, thoughtful eyes and delicate features which yet retained a hint of the strong Oliver characteristics in determined mouth or firmly moulded chin. There was one portrait which reminded her of a snapshot she had seen of Kenneth's youngest sister, a laughing, vivacious schoolgirl with a slightly rebellious mouth and masses of dark hair framing a perfect oval face.

She stood for a moment before the portrait, passing on at last to wonder about that distant ancestress of her dead husband's, and then, at the end of the corridor she stopped short. All the colour receded from her cheeks as her eyes were lifted to meet the pictured gaze of the man she had married so far away from his home that their little time together seemed to have been in another world.

The portrait had evidently been painted from a photograph Ken had sent home—a copy of the one she had begged him to have taken when they had first become engaged and which she still carried with her in its original leather frame, and the young soldier with the deeply penetrating eyes was Ken in his most thoughtful mood. She stood there motionless, looking and looking, reliving the happy past until the tears she had refused to shed for weeks dimmed her eyes at last.

'Oh, Ken,' she whispered, 'I've come! I've come to the Keep, but it isn't the same because we planned to be here —together.'

To her tear-dimmed vision, it was almost as if the firmly moulded lips of the portrait parted in a compassionate smile. What did he know? There was wisdom in those eyes, and suddenly words sprang into her heart, words from the storehouse of childhood knowledge, yet words that seemed to have been spoken there in the dim silence of the lonely gallery for her alone, for her present comfort and future hope. 'Let not your heart be troubled . . .'

They came and passed, words old as the Christian faith that had brought comfort to many a burdened soul down through the ages, and with them came peace and Helen Oliver knew that she would never feel utterly alone again.

She turned slowly in the direction of the stairway, going down into the hall to find her husband's cousin standing waiting for her at the end of the wide stone passage beneath with a look in his eyes which told her that he had guessed how she had spent these last few minutes, that he had been coming in search of her but had halted there, feeling that another step would have been an intrusion.

'I've drawn our chairs up to the fire in the hall,' he said, leading her back towards it with a smile. 'It's warmer here than in the round room which the family used.'

She wanted to ask him all about Kenneth's family, where they had gone, how she could get into touch with them now that she had discovered they were no longer at the Keep, but for a moment she would let herself dwell in this new atmosphere of perfect peace which encircled her, feeling the security of Kenneth's old home wrapping her round in its timeless spell which questions might break or endanger.

'You must be tired,' he said as she sank into the depths of one of the big hide arm-chairs and pulled its red velvet cushion into position at her back with a sigh of contentment.

'I'm not tired, really. It's just so marvellous to be able to relax and not have to think of tomorrow and where one has to go on from here.'

He said, 'I'm glad you feel that way about it. You'll bring the boy up here, of course.'

Her eyes, which had been lazily half closed in the warmth of the fire, opened wide to look at him in some surprise.

'Tony?' she questioned. 'But how could I?'

'It is your home.'

She sat forward in her chair, the slow smile that made

her face suddenly so attractive lighting it as she shook her head.

'You are being very kind, Commander Oliver, but that is impossible.'

'Will you call me Fergus?' he asked. 'After all, we are cousins by marriage.'

'I'd like to—Fergus. Ken talked about you quite often — telling me tales of the old days here at the Keep. That's why I feel I know every inch of it and'—her eyes were very steady on his—'why I am glad you are here to carry on.'

A slow flush rose and spread over his thoughtful face.

'Why did you say just now that you would not wish to bring Ken's boy up at Oliver's Keep?' he asked abruptly.

'Because he is not Ken's son.'

He could only stare at her speechlessly.

'I've been trying to adopt him since I came home—legally, I mean. It's a long story and perhaps—'

'I shall be interested,' he said quickly, although to Helen the disappointment which her confession had been to him was clear in eyes and voice alike. He had *wanted* Tony to be Ken's child; he had wanted Oliver's Keep to have its rightful heir—a son in the direct line—and her original liking for this cousin by marriage was increased a thousand-fold by the knowledge.

'It goes back a long way,' she began slowly. 'To nineteen forty-two and the days just before the surrender of Singapore. They are years away now, but the events of those days are still terribly vivid.' She drew in a deep breath and continued more quickly, 'We were a hospital ship, but we had taken on a good many civilian refugees from the Peninsula—people from Penang and Malacca mostly—and we were getting out as fast as we could. We had wounded from the Peninsula fighting on board and air-raid casualties from Singapore, and we were hopelessly short-staffed. We didn't mind that, of course, because we had been working that way for weeks past . . .' Her eyes were focused on the blue flames leaping up from the half-burned logs as if she saw the reflection of the things she spoke of pictured there in the fire. 'Then we had an SOS from another ship. She was burning. They said she had been dive-bombed and there were casualties on board and could we come alongside and take them off. We were pretty well full up, but that's the sort of call one doesn't ignore on the high seas, so our skipper put down a boat when we sighted her and the surgeon called for volunteers. I was on duty, so I went,' she continued with no suggestion in her quiet, almost matter-of-fact tone that she had done anything heroic or outside the bounds of her duty as a nurse.

'And you got them off?' he ventured.

'All the casualties—yes. There were also two children on board.'

'Tony?'

'Yes.' Her voice was suddenly constricted. 'He was only a baby—about eighteen months old. He couldn't have been more.'

'And you have no idea who his parents are? You said you wanted to adopt him.'

A shadow crossed her face, an old, poignant memory.

'His father handed him down as the lifeboat left the burning ship, but he stayed behind with the other men because there was just a chance that the fire might be got under control. I suppose they had some idea of fighting it and following us to Australia if they failed to get into Singapore. Anyway, they had done all they could for the wounded and the children. He put Tony into my arms and asked me to take care of him . . .'

'They didn't get through, then?' he asked, conscious of yet another tragedy of the war years, a little ship lost at sea and a child's future curiously changed.

'Neither of us got through,' she answered briefly. 'We were torpedoed before we reached Borneo and—Tony's father's ship was never heard of again.'

He said, 'I'm sorry,' because it seemed to him that she had taken this as a personal loss for the child's sake. Presently she continued,

'Apparently Tony's mother died before they left Malaya. His father had just time to tell me that before we pushed off.' Her eyes dimmed again. 'It's a cruel thing—a man parting with his child like that—all he had left—the memory of his wife and all their love.'

Somehow he knew that she was thinking she hadn't even that consolation, but not thinking it bitterly, as some women might have done. Instead of indulging in such self-pity he could well imagine her giving all her love to this unknown man's child, mothering it as she would have done her own—Kenneth Oliver's son. And he had taken it for granted that the boy was his cousin's legitimate heir and had been glad of it, seeing in this unexpected turn of events release for himself and justice for Oliver's Keep! Release? Yes, he had wanted that. Suddenly he looked up and met Helen Oliver's eyes.

'It's tough luck,' he said. 'I thought the boy was Ken's and I should have liked nothing better. Believe me when I say that, won't you?'

Her dark eyes searched his for an instant before she replied, and when she finally did so it was to ask a question.

'But why do you say it? Don't you feel that you have an obligation to Oliver's Keep?'

The question was in no way critical: she had asked for his reason in an endeavour to understand his attitude towards his inheritance and he gave it unfalteringly,

'I feel that I am not here by right. Maybe I should say that I have been made to feel a usurper.'

He saw her stiffen a little at the implication which she could not fail to see, but her tone of kindly interest in his affairs had not altered when she asked,

'By Ken's sisters, do you mean?'

'Not altogether, although they have helped the impression along, I suppose. It's mostly a mental attitude, I'm afraid. I feel that I have no right to be here.'

'But that's ridiculous!' Her tone was vigorous now, plainly discounting his attitude. 'Oliver's Keep is yours, as next in entail, as surely as it was Ken's.'

He smiled wryly.

'It's fine of you to be able to say that, and I really think you mean it, but after all you should feel the same way about it as—the others.'

'Jean and Isobel?'

'Jean mostly,' he nodded. 'She's the head of the family now, you know.'

'Is she an ogress?' There was a twinkle in her eyes as she asked the question and he recognised it instantly, feeling curiously ashamed.

'I've made her sound one, haven't I? But, honestly, she's pretty grim. It's a matter of pride, I suppose, and pride can take so many different forms.'

'You think it has become warped in Jean Oliver? What exactly has she done?'

'Nothing that she shouldn't have done about the Keep. I mean, she has left nothing undone.' He glanced about him at the relics hanging everywhere which had been Oliver property for generations. 'She left everything that belonged here.'

' But wouldn't stay herself.'

He looked up, searching her eyes.

'That's one thing I want you to believe,' he said earnestly. 'I didn't turn them out. I would have been much happier if they had all stayed at the Keep—Jean and Hattie and Isobel.'

'Wasn't there another sister?' she asked, suddenly remembering the girl's portrait in the long gallery.

' Yes—Margaret.'

There had been a queer, half-strangled note in his voice as he had uttered the name and he looked swiftly away from her questioning eyes.

'She was the youngest daughter, wasn't she?' Helen mused. 'Are they all living together now?'

'I wish I knew!' He got up, as if action was vitally necessary to him of a sudden, and strode to the far side of the big fireplace where he stood staring gloomily down into the heart of the fire. 'I've done all I possibly can to trace them, but my only contact with them has been through our respective lawyers. Jean Oliver won't have it any other way. When—your husband died I wrote offering them a home here, telling them that it was to make no difference to their settled way of life, but all the reply I received was through their lawyer in Edinburgh to the effect that they were vacating the Keep immediately and that I could not fail to accept it as next in entail.'

'And you do see that now, of course?' she asked earnestly.

'In a way—yes, but I'd far rather be out—back in my own small place in the south. Quite frankly, I can't afford Oliver's Keep. I could never do it justice.'

'Is that your only reason for not being very happy here, Fergus?'

The gentle question could not be regarded as an intrusion, and he answered it with simple truth.

'No. There's something else. Margaret and I were engaged to be married.'

She gave a small start of surprise and he saw that this was something which had not been discussed between her and Ken. Of course, they had met and married long after it had become stale news to everyone except himself, he thought bitterly.

'Do you want to tell me why it was broken off?' she asked. 'You needn't if it's going to be painful to you.'

He laughed abruptly.

'What does that matter! I've become used to the idea, and maybe a man isn't supposed to feel "pain" over these things.'

She chose to ignore the bitterness in him, sensing in spite of his defiant attitude that he wanted to talk and thinking that, by discussing this thing with him, she might help to get some of the bitterness out of his system. He had evidently been bottling it all up far too long, alone here in the Keep, with only the two servants for company.

'What happened?' she asked.

He moved uneasily, shifting his weight from one foot to the other, and then he felt for his pipe and sat down again in the chair beside her.

'It goes back a long way,' he said almost gruffly. 'I came to the Keep a lot as a child because my father was in the Indian Army and my mother was with him and I was at home in England at school. I spent all the vacations with my uncle, Walter Oliver, who was a remarkable man in many ways and one whom I admired intensely. He made the estate what it was, and he had a positive genius for making money. I needn't tell you about his rubber interests in Malaya, because that was why Ken went out there in the first place, but here in Burndean he spent freely, buying new land, farms, stock, and improving the old. It was a wonderful experience for a boy, coming up here among them all for the long vacations, especially for an only child, as I was. I loved every minute of it—the freedom, the companionship and, above all, the sense of "belonging."' He paused, letting memory hold the door of the past wide open. 'Margaret and I were of an age and we were always together. We climbed the hills, we got into scrapes together, and we made plans apart from the others. In later years we fished the burns and rode across the heather and went to Hunt balls and the Riding of the Marches, and still we made our plans. One day we would be married!'

Again he forced a laugh, but the bitterness of it was tangled up in a deep hurt this time.

'Surely there could be no opposition to your engagement,' Helen said. 'Unless it was the fact that you were related. But, even then, you were not first cousins.'

'There was no opposition to our engagement. Nothing ever went more smoothly. Our marriage was arranged to take place in the late autumn of '39 when I could most conveniently leave my smallholding in the south to take a fortnight's honeymoon.' He got up again, prowling restlessly across the hearthrug. 'Then, in August, when it became obvious there was going to be a war, I knew I wanted to join up—'

He paused awkwardly, but she made no comment, waiting for him to continue.

'It was then I knew that I couldn't go through with our marriage. I was determined to fly and I knew the risks to be taken in those early days. If I could have been sure that I would go out to a clean finish I would have gone on with it, but the thought of binding a spirit like Margaret's to someone who might come back to her an invalid for life—who might be blinded or bruised so badly as to be no more than a human hulk, wouldn't bear examination. I tried to explain it to her, and I think she understood up to a point, but she called it quixotic and wanted to risk everything. I was sorely tempted, but I held out—'

'And she finally broke off the engagement?'

He laughed grimly.

'I don't suppose I'll ever know who broke it off, but she sent me back my ring and that was that.'

'You mean that you—lay down to it as easily as that!'

'Oh, there were arguments, but nobody could ever get the better of Jean Oliver, and the others backed her up magnificently—even Margaret.'

'But did you *never* see her?' she protested. 'Surely you made an effort to come to some sort of understanding—that if you came back all right . . .'

'Oh, I tried, but the barriers were too formidable. You haven't come up against the Oliver pride yet or you would know!'

To Helen Oliver, who had lost the one love of her youth, who had come through so much and endured, the whole position seemed suddenly ridiculous, yet she knew that he did not consider it in such a light, that he had been gravely hurt and his own pride trampled upon. He was also an Oliver and it was well within the bounds of possibility that a touch of the famous pride was mingled in his own make-up.

'You have never seen Margaret since?'

'Never. I've done everything I could to get into touch with her, but it's all been no good. One thing you have to give the Oliver women credit for,' he added acidly, 'they stick together like limpets.'

'And a clam has nothing on them for secrecy!'

'That's about it, but I thought Margaret would understand.'

'She hasn't married?'

His mouth set tightly.

'Not that I know, but would I know if she had?'

Impulsively she rose and put a hand on his arm.

'Fergus,' she said, 'you haven't stopped trying just because you've come up against a blank wall, have you? It's not what I'd expect from a man who's done all you have in this war and come through. It's not what I'd expect from anyone who really cared about me if I were the girl you loved.'

He stared at her, thinking that he ought to feel resentment at being spoken to as if he were a small boy, but he couldn't feel resentment at Helen Oliver's interest. He felt it about him, wrapping him round warmly, and he smiled.

'Will you stay at the Keep,' he asked, 'at least until you've grown tired of me? I'd like to get it as it used to look—as it should look.'

Bright tears were behind her eyes as she nodded.

'If you'd like it that way,' she said. 'And perhaps I'll be able to feel that I'm doing it for Ken as well as for you—and Oliver's Keep.'

They went in to dinner, a simple meal served in the round room, which was lit solely by a glass-domed roof and was perfectly circular in shape, forming part of one of the four turretted columns which rose at each corner of the Keep. High up in the stone walls the narrow arrow-slits let in thin fingers of moonlight that lay along the old grey stone like silver thread, far above the artificial candlelight on the gate-legged table at which they sat. Fergus Oliver explained that the family had used this room more than any other in his uncle's time, and Helen was quick to see its possibilities.Somehow, she was glad she had promised to stay.

Fergus was pouring their coffee when the telephone in the hall rang shrilly through the stillness, and presently Bessie came to the door.

'It's a call frae Edinburgh for Mistress Oliver,' she announced. 'Miss Jean Oliver would like to speak to you, ma'am.'

Fergus Oliver jumped to his feet, facing Helen across the table.

'It isn't possible—'

Helen laughed.

'Evidently it is, and news seems to travel in this part of the world even more quickly than the bush telegraph! I wonder how my in-laws knew I was here?'

'You'll get their address?' he asked. 'It sounds as if they want to see you.'

'I'll do my best,' she promised with a smile, making her way towards the door where Mrs Michie was waiting expectantly. 'I've an idea I'll have that address for you within the next three minutes!'

The smile faded, however, as she walked briskly across the hall to where the telephone was hidden away in a stone alcove, this modern instrument that was somehow out of keeping with the rest of the old house, yet a necessity in its remoteness.

A certain nervousness had taken possession of her, coupled with an excitement at the thought of meeting Ken's sisters at last, and the nervousness predominated more than it had done before her arrival at the Keep. Was it, she wondered as she lifted the receiver, because Fergus Oliver had conveyed an impression of the three elder Miss Olivers which was not entirely reassuring?

'Hullo!' she said into the mouthpiece, hoping that her nervousness would not be detected at the far end.

'Hullo! Hullo!' came the reply in a voice bristling with vigour. 'I am waiting to speak to Mrs Kenneth Oliver, please.'

'This is Helen Oliver speaking.'

'Ah! how are you? I'm Jean Oliver, Kenneth's eldest sister. It seems a rather strange way to introduce ourselves, but, of course, I had no idea until this afternoon that you were even in England.'

There had been definite accusation in the tone and Helen felt the colour mounting in a swift wave to her cheeks even although she could not be seen. The voice that came across the wire was so forceful that there could be no doubting its owner's characteristics, and they seemed to add up to Fergus Oliver's impression of her.

'I really would have tried to get into touch with you, Miss Oliver,' Helen explained, 'if I had thought you were not at the Keep, but I took it for granted that you would be—'

Because she knew she was saying the wrong thing, blundering foolishly, she paused, biting her lip and waiting for the woman at the other end of the line to reply. There was a short interval of absolute silence before the vigorous voice sounded once more.

'I think you had better call me Jean,' it said decisively. 'After all, we are sisters-in-law, even although we have not yet met each other. No,' she went on steadily, 'we are no longer at the Keep, as you have now discovered, and really that is my reason for calling you this evening. I'd like you to come to Edinburgh to-morrow—if you are not too tired after your journey from the south.'

'It was rather a tiring journey,' Helen admitted.

'Then, perhaps we'd better make it Friday. Do you know Edinburgh?'

'No, I'm afraid I don't.'

'Well, then, listen carefully and I'll give you some directions. You'll get a train from Burndean shortly after eleven o'clock—eleven twelve, to be exact—and that will bring you into Edinburgh before one o'clock. You'll come down Princes Street to Macey's restaurant, where I shall be waiting for you in the ladies' lounge. Is that perfectly clear, for I'm afraid our three minutes are almost up?'

'Yes, thank you, it seems clear enough,' Helen agreed, 'but I hope you are not putting yourself to a great deal of trouble, Miss— Jean.'

'Not at all.' The expected time signal rang out between them. 'These are my arrangements. By the way, what is the boy's name?'

'You mean—Tony?'

There was an instant's pause.

'Tony? Tut! Tut!' The clicking sound indicated Miss Jean's intense disapproval, although she made no further comment, ringing off with a final brisk, 'Until Friday, then!'

Helen was left with the dead line in her hand and the conviction in her heart that the woman she had just been speaking to was under the impression, as Fergus Oliver had been, that Tony was Kenneth's son.

How stupid she had been not to correct that impression right away, she thought, although Miss Oliver had hardly given her the time to do so. A telephonic conversation on first acquaintance was never a very satisfactory affair she mused as she retraced her footsteps to the round room where Fergus Oliver was waiting for her, and then she remembered the fact that she had laughingly promised to bring Fergus his cousin's address which he had long sought, the address of Margaret, the girl he loved.

Well, at least she had made contact with the family, and on Friday she would actually meet one of them!

The prospect presented a doubtful side. Would she and Jean Oliver like each other, and would the interval be easy when she was now thoroughly convinced that Jean Oliver disapproved of her visit to the Keep in the present circumstances? She wondered how she knew that, but the impression was very strong. Even over the telephone Jean Oliver had managed to convey her censure upon this wrong step, and it was evident that she considered Helen's first action on reaching England should have been to seek her out personally and not take the Keep or anything else for granted.

But how could I have known? she thought. It was the most natural thing in the world that they should all still have been at the Keep. One big, happy family! She tried to laugh, but it rang hollow and she knew deep in her heart that this was a serious matter which no amount of laughter could ever dismiss.

Fergus Oliver was on his feet, standing looking down into the wide fireplace with hands thrust deep in his pockets when she opened the door, but he wheeled round immediately, hope and resignation struggling in his eyes.

'What news?' he asked.

She smiled at him, trying to soften the blow.

'I haven't exactly got their address, but I have an appointment to meet Miss Jean in Edinburgh on Friday.'

'How like her!' he exclaimed bitterly. 'I expect she knows I'm here and she wouldn't give me the satisfaction of having caught her even a fraction off guard.'

Helen felt sorry for him, but she was still determined to treat the matter with the utmost optimism.

'We're on the right track, though, aren't we?' she pointed out. 'And at least you know they're all in Edinburgh.'

'We know Jean's in Edinburgh,' he corrected, 'and probably Isobel and Hattie—'

'If I'm going to meet them I can ask—judiciously, of course!—about Margaret. If you want me to?'

He moved restlessly back into the shadows away from the firelight.

'Maybe I'm just being a fool,' he said, 'probing like this. What guarantee have I got that she isn't—married or something?'

'None,' she admitted into the shadows, 'but at least you don't know she is, at present.'

'I suppose you think me a queer sort of moral coward—'

'Not one bit, but I think you should go on trying till you are *sure* it isn't any use.'

She heard him fumbling with the china on the table and presently he came back with fresh coffee to replace the cup she had left when she had been called to the telephone.

'What did Jean say?' he asked.

'Just the conventional sort of thing—how was I, and some remark about the journey, chiefly, I think, the journey from London to here!' She would not repeat what he already knew, and what had been conveyed to her so strongly over the distance separating Jean Oliver from her family home, the sense of resentment that was so strong in this displaced Oliver woman that it could be felt almost in every breath she drew. It was a resentment which she still felt, in spite of Fergus's explanations about the broken engagement, largely hinged upon their own removal from the Keep, but in this respect she was soon to learn that she did Jean Oliver a grave injustice. 'She even asked me to call her by her Christian name,' she added whimsically.

He smiled faintly.

'That's always something!' He drew a deep breath, bending forward to search her face intently. 'I expect you think me an awful boor, serving up your in-laws to you in such a poor light, but from the beginning we seem to have got down to brass tacks . . .'

'I like it that way,' Helen said. 'After all, you are one of my relations, too, aren't you?'

'Yes—related by marriage.' He stirred his coffee thoughtfully. 'It's been deuced lonely here at times—not having anyone to talk to—and I've wished over and over again that Jean and the others had been able to put their pride in their pocket and come and live here again.'

Helen said without a great deal of conviction,

'She may change her mind one day.'

'Who? Jean Oliver?' He laughed abruptly. 'You might just as well expect the Atlantic to roll back and let us walk to America! Jean Oliver never changes her mind once it is made up.'

'What are the others like?' Helen asked. 'Isobel and Hattie?'

'Oh—satellites.'

'Revolving about Jean?'

'More or less.'

'What a lovely prospect! I hope they won't expect me to —revolve!'

'Don't let it scare you if they do, but I don't think they'll be like that with you. They'll be friendly and welcome you into the bosom of the family, I expect, for after all, they have nothing against you.'

She flushed.

'I'm not so sure of that,' she said slowly. 'They'll have Tony, for one thing.'

'Tony?'

'Jean highly disapproved of his name, for one thing, and she didn't give me a chance to explain that he isn't Ken's son.'

He whistled.

'Good heavens! so she thinks that?'

'So did you,' Helen pointed out.

'Yes, I must admit I jumped to conclusions there because I wanted it to be that way. And Jean must want it that way, too! Good God! what a situation!'

'It sounds as if it might be an uncomfortable one for me,' Helen said, 'but there's really nothing I can do about it. I can't pretend the boy *is* my son—'

She broke off, but he had heard that note in her voice, the longing she could not quite suppress, and a mad idea rushed through his brain.

'Why not? Wouldn't it solve all our problems, and make everyone so much happier? You've brought him up—you say you don't know anything about his parents—that the father may have been drowned at sea. He's yours, Helen, almost as surely as if he had been Ken's son . . .'

In the wavering light of the candles he saw her pale face and was instantly sorry he had ever made the suggestion, although in that first wild moment it had seemed the answer to a good many things.

'I'm sorry,' he said. 'And I'm more than sorry he isn't yours, Helen—for your own sake. Still, you said you were making every effort to adopt him legally—'

'I've been trying to set some of the wheels in motion, but I must make a more determined effort to trace his father first,' she said. 'It all takes time.'

'There's absolutely no chance of the mother being alive?'

'Oh no. I gathered she died soon after Tony was born.' She set her empty cup down on the stone kerb round the fire, her eyes remote for a moment as her thoughts dwelt in the past, lost among its poignant memories. 'As for—the man who gave me his child to look after, there's simply no hope that he could have survived.'

'But he may have got through,' he suggested. 'So many queer things happened—strange, almost providential escapes . . .'

'I wish I could think that, for Tony's sake.' Her voice was suddenly broken up with emotion. 'What a queer specimen I am! I love Tony and I know his father has the only true claim to him, yet one part of me hopes he will never be claimed—the part of me that nursed him through pneumonia, and told him his first bedtime story and tucked him up at night, and taught him to say his prayers.' She smiled through a mist that was unshed tears. 'Don't think you're alone about being a coward mentally! I want Tony and I know it isn't right, and still I want him, yet if his father were to come for him tomorrow I'd try to let him go gladly.'

They sat in silence because he could find no adequate words in which to answer this confession straight from another lonely heart, and words were no longer needed, for Helen Oliver felt that he understood.

'Tony thinks, of course, that you are his mother?'

'Yes. I often wonder if I did wrong in that, but it seemed so natural. All the other children in the camp were with their mothers and Tony is a sensitive child. I did not want him to feel odd—left out.'

'I think you did the very best thing under the circumstances,' he told her definitely. 'There will be time enough in the future to tell him the truth, when he is older and can understand.'

'I often wondered what a man would think about that sort of thing,' she confessed with a faint smile. 'Sometimes, when you are entirely on your own, it is difficult to know if you are doing right or not.'

'You have no family in England?'

'None at all. My mother died when I was very young—not much older than Tony is now—and my father was killed during the war while I was out East. He was an air-raid warden and was killed in one of the blitzes. He was fifty-seven—not old, really. Perhaps that's why I feel Tony's position so keenly—knowing what it is like to be without my parents.'

He sat forward in his chair, taking his pipe from between his teeth and meeting her eyes with an earnest expression which added weight to his words.

'I don't want you to feel that you are alone in the world as long as I am at the Keep,' he said. 'I have asked you to make it your home and I really mean that. If you have nowhere else to go—'

'I stayed with an aunt in England before I joined up,' she said. 'I would like to go and see her again—in a week or two, when Tony has settled down after all our travelling.'

'I think he will settle here very easily. It's a grand life for a boy and he can be with me most of the day going round the various farms.'

'I'd like nothing better,' she confessed, and he saw her

eyes shine and the tender smile on her lips, knowing that the love she bore for the sleeping child upstairs was as tender as any mother's, knowing, also, that she was glad to have found an anchorage for a little while after the storms and stresses of the past six years and was genuinely grateful to him for having offered it.

It had been evident from her surprise when he had first suggested a prolonged visit that she had not expected to stay in the Borders more than a day or two, and he was glad that he had been able to persuade her to change her plans, for his own sake as well as for hers. He had been far too much alone of late, thrown back upon moody thoughts and bitter memories, and he was sensible enough to realise that such things can be destructive. Where regret and bitterness dwelt, there could never be peace of mind, but at least he could forget for a little while.

'Tony will love it, too,' she said. 'Animals are more or less new to him, but I think he will be very fond of them. There was a cat on board ship coming home and it followed him everywhere, so I can quite imagine his delight at cows and horses!'

'Will you take him to Edinburgh with you on Friday?' he asked suddenly.

'I hadn't thought about it,' she confessed, 'but really there doesn't seem much point in taking him all that way, only—'

'If he'll stay, you can leave him with me. Mrs Michie will see to his meals and I'll enjoy having him.'

'It's far too kind of you,' she protested, 'but I had been thinking he'd had enough travelling for a week or two. After all, he's come right across the world.'

'It will leave you more free to talk to Miss Jean,' he said, 'and I don't think he'll be unhappy here.'

'Don't worry about Tony,' she assured him. 'He's a singularly amenable child and will go with anyone—once approved!'

'And you think I'm approved?'

She smiled softly at the eagerness in his voice.

'Very much so! He almost talked his head off after tea. Didn't you notice?'

'What he said was interesting. I'm sure we shall get on famously together.'

Helen rose to her feet.

'I wish I could say the same about my interview with my in-laws!' she laughed. 'Somehow, I think it will be an interview.'

'You'll hold your own,' he said confidently—even admiringly.

CHAPTER THREE

IF I could be *sure* that I would hold my own! Helen Oliver thought two days later as she set out on the first stage of her journey to meet her sister-in-law. But why should I feel nervous at the thought of Ken's sister? After all, we should get on well together, if only for the reason that she *is* his sister. Strange, though, how she had always felt, even from the beginning, that Ken's thoughts of his eldest sister were more respectful than loving! And that impression of Jean Oliver's dominating character had been gained long before she had arrived at the Keep and heard what Fergus Oliver had to say.

She thought about Fergus now, sitting back in her corner of the carriage where he had settled her comfortably for the journey, thinking that they might have known each other for a lifetime instead of for the short span of two days. He had been easy to know because of that genuine quality about him that shone through his shyness, and she still could not understand how things had gone wrong between him and Margaret Oliver.

It made her all the more eager to meet Margaret, who had been Ken's favourite, and she wondered if she would do so before the day was out. Fergus had not repeated his plea of that first evening under his roof that she should try to obtain the Olivers' address for him, but she knew that he still hoped she would bring it back with her. The desire had been mirrored in these frank eyes of his when he had stood back from the carriage door as the train had moved away, and she was determined to do what she could for him. She wondered for a moment if Jean Oliver was the sort of woman who would respond to a direct appeal and then considered it unlikely. More than once, Fergus had told her, he had appealed to Jean Oliver in vain.

It was strange, especially when they had known each other for so many years, she mused, thinking that Fergus was the type who would very soon gain everyone's liking and sympathy in his cause—as she herself had been pressed into service!

Smiling at the thought, she accepted the role of go-between because it now appeared that she was definitely committed to it—at least, in her own mind!

Thinking so much about Fergus Oliver's affairs and the future of the Keep had given her a new interest, and all day yesterday she had watched happily while Tony had light-heartedly adopted the Keep as his new home, showing a child's instant delight in everything—running down the road to meet Fergus when he came in for a meal; shouting from high, unexpected places with the joyful, carefree spirit that is every child's birthright and had been subdued in him too long, and racing across the heather and young bracken with an abandonment which delighted the watching Helen. All these things personified freedom in her mind, and she saw with a sigh of thankfulness the wild rose colour which the winds from the hill painted on his cheeks. This, indeed, was recompense for many things, and these wide spaces were clearing her mind of the cramped thoughts born in a prison-camp and the fresh winds blowing free across these hills which Ken had loved were as balm to her bruised spirit, but above all, they were health to Tony and that was everything. Here she would rest for a little while before she took up her journey again.

Lying back in her corner as the train sped quickly northwards, her thoughts of the future were vague because she had accepted the peace of the present for the time being. One day she would go south and visit Aunt Anna in Yorkshire, who was her sole remaining relative, but that day was in the future. Perhaps she would call there on her way to London, or somewhere else in the south, if she decided to settle in England, but just at present she could not make up her mind. Unlike most of the other women in the home-bound boat, she had had no roots in England—only the vague feeling that she must go to Oliver's Keep—and that feeling had mercifully kept her from brooding over the fact that she was entirely without a plan for the future. She was free in a sense that she did not want to feel free. She was alone.

But that wasn't strictly true, she reminded herself firmly, as the train drew steadily nearer her destination. There was Tony. Passionately she hugged the thought to her, and as she closed her eyes for an instant she could see again a swaying lifeboat and a man bending over the side of a burning ship to place his child in her arms. Vividly she could see the face above her as a searchlight flashed across the water catching them both in its cold, revealing light; she could see the marks of fatigue, and the lean, hollow cheeks and the firm line of the mouth, but above all stood the memory of the keen, searching eyes which had held hers for an instant and had seemed to go probing down into her very soul to find the goodness in her and the compassion.

'You'll take care of him? His name is Tony. His mother died when he was born. There are some papers—wrapped in the blanket . . .'

One last look at his child and the dark waters were widening between them. For ever? Helen gave an involuntary shiver, forcing her mind away from the thought as she had done so often in the past. There had never been any contact between them and the bundle of papers must have slipped from the child's blanket as he was passed down into yet another lifeboat. She knew nothing of Tony except that he belonged to a man who would have loved and cherished him all his life. Somehow, she felt sure of that, although the knowledge had been born of a moment's contact only, for such moments can be more revealing than the accumulated. knowledge of years. And Tony had come to her to fill a gap in her life at a time when she most needed him.

Once more she wondered what she would have done without him during all those long years of captivity. The women in the camp who had had children to care for had been more than blessed.

'We're nearly at Waverley now,' she heard the girl in the far corner of the carriage explaining to the young Canadian airman at her side.

They had sat together all through the journey with fingers interlocked and glances crossing so frequently that it had scarcely been necessary to look at the girl's ungloved left hand where a narrow gold band gleamed brightly on the third finger to discover that they were on the first stage of a honeymoon, and Helen's thoughts rushed headlong back to just such another journey in a local train on the other side of the world when she had sat hand in hand with Kenneth Oliver, looking into his eyes with the same smile as the girl in the corner turned upon the young Canadian now.

She rose to put on her coat, the sharp pain of memory stabbing into her heart, and then her chin lifted determinedly and she turned her thoughts to the coming meeting with her sister-in-law, wondering if the Oliver women were living in Edinburgh and, if so, why Jean Oliver had not asked her to come direct to the house.

The sun was shining as she walked up from the dim cavern of the station on to Princes Street and she looked about her with interest. Often, in that far corner of the world which had been their home for a little space in time, Ken had described Edinburgh to her, vividly, as all true Scotsmen see it, Edinburgh that is like no other city in the world, with its contrasts of old and new backed by the green massif of Arthur's Seat and dominated by its grey castle, bold in strong sunlight or dreaming through mist, gaunt and austere against a grey sky, or smiling in the gloaming hour a little wistfully, as if regretting the passing of all the pageant and pomp of which it had once been part. She had envisaged Princes Street in many a dream as it stood now before her, the gardens resplendent in new green, the beds flaunting their gay colours in the sunlight, and always the castle gazing down from its craggy eminence, but she had never dreamed to come upon it alone, and from somewhere, unbidden, came the thought that Jean Oliver might have made the effort to meet her at the station.

She found the restaurant her sister-in-law had mentioned without difficulty, however, and made her way up the thickly carpeted staircase to the ladies' lounge where, the moment she entered and without any hesitation, a tall woman in dark tweeds came straight towards her.

'You're Kenneth's wife,' she said decisively, holding out a gloved hand. 'I am Jean Oliver.'

'Oh—how do you do?' Helen felt her fingers crushed in a firm handclasp which might have been a man's. 'I wasn't quite sure how we were going to recognise each other.'

'Kenneth sent us a snapshot of you when you were first married and I never forget a face.' Jean Oliver made the statement as her glance travelled beyond her brother's young widow, and Helen saw her frown. 'Where is the boy?' she asked. 'Tony, I think you called him. A strange name for an Oliver and one I should hardly have expected Kenneth to choose for his son.'

A sudden hot flush spread over Helen's cheeks, receding instantly to leave her paler than before.

'I haven't brought him,' she said stumblingly. 'You see, I have something to explain to you, Miss Oliver. Could we —sit down somewhere?'

Conscious of a swiftly penetrating glance from the vivid blue eyes of the older woman, Helen followed her across the lounge into the restaurant beyond where a waiter escorted them to the table which had been reserved for them. Jean Oliver picked up the menu card and handed it across the white cloth to her sister-in-law.

'Will you order what you would like?' she suggested. 'I'll have my usual, Fothergill,' she added to the waiter, who took Helen's order, remarked that Miss Oliver was getting a nice day for her visit, and moved silently away.

Which meant, Helen thought, that the Olivers were living out of the capital, which was something to be going on with. No doubt she would know just where before they parted this afternoon.

'I am disappointed that you did not bring the boy,' Jean Oliver said. 'I have been looking forward very much to seeing him and, of course, you realise that your coming home with a son will make a great deal of difference to Oliver's Keep.'

The waiter was approaching with their soup and Helen could not immediately reply. Instead she took the time to study her sister-in-law, seeing a vigorous and well-preserved woman in her late forties with hair severely cut in a style once known as 'the shingle,' which gave her a rather masculine appearance, added to by her strictly tailored jacket and high-collared blouse. She had unpinned the scarf which she had worn like a stock, and Helen recognised the Oliver crest on the brooch with which it had been fastened, seeing reflected therein all this woman's pride of lineage, her hopes and fears and plans for Oliver's Keep, which she was now about to shatter by a few brief words of explanation.

In that moment she felt sorry for Jean Oliver, and never in the days which followed was she to lose that first sense of pity which understanding brought. Jean Oliver was, in truth, one of those unfortunate people who are destined to go lonely to the grave because of some flaw in their nature that will never wholly admit another into absolute confidence, a woman whom the thoughtless might dismiss as being without a heart or any genuine feeling, but Helen recognised that all her capacity for loving had been bottled up within her to be shed eventually upon Oliver's Keep, as it might have been shed upon the husband and family which had been denied her. She had become possessive and proud and aloof, carrying her loyalty to family tradition and the past to fantastic lengths which might have warped a mind and character less strong than her own, but which had only turned her bitter and a little scornful of the softer emotions of the world.

'You said you had something to explain,' she prompted, frowning over her soup. 'Would you rather talk now or wait until we have our coffee in the lounge?'

Helen met her eyes squarely.

'It's something I think you should know right away,' she said. 'It's—about Tony. He's not my son. He's a child I brought home from Singapore.'

The blue eyes registered Jean Oliver's shock and disappointment, but she said steadily,

'Go on.'

'He—I think he is an orphan and I am trying to adopt him, but I'm afraid I have no proof that his father is dead.

All I know about him is that he was on a boat going into Singapore as we were coming out and he handed Tony to safety when our lifeboat was pulling away. He asked me to take care of him.'

'And you have no idea whatever who or where this man may be?' The blue eyes were searching, indecisive. 'But surely he gave you some clue to his identity?'

'There were papers,' Helen explained, 'wrapped in the baby's blanket, but we were in rough sea and all I can think is that they must have fallen overboard in the darkness and drifted away. But that doesn't make any difference,' she declared stoutly. 'It only makes it more imperative that I should stand by Tony for always now.'

Jean Oliver said, 'Of course,' but much of the warmth had gone out of her. There was no hint of the suppressed excitement which had burned in her eyes at the first moment of their meeting when she had hardly been able to wait before she inquired about the child, and it seemed to Helen as if something cold and almost tangible had risen between them, an indifference so utterly chilling that she did not know how to contend with it and was silent.

The older woman drew in a deep breath.

'I must admit your news has dealt me a severe blow,' she confessed at last, 'and I can't quite think how my—informant in Burndean could have made such a mistake.'

Helen smiled wistfully.

'Perhaps it was the most natural mistake anyone could have made,' she said, and then added deliberately, 'Fergus made it too, you see. When he first saw Tony he felt sure he was Ken's son, and welcomed him gladly.'

Jean Oliver stiffened, her blue eyes becoming suddenly watchful, and it was apparent that she was not prepared to discuss her distant cousin or his reactions to a possible new heir, and suddenly Helen was convinced that this was not the trouble which lay between these two. Jean Oliver had accepted Fate's bludgeonings, her head unbowed, but she would never forget a blow to her pride, an injury to what she considered was the family honour, and such a blow had been dealt unwittingly by Fergus when he had listened to the voice of his own conscience and tried to explain it to the girl he loved.

'Tell me about your journey,' Miss Oliver commanded, 'and then we must have our coffee and a look at the shops before we go out to Collister to tea. My sister—Isobel—is confined to the house after a severe chill and Hattie is looking after her, but they would both like to meet you.'

Hattie and Isobel, but no word of Margaret! Well, thought Helen, all things could not come their way at once, and at least she would have an address to give Fergus when she returned to the Keep!

The fact made her feel a little more cheerful as she followed her sister-in-law into the ladies' lounge, where they were to take their coffee, and she wondered if perhaps Fergus had not been slightly exaggerating the position in defence of his own hurt pride. Then, quite abruptly, Jean Oliver turned to her and said,

'I must be frank with you, my dear. Neither myself nor my sisters think it very desirable for you to be staying at the Keep just now, and we should be pleased to offer you a home at Collister.'

Completely taken aback, Helen could only stare at her for a moment until she had collected her thoughts, and then she flushed scarlet.

'But what can be wrong about going to the Keep, or staying there on Fergus's invitation?' she asked.

' Not wrong—but undesirable,' Jean returned firmly.

'Because?'

'Since you press me, because, as a family, we are not in agreement and because, as long as you stay there, I shall feel that our relationship is going to be—slightly strained.' Jean Oliver pushed her coffee-cup aside, resting her arms along the table between them and looking intently across its glass surface into the eyes of this stranger her brother had married. 'I want you to make your home at Collister and, since you have decided to adopt this child, although you have no definite knowledge of his parentage, I shall undertake his education and accept him as one of the family for your sake.'

It was a generous offer, Helen acknowledged, but behind it she sensed a will of steel, the will that had broken down a young girl's resistance, chaining Margaret Oliver's happiness to the pillory of pride and condemning Fergus Oliver to a loneliness which would one day shatter the peace and prosperity that now was Oliver's Keep.

And because she was part of the Keep, because, through the man she had loved and married, she had become an Oliver, Helen was suddenly determined to fight this thing which overshadowed all their happiness. She knew that her task would be no easy one, nor the way made smooth for her, but she possessed a determination almost as strong as the woman's who sat facing her across the table awaiting an answer to her surprising proposition, and she gave her answer firmly.

'It's kind of you,' she said, 'but I have already promised Fergus to stay at the Keep. He has asked me to help him to get things straight, to make it as it should be, and I couldn't possibly go back on him. You see, he wants to keep it as it was before you left—as he always remembered it.'

She knew that she had been making an appeal on Fergus's behalf, and Jean Oliver also knew it, but she felt that the older woman would not despise it because it had lacked subtlety. The blue eyes, although they remained frosty, held a certain admiration for the way in which her brother's young widow had stood by her guns, even although they were part of Fergus Oliver's artillery. There was no softening about Jean Oliver, however, and she had no intention of letting anyone talk her into a sympathy with the heir to Oliver's Keep. Long ago she had made up her mind; the rules were laid down and there was no more to be said.

'For the Keep's sake,' she returned coldly, 'I can only wish him success, but you know, of course, that he hasn't the money to carry on as my father did—as we could have done if we had not been—uprooted.'

'At least he has the will to do all he can,' Helen answered, wondering if the loss of the Keep had exaggerated this woman's objections to Fergus, 'and I should feel that I was letting him down terribly if I went back on my word now. There's absolutely no one to help him to get the Keep straight—no woman—'

'I understood that he had employed one of our late servants,' Jean said mildly, not attempting to conceal the fact that she possessed up-to-the-minute information of all that went on at Burndean, as her knowledge of Helen's arrival amply proved.

'Yes, there's Mrs Michie,' Helen admitted, 'and she's a splendid housekeeper, but Fergus needs something more than a housekeeper. He needs the advice and understanding of a woman who will see the Keep as a trust—'

She broke off, although her eyes did not fall before the look in the other woman's.

'Forgive me if all this is—distasteful to you,' she went on impulsively, 'but I had to say it.'

'And I've let you have your say,' Jean Oliver returned. 'I've always maintained that everyone is entitled to their own opinion, however contrary it may run to mine—everyone, that is, outside the family circle.' She bent over the table, fixing Helen with a level, commanding look. 'And that brings me to my point. Whatever way you care to look at it, my dear, you *are* one of the family and, as my brother's wife, do you think it fitting that you should continue to remain at the Keep rather than come to Collister where we are prepared to make you welcome for Kenneth's sake?'

But not for my own! thought Helen, although she could think it without chagrin.

'I should like to come to Collister,' she said, 'and perhaps you will let me visit you quite often while I am so near Edinburgh, but Tony has just got nicely settled down at the Keep and I think I shall stay there for a week or two until he is rested after our long journey. I don't think—Ken would mind me living in his old home.'

Even with Fergus in possession! The words had been on the tip of Helen's tongue, but she would not utter them, preferring not to add anything further to the embitterment between these two. She considered them unkind, too, because subconsciously she knew that Jean Oliver had risen above her disappointment and sense of loss over the Keep, and that it was a personal issue that alone rose between her and Fergus, the insult which she considered he had inflicted upon their family pride. Although she could have quite cheerfully shaken Fergus for his part in the blunder, she knew it was not going to be so easy to approach Jean Oliver or attempt to explain matters away to her.

But why was she constantly thinking in terms of Jean when Margaret was the real one concerned? Surely it could not mean that she had subconsciously accepted Jean Oliver's as the final word on all things, as her entire household seemed to do? Surely she had not already succumbed to this dominating personality who ruled the Oliver fortunes and—presumably—the lives of all the Oliver women under her roof? She had no intention of becoming one of those women, and although Jean Oliver had nobly taken up the burden of family responsibility after her father's death, Helen considered it was no reason why she should have become hard and unbending and so terribly overbearing.

'My brother was very proud of his home,' Jean Oliver said, rising from the table, 'and unfailingly loyal to his family.'

A tremor ran through Helen at the stern implication in the quietly-spoken words. Her sister-in-law evidently considered it disloyalty on her part to stay at the Keep, but in her own mind it would have been equally disloyal to desert Fergus after she had given him her word to stay. She knew that her promise had given him a strange sort of courage. He was no longer alone; there was someone else who cared about the old place, who would help him to get it straight, someone to whom he could turn for companionship and a woman's understanding of these things.

Helen glanced at her companion. She was drawing on her gloves, substantial leather gauntlets that had seen many a day's wear and were good for many more. Like all Scotswomen, she carried her tweeds with an air; they were worn but not shabby, and her sports felt hat was enlivened by a jaunty sprig of feathers fastened in with a miniature silver dirk. She was a grand type, really, one of an older generation whose poise and standards Helen had always admired, and she felt it a pity that the bitter misunderstanding of so many years ago should threaten to spoil their friendship.

'I thought you would like a look at the shops,' Jean suggested, apparently dismissing the subject of the Keep, although Helen was sure it must still be well to the front of her agile mind, and for the next hour they wandered along the wide pavement of Princes Street on the shopping side, Helen making a few small purchases for Tony here and there, while her sister-in-law looked on without comment.

'How old is this boy?' she asked as she led the way to the square where she had parked her car.

'About six, I should say.' Helen's voice softened. 'It's strange not knowing his birthday—and rather sad, but we've invented one for next week. Hence the toys!'

'You've taken on a great responsibility,' Jean Oliver observed, unlocking the car door, 'but perhaps you're very fond of children? It's a great pity the boy was not your own.'

Helen swallowed hard.

'Nothing would have pleased me better,' she said, 'but I don't think Tony need ever feel that he has missed anything.' She got into the car. 'He's a grand little fellow—older than his years, I suppose, but I'm sure you would like him. If I may, I would like to bring him to see you next time I come to Edinburgh.'

Jean Oliver did not seem very interested, but perhaps it was just because she was a careful driver and was watching the traffic as she made her way with the stream towards the city's outskirts.

They went by way of the Braids, and Helen looked about her with interest. Now and then her companion flung her a word or two of explanation as they passed this landmark or that, but it was evident that Miss Oliver did not believe in committing herself to long conversations while at the wheel, and this arrangement Helen found satisfactory enough, because to talk pointlessly was not her way and when there was scenery to be enjoyed she generally preferred to enjoy it in silence.

The houses began to thin out and they were almost in open country before the car was pushed into second gear and guided up a winding hill. Half-way up Jean Oliver turned expertly in between two ivy-crowned gate-posts and brought the car to a standstill at the end of a gravelled sweep of drive with a sigh of satisfaction.

'I must confess it,' she remarked. 'I'm never wholly at ease driving through traffic, but one has very little choice these days with a chauffeur out of the question and Margaret away from home.'

It was the first time she had directly mentioned her youngest sister and Helen said eagerly,

'I had been hoping to meet Margaret.'

'She's nursing,' Jean Oliver replied abruptly. 'She spends very little time at home now. Sometimes we get her to tea—always very unexpectedly.'

It almost seemed as if Margaret was bent on making her own life, at last, Helen mused, and behind the thought lay a strange urgency, so that she felt she must meet Margaret Oliver soon. There seemed no time to be lost.

'Nursing is still her war job, I suppose?'

Jean Oliver smiled as she inserted her latchkey into the lock of the massive studded door at the top of the flight of stone steps.

'Yes, but she's always been interested in that sort of thing and at one time she wanted to study medicine. However, I firmly disapproved. I have no use for women doctors, and no faith in them.'

And so Margaret had been forced to become a nurse so that she might satisfy the urge in her to serve her fellow-men! Away at the back of Helen's mind a sudden impatience stirred, yet as suddenly she was remembering that portrait in the long gallery at the Keep, remembering the determined chin and proud lift of the head that characterised it and knowing that she had seen it all reflected, feature for feature, in the snapshot of Margaret Oliver which Ken had carried about with him. No, she could not imagine Margaret as weak, as giving in easily even to such a strong will as Jean Oliver undoubtedly possessed, and probably the determination in Margaret was latent and had not yet exerted itself in full measure. What would happen when it did she could not guess, but something about Jean Oliver's tight-lipped mouth as they entered the hall told her that there had already been signs of rebellion—probably promptly dealt with but distinctly annoying for all that.

They were in a large, square hall lighted by a high, stained-glass window half-way up a broad staircase, circular in shape, with finely-wrought iron supporting a gleaming brass handrail which seemed to reflect back all the light from the windows in a golden glow. Jean Oliver grasped it and motioned her sister-in-law to follow her upstairs.

'I've given orders that tea will be served in Isobel's room,' she explained, and to Helen that remark seemed typical. 'I've given orders'!

The thickly-carpeted stairs led to a broad landing with a corridor branching right and left and a wide oak door immediately facing them, on which Jean Oliver tapped briskly and went in.

'I hope you're not asleep, Isobel,' she said in a tone which suggested the act would have been an offence, and the occupant of the room laughed.

It was a queer, conciliatory laugh, Helen thought, half-apologetic, as if the owner of it was ashamed to have been caught on the point of sleep when it was not expected of her.

'Of course not, Jean. I was expecting you back for tea. Millie has just been up with the tray.'

Jean Oliver drew her visitor forward.

'Isobel, this is Kenneth's wife.'

Helen found herself looking across the width of the room into a pair of pale grey eyes which at first she thought entirely expressionless. They gave Isobel Oliver's face a curiously blank look, as if she had withdrawn into herself, nursing some vague grievance which she had never been strong enough to put into words, yet they were eyes which were quick to perceive and ready to criticise, Helen realised, as she felt their keen scrutiny bent upon her.

'We expected you to bring the boy,' Isobel said, her tone frankly accusing as she looked towards her elder sister for confirmation.

'I have been explaining to—Jean about Tony,' Helen said, sitting down on a chair facing Isobel's across the hearth. 'I know you must all be frightfully disappointed, and I'm so very sorry—'

'The child apparently isn't Kenneth's,' Jean Oliver cut in abruptly as she discarded her hat and gloves, 'so we must just face up to our disappointment in that respect, Isobel.'

'But I don't understand,' her sister began. 'We were told on the very best authority that you had arrived in Burndean with your son—'

'As I have explained, Isobel,' Jean Oliver broke in impatiently, 'he is not Kenneth's son. He is a child Helen intends to adopt. She rescued him in Singapore at the time of our defeat there, she tells me.'

The flush of excitement which had coloured Isobel Oliver's cheeks at their entry receded, leaving her very pale.

'What bad luck,' she said. 'We thought your arrival had changed a great many things, but now—'

'Wallowing in regret won't make the situation any different,' Jean Oliver cut in sharply. 'We must face the facts, and after all they are no more unpleasant now than they were a week ago. A mistake has been made. That is all.'

Helen was beginning to feel uncomfortable. It was almost as if she had cheated these people. At least, that was how Isobel made her feel, because the blank look had now given place to one of definite hostility and Isobel Oliver's rather thin lips were tightly compressed.

'If you have not brought the child with you, where is he?' she asked.

'I've left him at the Keep,' Helen explained. 'He's with Fergus.'

The name had the effect of electrifying Isobel, but once more it was to her sister she looked, as if for guidance.

'Helen has decided to stay at the Keep for a week or two on our cousin's invitation,' she was told acidly. 'Of course, I have explained that I should prefer her to make her home here with us, but that must be entirely her own decision.'

Isobel's eyes filled with surprise, and then she looked past them both to the opening door.

'Well, Hattie,' she said with a queer sort of satisfaction in her brittle voice, 'you're just in time to hear the news!'

Helen turned to greet Kenneth's third sister, knowing that, next to Margaret, he had liked Hattie best. She was but eleven months his senior and they had always been friends, but it was difficult for Helen to imagine this Hattie as her husband's gay and youthful companion. She was a true Oliver—more like Kenneth than any of the others—with the characteristic high-bridged nose that was an asset in the men of the family though scarcely an attribute to a woman. Jean Oliver had also inherited it, but its boldness became her, somehow, or perhaps it had even moulded her character along those strong lines, bringing out the determined streak in her nature that was so curiously mannish. In Hattie it was a lost feature, apologised for by soft brown eyes and full, childish lips, and a chin that just missed being firm. There was a subdued sweetness about Hattie Oliver that Helen recognised and liked immediately, hoping that one day she could draw it out. At present Hattie looked crushed, although not unhappy.

'Hattie is our housekeeper,' Jean explained. 'She enjoys being in charge in the kitchen and the sick-room, don't you, Hattie?'

'Very much.' Hattie came towards Helen, her hand outstretched. 'I've been looking forward to meeting you,' she said, stretching up to place a shy kiss on her sister-in-law's cheek.

It was the first attempt at an embrace Helen had received since her return to Britain and sudden, foolish tears stung her eyes as she looked down into Hattie's apologetic face.

'I'm glad, Hattie,' she said, and then could say no more because of the sudden constriction in her throat and the reflection of her own tears in Hattie Oliver's eyes. This was Hattie. This was Hattie, whom Kenneth had loved . . .

'The wee lad? Have you got him with you?' Hattie asked eagerly, while from behind her came a small exclamation of impatience.

'This must all be very embarrassing for Helen, I'm sure,' Jean said. 'The child isn't hers, Hattie. Helen is merely adopting him. He's an orphan laddie she picked up in Singapore. It's very noble of her. I'm quite sure we all agree about that.'

There was a murmur of assent, but only Hattie's eyes were on Helen's face and they were full of a deep sympathy and understanding.

'It's wonderful for you,' she said, 'having something to hold on to out of the wreckage.'

'Yes, yes, Hattie,' Jean interrupted before Helen could speak, 'we all realise that, but there's no need to be melodramatic about it. Helen's life isn't entirely wrecked. She is young enough to marry again, although naturally not for some time yet.' She fixed Helen with a steady glance, as if to impress her will upon her in that direction, at least. It would not, in the eyes of Jean Oliver's world, be correct for the young widow of her brother to 'forget' him before a year or two had elapsed which would be duly hallowed by his memory. 'And now,' she added briskly, 'do you think we might have tea, Hattie?'

Her sister crossed to the window, hesitating as she looked down on to the short sweep of drive which led up from the front gates.

'I was wondering if Margaret might be coming this afternoon,' she said in a tentative attempt to hold up the meal for half an hour longer. 'She often drops in on a Friday.'

'She phoned yesterday to say she didn't think she could come,' Jean informed her abruptly.

'But, surely—if she knew about Helen's visit—'

'Margaret, I'm afraid, has her own interests these days and has very little sense of duty,' her sister said calmly. 'No doubt she has arranged to go somewhere with Hamilton Purdie.'

The remark, although it was ostensibly made to Hattie, seemed to be directed towards Helen in some peculiar way and Hamilton Purdie's name—whoever he might be—rang in her mind like a warning bell as the conversation drifted to her experiences in the East before and during the war and Hattie went off to attend to the tea.

Ten minutes later she came back into the room, followed by a young maid, who seemed immediately nervous in Jean Oliver's presence, although she looked slightly reassured when Hattie turned to her with a smile.

'All right, Millie, I'll manage now. We'll boil the kettle up here. On you go and have your own tea, and if Miss Margaret comes, send her straight up.'

'Yes, miss,' agreed Millie and departed with a sidelong glance in Jean's direction.

'You'll never train that girl,' Jean remarked, seating herself at the head of the small table Hattie had moved in towards the fire where Isobel and Helen were already seated. 'She'll learn to think of herself first and us afterwards. Better leave her to me.'

'All right, Jean.' Hattie sighed. 'But I thought she was doing fine.'

'She's been doing absolutely as she likes round here for weeks,' Isobel put in unpleasantly. 'And turning insolent into the bargain. When I asked her to bring me up the *Scotsman* this morning she said she had something to get for Hattie out of the linen-room first and that she'd bring the paper up next time she came!'

Jean lifted the massive silver teapot Hattie had placed before her from its stand and glanced across the hearth at her sister.

'You know I bring the *Scotsman* up as soon as ever I have finished it,' she said, 'and Hattie and that girl are running this house between them where several maids would have been employed before the war. You can't expect miracles of people, Isobel. I'll see that you have your papers, and anything else you need to read.' She turned to their visitor, seemingly oblivious of the painful flush mounting to Isobel's face and the twisted, bitter mouth as her sister suppressed the retort that had been on the tip of her tongue. 'Sugar, Helen?' she asked. 'Or did you learn not to take it in your prison-camp? I haven't touched it myself since the last war.'

'I'm afraid I've learnt to take it again,' Helen apologised, feeling the strained atmosphere like some dark cloud descending on a sunny day. 'I always did love sugar.'

'Was it very dreadful in the camp?' Hattie asked, coming close to sit down beside her. 'I shudder every time I think of you there—and that poor child! Whatever must it have been like for him?'

'He was little more than a baby when he went there,' Helen explained. 'He knew nothing else, and, on the whole, we weren't too badly treated.'

She went on to describe the lighter side of camp life, laughing as she lived again these brighter moments when some brave spirit had rallied them all under the banner of humour, reminding them that they were women of Britain and stirring all their pride in the fact so that it overcame frayed nerves and loneliness and worry about loved ones in the world outside and brought back to life again the will to endure.

Jean listened intently, deeply interested, putting in a word of comment here and there and asking a question or two until voices were heard in the hall below and the slamming of a heavy door.

'That must be Margaret!' Hattie exclaimed eagerly, jumping to her feet. 'I'll run and get another cup.'

'Margaret knows her way upstairs,' Jean said mildly, 'and Millie can bring the extra cup,' but behind the mildness of the tone lay an undercurrent of command which Helen could not fail to recognise. Hattie sat down again with a sigh.

Presumably they were not allowed to make a fuss of Margaret on her odd visits home, Helen mused, sipping her tea while she became conscious of a swift stirring of excitement at the prospect of meeting Margaret Oliver at last.

The room was suddenly very still: Isobel lay back among

her cushions looking intently at Jean, while Hattie bent to plug in the electric kettle at the side of the fire and Jean herself sat stiffly upright in her chair looking towards the door expectantly. Then, quite clearly, a man's voice drifted to them along the corridor, a deep, incisive voice, low and wholly attractive.

'This may appear an intrusion on my part, Meg—'

'Of course, it won't! You know Jean adores you!'

The girl's voice was teasing and full of laughter. Margaret's voice! Helen found herself smiling involuntarily and looked up from her teacup to find Jean Oliver smiling, too. It was a little, indulgent smile which said she was pleased and immensely gratified at the thought of her second visitor, and before the door opened to admit him she had just time to say, looking across the hearth at Isobel,

'This is the first time Margaret has brought Hamilton Purdie to tea without letting us know beforehand. I wonder if that means she has news for us?'

'That—they are engaged?' The words left Hattie's lips like a signal of alarm. 'But—'

Jean silenced her with a look as the door swung open and a small, dark girl in nurse's uniform stood framed in the aperture.

'Hullo, everyone!' Her bright eyes swept across the room to the invalid. 'Better, Isobel?' she asked. 'Anyway, I've brought Hammy to have a look at you.'

Jean Oliver rose stiffly to her feet, her heavy brows drawn swiftly together, and it was evident that 'Hammy' was the greatest form of disrespect in her eyes. Helen looked at Margaret's companion, seeing a man in his early forties, dark and distinguished-looking, with calm grey eyes and a thin, clever face, the gravity of which was redeemed by a mobile mouth, turned up now in a whimsical smile as he looked in on the little tea-party.

'You'll forgive me for coming in uninvited?' he asked Jean in his pleasantly deep voice. 'I met Meg in the library and she demanded a lift out. The buses were crowded.'

'You know you are welcome at any time,' Jean assured him, smiling. 'Come away in and Hattie will make us some fresh tea. Margaret,'—she turned to Helen's corner—'I've a surprise for you. This is Kenneth's wife.'

'Helen!' Margaret's eyes were warm and friendly as they faced each other across the room and then she came forward and kissed Helen as Hattie had done. 'But this is wonderful! When did you come? Have you just arrived—and why wasn't I told? But Jean probably met you. Have you just arrived in England?'

The eagerness in Margaret was like a fresh, invigorating wind blowing across parched grass in that quiet room and Helen knew that this was what she had expected Ken's youngest sister to be like.

'I've been in England about a fortnight,' she said, and then, on a sudden impulse, 'I'm staying at the Keep.'

She saw the colour flood into Margaret's cheeks and some of the laughter die in her eyes.

'Oh,' she said uncertainly, 'I had no idea.'

Desperately Helen wondered if she had done the wrong thing to mention the Keep, but Margaret had to know that she was staying there, and once this girl with the deep-set eyes and proudly held head had loved Fergus Oliver. Helen found herself looking at her present escort and wondering what part Hamilton Purdie now played in her life. Could Margaret have changed? And was this the man who now held her heart, this successful, dignified man who surely belonged to one of the professions and who looked as if he had already attained the top on his chosen one? Vaguely the name seemed familiar. Hamilton Purdie. Should she have recognised it—known who he was?

Margaret turned towards him.

'Helen,' she said shyly, 'this is—a great friend of mine—Mr Purdie. Hamilton—my brother's wife.'

Purdie came across the room to shake Helen's hand.

'I've heard about your ordeal, Mrs Oliver,' he said, his eyes grave and slightly searching as they looked down into hers, 'and I'm glad you have come home. It won't be long before you will be able to put most of your unfortunate experiences behind you, I hope. Fortunately, we forget these sort of privations easily when we are young.'

'It wasn't so very bad,' Helen said, looking up into his

keen, strong face and struggling with a memory. 'There were—compensations and so many of us in the same boat that one couldn't really squeal too loudly!'

Hamilton Purdie? The name was linked with something in her mind, something which had held her interest long ago. It seemed to be connected with her own profession . . . And then she remembered! A paper in the *Lancet* read in the shade of a banyan tree and, under the heading, this man's name! That was it! Hamilton Purdie, the eminent Edinburgh authority on diseases of the brain! And once, long ago, Ken had mentioned that Hattie knew him.

Helen glanced across the room to where Hattie was busying herself with the teapot, surprising an expression of pain in her quiet eyes from which she looked hastily away as after some unpardonable intrusion, and Hattie bent over the tea-tray with her back to Hamilton Purdie for a moment while he turned to say a few words to Isobel.

'You'll have to take more care of yourself . . .'

'Helen,' Jean commanded, 'draw in that chair beside yours for Mr Purdie and—oh, here comes Millie with some more scones. We might almost have known you were coming this afternoon,' she added as the tall man turned back towards the fire and sat down in the chair Helen had placed for him, 'they're your favourites!'

'Hattie's baking?' he asked with a smile in the direction of the tea-tray that was gentle and kindly, and Helen saw Hattie Oliver blush violently as she came forward with his teacup. It was a painful blush, spreading to the very roots of her hair, and Helen sensed that Hattie was angry with herself for not having been able to control it.

Hamilton Purdie's attention had been mercifully claimed by Jean, however, but Isobel, lying back in her cushioned chair, with her eyes half-closed like those of a drowsing cat who yet watches for the moment to spring, saw the blush and smiled a cruel, tight-lipped little smile of secret satisfaction. Helen saw the smile and hated Isobel for it. She also saw Hattie as the essential Martha, serving these others unobtrusively, with her own thoughts locked away in her secret heart. Would she ever rebel? She could not be much more than thirty, yet she had already been accepted as an old maid by Jean and Isobel, at least, drawn into their circle, one of the three unmarried Misses Oliver of Collister, handsome, admirable women, good in their own way, and thirled to each other by strong family bonds which Jean firmly believed nothing could ever break. If she had her doubts about Margaret's allegiance, she rarely expressed them, but she was sure of Hattie and Isobel.

Gradually the conversation swung round to Margaret's hospital work, and Helen found herself involved in a long and interesting discussion with Margaret and Hamilton Purdie, forgetful of time and the fact that she had to make a journey back to the Borders. It was Jean who finally reminded her that her train left in less than an hour.

Margaret jumped to her feet.

'Goodness! is it that time already?' she exclaimed, looking about for the cap she had discarded when she came in and seeming to avoid her eldest sister's eyes as she did so with a strange sort of determination which suggested that there might be a silent battle of wills in progress. 'I'll come to the train with you, Helen,' she offered. 'I'm going that way.'

Jean Oliver rose to her feet.

'That will be fine, Margaret,' she observed dryly. 'Mr. Purdie will see you as far as the station, I'm sure.'

Margaret looked across the room in Hamilton Purdie's direction and flushed.

'Of course—I'd forgotten,' she said.

Instantly Helen felt that Margaret had wanted to make the journey with her alone, and as surely she knew that, had Hamilton Purdie not been available to make a third, Jean Oliver would have come to the station with them herself. But why? Why? Could it possibly be because she suspected that Margaret sought news of her cousin? Helen's pulses quickened at the thought. Perhaps Hamilton Purdie meant nothing to Margaret, after all. Perhaps she still cared for Fergus deep down in her heart where even Jean could not reach with all her talk of pride and allegiance.

She *must* care for him! Helen's mouth was suddenly determined. But how could she find out short of asking Margaret point-blank? Well, maybe she could even do that one day, although today Hamilton Purdie would be an undoubted obstacle.

She could not dislike him, however, even on that score. He was that rare thing, a modest genius, and there was no doubt that Margaret, with her sparkling vitality and keen wit, held a deep attraction for him, yet sometimes as he had looked at her he had seemed to draw back within himself, as if some invisible barrier had suddenly been raised between them. Was it, Helen wondered, that barrier of years which no thinking man could ever deny? Margaret was twenty-five: Hamilton Purdie might be twenty years older than that, yet the years sat lightly upon him, and his personal magnetism was a thing which even Helen had felt on sight.

She said goodbye to Isobel with a few conventional words, hoping for her quick recovery and realising that she liked Isobel least of all Ken's sisters. There was something hidden about her, a grievance nursed in secret, perhaps, and her thin lips did not part as she smiled.

'We'll be seeing you again, I suppose,' she said stiltedly and without any warmth in her voice. 'I may be well enough to meet you in Edinburgh with Jean next time, although we don't go very often to town.'

Jean held out her hand, saying abruptly,

'Well, you know how I feel about the Keep, Helen, but even though you continue to stay there we expect to see you in Edinburgh sometimes. I shall continue to make you welcome—so long as you are not a carrier of news from point to point.'

There could be no mistaking the implication in her words, Helen thought. Indeed, it was no implication at all, but she felt that she could not take exception to it for that very reason. Jean Oliver had called a spade a spade in her own blunt way and she had to be admired for her straightforward principle. The fact that she had invited her brother's widow into the family circle was to be no excuse for Fergus Oliver finding his way there!

Swiftly Helen glanced in Margaret's direction, but it was hard to tell what Margaret was thinking. She was drawing on her gloves with her lips slightly pursed and when she had collected her bag and a parcel Hattie had made up for her, she said briskly,

'Well, children, on our way! We've plenty of time now that Hammy is running us to the station, but sometimes it's difficult to find a seat in the trains these days. You've generally got to be there in loads of time or you stand in the corridor all the way!'

She blew a kiss to Isobel, hugged Hattie and said, 'Cheerio, Jean, I'll phone you sometime next week,' crossing to the door to wait for them to make their final goodbyes.

Hattie held Helen's hand, saying in a low voice,

'You will come back again, won't you? And bring the wee lad with you next time.'

'I will,' Helen promised. 'He'll like Edinburgh and all the traffic. If it was a fine day we might even get over the castle.'

'There are other places he would love, too,' Hattie said. 'Arthur's Seat and out along the Braids—'

'We can make these arrangements when the time comes,' Jean broke in somewhat impatiently. 'You will write, of course, Helen, when you wish to come through again and one of us will meet you.'

Going downstairs Margaret said,

'What did Hattie mean about a boy? It isn't—you haven't a son, Helen, have you?'

Helen looked away from the shining eagerness in her eyes.

'I am trying to adopt a child I took charge of out East,' she explained, and on the way to the station, seated between Margaret and Hamilton Purdie in the front of his long, black Jaguar, she told her sister-in-law the story of Tony, unconsciously conveying to both her listeners the fact that he had become the most precious thing in the world to her.

'And he's at the Keep now?' Margaret asked.

Deliberately Helen turned to her.

'Fergus has asked us to stay there until I decide what I want to do. I thought the Keep would be good for Tony, so I accepted. The Keep and Fergus! A boy needs a man's influence and the stimulus of a man's outlook in life and Tony has been brought up exclusively among women so far. I think it tends to make a boy soft.' She paused, her brows closely drawn together in a perplexed frown. 'That's not exactly the right word, though—'

'I know what you mean,' Hamilton Purdie said, 'and I think you are being very wise, Mrs Oliver.'

Helen could sense Margaret sitting tensed in the seat beside her, knowing that she wanted to ask about her old home and about Fergus, yet would not.

'Fergus has felt very lonely at the Keep,' she volunteered. 'I think that is why he wants Tony and I to stay there,' she went on deliberately. 'No man can live long in a big place like that with all its memories of happier times and be—content.'

'Why shouldn't he be content?' Margaret asked rebelliously. 'He has everything.'

'Not everything.' Helen turned right round to meet her stormy eyes, surprising a look in them which she could not fathom. 'I've never known a man more lonely—lonely of heart, Margaret—missing everything.'

The eyes which she had forced to meet hers filled with sudden tears, but Margaret turned her head away to look out at the busy pavement, and Helen was left to wonder compassionately what visions were superimposed upon the hurrying crowd of mortals bent on their own amusement or upon some other sober journey which took them hurrying onwards out of sight. She could not know what Margaret was thinking, but surely it was about Fergus as he had been in the days not so very long ago when they had confessed their undying love for each other and made their plans for a perfect future in the lovely surrounding of Oliver's Keep.

If they had been alone Helen felt that she could have said so much more, but Hamilton Purdie was sitting on her other side, tall and distinguished, his fine, strong hands gripping the steering wheel with a light, sure touch as he guided the car down into the cavern of the station and she could say nothing further in his presence.

It seemed that he cared for Margaret, and perhaps Margaret even cared a little for him, too, but Helen was too romantically inclined and had become too fond of Fergus Oliver to want to believe that Margaret had completely transferred her affections to this distinguished stranger. It was entirely outside her scheme of things. It just couldn't be! Fickleness was something she had never understood, and in Margaret Oliver's eyes there had been a gleam of deeper things.

There was little time to probe further, however: her train was standing at the platform and Hamilton Purdie had already found her a corner seat with her back to the engine.

'Helen, when will you come again?' Margaret asked. 'Don't stay away too long.'

'I won't,' Helen promised. 'Can I phone you somewhere, because I may just come on the spur of the moment next time?'

Margaret searched in her handbag, producing an old envelope on which she scribbled a number.

'That will find me for the next week or two,' she said. 'My career's in the melting-pot,' she added, with an attempt at a smile. 'Anyway, they'll be able to tell you where to find me, although I hope it won't be all that long before you come back.'

'With that invitation, Mrs Oliver should be back next week!' Hamilton Purdie observed pleasantly. 'Indeed, it will probably do you good to come to Edinburgh quite often, Mrs Oliver,' he added to Helen. 'You have had enough semi-solitary confinement to last you a lifetime.'

'Yes, I feel that too,' Helen confessed. 'I loved that hour's shopping this afternoon, and I must admit I was glad to have Jean's advice about prices and coupon values. They have me all at sea at present!'

'You'll soon learn!' Margaret smiled as Hamilton Purdie closed the carriage door.

As he did so, his eyes met Helen's and she surprised a vaguely questioning look in them.

'Perhaps Margaret and you will find time to lunch with me on your next visit?' he suggested. 'Margaret can phone me and I'll make all the arrangements.'

'That would be nice,' Helen said, really meaning it, yet feeling that perhaps she should not have accepted his invitation so readily when she fully intended to do everything in her power to supplant him in Margaret's life.

The friendship which undoubtedly existed between these two was dangerous—dangerous to Fergus's cause, which she had promised to champion!

The guard blew his whistle and Margaret stretched up to kiss her.

'Au revoir!' she said. 'You see, I'm determined this isn't going to be goodbye! Why don't you come and stay in Edinburgh?'

'And why don't you come to the Keep?' Helen countered.

'I—couldn't do that.' Margaret stepped back, her face very white. 'No, Helen, I couldn't.'

The train was moving away, but Helen stood to wave at the window.

'She's lovely, isn't she?' Margaret Oliver said with a sigh when it had finally disappeared from view.

'Very. But why the sigh?' her companion asked.

'I was thinking how strange it is—someone like Helen, with all the world in her grasp, suddenly bereft of it through no fault of her own—because of the war.'

'That's life,' Hamilton Purdie said gruffly, 'and your Helen knows how to meet it.'

Her wide eyes were lifted to his.

'You don't think her—hard, do you?'

'Not in the slightest. She is competent—and very wise.'

'I'm sure Ken and Helen must have been very happy. He was fairly old not to have fallen in love before—twenty-nine. Do you believe in first love?'

'Believe in it? Are you asking me if I think there can't be anything quite so strong—afterwards?'

'I suppose that's what I mean,' she confessed in a whisper which barely reached him.

He seemed to be considering the point as he guided her out through the barrier towards his waiting car.

'I believe that it always leaves its fragrance behind—or its sting,' he said at last. 'But if it is a hopeless love we are best to try to forget it.'

'Forget!' Her laugh was a small, choked thing bearing no relation to mirth. 'Did *you* find it easy to forget?'

'I was never in love like that—when I was very young.' He got into the car beside her but did not start the engine immediately. 'Before I graduated I learned just how many sacrifices my mother had made to see me through to my degree and—afterwards—I tried to make it up to her.'

'How proud she must have been of your success! I've often wished I had known her.'

'I wish you had. She was a very simple person, Meg, with a rigid code for living which never once let her down as far as I know. I've never known her hurt anyone by a harsh word or the truth bluntly spoken, and I often think she softened it and drove it home far deeper that way.'

'Hattie knew her, didn't she?' Margaret's eyes were suddenly dark. 'I wish we could do something about Hattie. She's not the same these days.'

'In what way?'

'Oh, I don't know. I can't find the exact word for it, but she's changed—grown old terribly quickly. She doesn't laugh so much now, or—or care about the things she used to care about, and she ought to go out more. She just seems content to sit at home with Jean and Isobel all the time.'

'We could remedy that for one afternoon,' he suggested, 'by asking her to the luncheon party.'

'When Helen comes to town? Oh, Hattie would love that! And I'm sure she liked Helen. One always can tell when Hattie likes a person because she's much more natural in their company, not—not sort of stuffed as she is when we're all alone at home.'

'You're not very often at home these days, Meg,' he pointed out.

She looked away from his probing eyes.

'No.'

'Not very happy?'

'There's no reason why I shouldn't be happy.' The reply had come instantly, yet he knew there was something else at the back of Margaret's mind. 'They're a good family, Hammy, really, and they're all terribly fond of me.'

'Then, what's the trouble?'

'Possessiveness, I think. Sometimes when I'm with them I feel as if I can't even breathe freely—that I should ask Jean which way! Oh, I'm a positive disgrace to them all—talking like this, but I know you'll understand. Jean has been this way ever since we were all children together, but it has grown worse since Daddy died and she took over the family responsibilities—all of them, every single, individual care—the things that should have belonged to us all separately . . .'

'Like being in love for the first time, Meg?' he asked quietly.

Margaret flushed crimson and was glad that he could not see her face in the dimness of the car's interior, although she answered him frankly enough,

'That—and finding one's own solution.'

Abruptly he bent forward and switched on the engine.

'Is it too late to find a solution now—or even to reverse an old one?' he asked.

'I don't know. Oh, it must be! It was six years ago, and since then—'

'Since then—?'

'We've forgotten. We must have forgotten.'

'Have you forgotten, Meg?'

'Almost.'

He took his hand from the steering wheel to cover her clenched one where it lay in her lap.

'Forgive me, my dear,' he said gently, 'but is that quite true?'

She drew in a long, deep breath.

'No, it isn't exactly true, Hammy, but it's too late now to do anything about it. Besides, I've given my promise.'

His dark eyebrows were slightly raised when he asked, 'What have you promised—and to whom?'

'Oh, to Jean, I suppose.' Impulsively she turned towards him. 'Don't let's talk any more about it tonight, Hammy, please. I never dreamed I should ever feel—like this again.'

And you feel it, Hamilton Purdie thought, because your sister-in-law came to Collister from the Keep! Was it someone in those far-off days, Meg—someone young and gay like yourself who taught you the meaning of first love so that you have never been able to forget? The rather wry smile deepened about his fine mouth. And I was fool enough to imagine that I could make you love me! Ah, well, what matter? Friendship has put a warm cloak about love before now!

'Where to, Meg?' he asked lightly. 'We're dining together, of course.'

'Why "of course"? Are you beginning to take me for granted?' she challenged with an upward smile and a return of her old gaiety.

'I could never do that, simply because I am never likely to find you in the same mood twice!'

'Which is good for you,' she asserted. 'All you eminent professors take everyone far too much for granted.' She slid down in her seat, her eyes suddenly alight with laughter. 'And how I should love matron to overhear me telling you that!' she confessed. 'She'd swoon with mortification, I'm sure! D'you know, Hammy, I don't think anyone at the Home knows about our little "go places." We've kept it a marvellous secret, though I often long to laugh—or wink!—when I pass you and matron in a corridor on consulting days!'

'My dear child,' he remonstrated, laughing down at her, 'I don't even see you on these occasions! Anything less than a staff sister pales into insignificance once matron takes one in tow! Seriously, though,' he added, 'what do you propose to do about your nursing? Are you going to go on in the profession or will you quit?'

'Quit! What a beautiful word to use if you want to make

me feel a worm! I'm not quitting. I've served my time. The war's been over for more than a year.'

'But the need for nurses is as great as ever. What has Jean got to say about it?'

'How did you know it was Jean?'

'Oh—a shot at random.'

'She thinks that sort of thing is all right in wartime—doing one's bit, and all that—but now that the emergency has ceased to exist she thinks I should do something else.'

'Such as?'

'That's just it. She's not very helpful. She thinks I should go home for a while.'

'And you'd hate that?'

Margaret nodded emphatically.

'I've learned to work, and I love it. Hammy, I'm not going back to being just an ornament!'

'Nobody is, my dear. That sort of thing is over and done with.'

'Yes, I think it is, and I'm glad. Hammy, I'm still going to be a nurse!'

'Good for you! And when do you propose to announce your revolt?'

Her eyes clouded a little.

'It is revolt, isn't it?' she said thoughtfully. 'And the awful part of it is that I don't feel in the least guilty about it!'

'Why should you? We all have to live our own lives.'

'Yes,' she said, her eyes shadowed by that look of regret he had so often seen in them and wondered about, 'we should all live our own lives.'

'And it's rather up to us to snatch at what happiness we can in the process,' he remarked lightly, 'so let's forget about momentous decisions and dance!'

'I've often wondered how you became so proficient in the art of dancing, Hammy,' she observed, waiting for him as he parked the car outside the restaurant. 'It rather undermines your dignity, I think.'

'Sometimes I try very hard to forget my dignity,' he said. 'I find it easy, by the way, when I'm with you.'

'I'm not very sure whether to take that as a compliment—or the reverse,' she told him as they went through the revolving doors. 'I know you relax in my company, but I always thought it was a relief rather than an effort.'

'One shouldn't have to make an effort with the people one likes.'

'Hammy,' she said suddenly, thrusting a hand through his arm, 'always like me!'

'I'll do my best,' he promised, squeezing her hand, and if his smile was suddenly grim she did not notice it.

They spent the next two hours dining and dancing afterwards, arguing and laughing and making confessions, which had always been their free and easy way when they were out together, and if their conversation in the car on the way from the station had slightly tempered Hamilton Purdie's enjoyment of the evening with regret, there was very little in his manner to show it.

And regret seemed far from Margaret as she danced round the room in his arms humming the tune of the latest waltz.

'I'm not going to dance again till there's another waltz!' she declared as he guided her back to their table. 'It's easily my favourite. I could go on waltzing all night!'

He glanced at his watch as they sat down.

'We've just about time for another one and that's all,' he said. 'Pity they lock you up so early!'

'And you have just been advising me to stay on and be locked up early for the rest of my life!'

'Not for all of it,' he returned. 'You'll marry, Meg, and there will be plenty of other dances.'

And plenty of men to dance with, he thought, wondering if he was being a fool to stand aside now when he had her complete confidence and her liking and respect. What were a score of years when they had so much in common, when their minds were in tune and they were good companions? He had missed a lot in life that Margaret Oliver could teach him even yet.

A selfish way to look at it? Perhaps, but a very human way, and but for the memory of that look in her eyes when they had discussed the measure of first love he might have swept all indecision aside as he had meant to do quite soon.

He was to see the same look once more before they finally parted that night and tell himself that no man, whoever he was, had the right to make another suffer like this.

He ordered coffee for two and they drank it before the next waltz struck up. Margaret was first on her feet, but as the opening bars of the tune drifted across the floor to them he saw her stand arrested, her face suddenly pale, her small, neat hands clenched firmly by her side.

The tall, slim girl who sang with the orchestra came forward to the microphone and he felt the wordless tune drumming in his ears as it must be in Margaret's, yet he could not put the appropriate words to the music and suddenly she had slipped her hand into his and pulled him on to the dance floor. They were circling the room together in perfect unison yet he could feel her body taut and stiff against his and her hand lay coldly in his warm grasp. Then slowly and leisurely the girl on the platform began to sing:

"The leaves of brown came tumbling down—
remember?
That September, in the rain . . ."

'Margaret,' he said softly, 'shall we go?'

'And spoil your dance!'

'I told you before, there will be plenty of dancing.'

He knew that she was struggling with tears, and he held her closer, guiding her towards the side of the floor. It seemed for a moment that she clung to him, hiding her face against his shoulder, and then she said calmly,

'I'm a fool. Let's go home.'

When he left her at the arched gateway to the nurses' home she was laughing again, but no reference had been made to the song which had so strangely stirred her memories, and only when she had reached the comparative sanctuary of the deserted bedroom which she shared with another girl did the bright mask fall from her face. Then, and only then, did the look Hamilton Purdie had detected in her eyes deepen, although she steadied her determined lips to whisper into the darkness,

'I'm being a complete fool. Just a silly, sentimental fool!'

She crossed to the window, looking out to where the bright street lamps twinkled at the far side of the square and away down the long road to the yellow haze in the sky above Princes Street, but her thoughts were far away from the city in a Border Keep, dwelling on the girl who must have reached there by now, wondering about her and envying her.

There was no way back, Margaret Oliver thought, and somehow she knew that Helen had recognised that truth, too. Helen had resolutely laid the past aside and was looking towards the future—a future planned about the child she had rescued and cared for all these years, and in her heart there could be no qualms of regret. All that had happened to Helen, all the heartbreak and sorrow, had been beyond her control—the pitiless bludgeonings of fate—and she had accepted them and fought back with all the weapons she had, but nothing could dispel the thought from Margaret's mind that once *she* had been challenged by fate and she had not fought back. Oh, yes, she had reasoned and protested, and deep in her heart she had suffered, but now she knew just how much she had merited this long-term punishment. Regret! Could ever word be more bitter! And there was nobody to blame except herself.

Event had mounted upon event and she had let pride trample across her heart—Jean's pride, the family pride—and her own. Yes, in the end she had succumbed to pride and let first love go. But how earnestly the memory of it had pursued her all through the years—with a word, in a thought or a look, and now the words of a song—a sentimental waltz refrain of half a dozen years ago—had reduced her to the point of tears. Why had she to remember like this when she had almost managed to forget! 'The leaves of brown came tumbling down—remember?'

Oh, it was intolerable! And she had thought sometimes that Hammy was the answer to it all—kind, considerate Hammy who had learned how to wait! Tonight he had known that something was wrong—probably guessing about that silly song—but he had not said anything, only been kind and patient and understanding. If there was anything to be found after love had gone surely this was the greatest thing? They were good companions, they liked the same books and the same plays, and now she had accepted his profession as her chosen career. Wasn't that enough? Mutual interests in all things. It should be enough—it should make life flow placidly . . .

'The leaves of brown came tumbling down—
remember?'

She covered her face with her hands.

'I mustn't remember,' she whispered. 'It's all over. The past is dead. I must bury the past.'

Firmly she drew the curtains, shutting out the night and the memories. She must forget. She *must*! She couldn't go on through life with her heart aching like this every time she remembered the Keep and thought of what might have been, and surely there was a limit to all heartache, a satiation point for all regret—a time when they began to grow less acute, when each waking hour was not filled by them, each dream less acutely poignant in its repetition of the past!

Tomorrow I must cease to think of him—and tomorrow, and tomorrow!

Why had Helen said that about loneliness? 'I've never known a man more lonely—lonely of heart, Margaret—missing everything.'

He had never married. She lay down on her bed, stretched out to her full length, her slim hands clasped behind her head, her dark eyes fastened upon the pool of light cast by the bedside lamp upon the ceiling. No, he had never married. For that old reason that was a thing of the past now? How young they had been in those days—blundering stupidly, and how expertly she would have handled the situation now if she had been given her chance over again! The heart-cry of half the world! But now was too late.

She turned over, burying her face in the pillow. This was one of the days that the past had claimed, brought back by Helen, and she had asked Helen to come again!

CHAPTER FOUR

THE train which carried Helen Oliver southwards to Burndean Junction was twenty minutes late when it arrived, but her cousin was on the platform to meet her. She saw him as the train slid to a standstill, scanning the carriage windows anxiously, and when she jumped down from her compartment he came quickly towards her.

'I wondered which train you would come by,' he said, his eyes holding hers. 'and I had an idea it might be the last one, although I've met them all since five o'clock.'

He was waiting for news, his eagerness in every line of him, and she found herself wishing that she had brought back some concrete proof of Margaret's fidelity and could offer it to him for his comfort.

'We've had a big day,' he went on as they passed through the barrier and out to the waiting car, which he had evidently driven over himself. 'We've been doing a complete tour of the farms—up to the Mains and across the hill to Burn Top and back by Toshiehill and Muckle Gates. You've got a grand boy, Helen, and he's certainly a stayer!'

Helen's eyes filled with happy laughter.

'You two are in danger of developing into a mutual admiration society,' she declared, 'and that can be a terrible thing to those forced to listen! You are quite sure Tony didn't get in your way at all?'

'On the contrary, he was a blessing. I just couldn't have concentrated on anything else all day.'

'Waiting for news?'

He nodded, opening the car door for her to get in.

'I met Jean in Edinburgh as we arranged,' she explained as he started the reluctant engine, 'and she's very much as you described her, only I think you've made one mistake. She isn't entirely heartless.'

'Then it must be fossilised—built into the stones of the Keep!'

'We can't blame her for that. It's a place to be proud of.'

He did not answer that direct thrust, asking instead,

'Are they living in Edinburgh?'

'Just outside—at a place called Collister.'

'It's funny—you getting all this information when I've been trying unsuccessfully for years. Is—Margaret with them?'

'She's not living at Collister, but she was there this afternoon. She's been nursing during the war and still appears very keen on it.'

'She isn't—married?'

'No.'

It was almost dark in the car and she couldn't see his face clearly, but she could imagine the relief on it because some of it had been in that swiftly indrawn breath of his.

'Not even engaged?'

She hesitated, remembering Jean's reference to Hamilton Purdie and Margaret's expected 'news,' and then she said firmly,

'No, she's not engaged.'

He had been quick to detect her momentary hesitation, however, quick with the sharp instinct of love.

'But there is someone? You met him this afternoon?'

'An old friend—'

'Don't try to make it easier for me, Helen—to soften the blow. I can take it!'

Swiftly she turned in her seat.

'That's just it!' she declared. 'You've been "taking it" for years and doing precious little about it, really! Do you *want* to lose Margaret? Are you preparing yourself for a lifetime of heartaches—accepting it without as much as a struggle?'

He slowed the car, negotiating a narrow bridge and difficult bend before he spoke.

'What can I do?'

'What have you done?'

'Nothing for a very long time—since I discovered how hopeless it all was.'

'Nothing's hopeless—not till you've come face to face

with finality. And even then,' she added almost to herself, 'there's sometimes—another road.'

'How could I use their address now?'

'Now? It was what you wanted, wasn't it?'

'Yes, when I thought that Margaret—'

She cut him short.

'How do we know what Margaret thinks—what she feels? I've told you that she's not engaged to be married, even though she happens to have a man-friend who, incidentally, is a great deal older than she is.'

She saw him frown in the sudden glare of the headlights from a passing car.

'His name is Hamilton Purdie, and he is a famous surgeon.'

'Hence Margaret's interest in nursing?'

'Not at all! I believe Margaret met him while she was nursing, but he knew the family before that. Fergus,' she said suddenly laying a hand on his arm, 'are you going to stand aside and let Hamilton Purdie walk in unopposed?'

His fingers gripped hard on the wheel and the car increased speed on the straight stretch before the Keep.

'No, by heaven, I'm not!' he said fiercely. 'But the first step is always the worst. I wish I knew what to do.'

'There are trains to Edinburgh, and petrol can't be so very short.'

'Helen! you're a wonder! You get things straight so easily. Or they look as if they might go straight . . .'

'Don't get off to a bad start by doubting them,' she warned. 'All I have done is brought you a telephone number and an address, but I do expect you to use them sensibly and to the best advantage.'

'If I bungle things now, I deserve to lose.'

'Yes, I think so, too!'

She made him laugh at that.

'What was Margaret like?' he asked.

'Very like the lady in the gallery upstairs!'

They had entered the Keep and she glanced up at the dim row of portraits and the faint, almost ghostly light filtering down upon them from the high, lancet windows above.

'She's young and lovely and still proud,' she continued after a moment, 'but love should laugh at pride as it laughs at locksmiths.'

'Helen, you talk like a philosopher and you're only a woman!'

'A woman has a good deal more sense than a man in these affairs,' Helen declared defensively. 'Besides, I think Margaret was made for you and I think she should be back here in the Keep.'

'But how to get her back!'

'Go out and find a way. She will never come of her own accord.'

'Did you speak to her—about me?'

'I hadn't a chance—apart from letting her know that you were alive and well.' She would not mention the confession of his loneliness which she had made to Margaret, fearing the resentment of his pride. 'We never really had any time alone.'

'Jean would see to that, I suppose.'

'No—circumstances.'

'Engendered by Jean!'

'Perhaps, but these things needn't daunt you if you're thoroughly determined. I'm seeing Margaret again—quite soon.'

'Alone?'

She remembered Hamilton Purdie's invitation, but thought she could manage to evade that when the time came.

'Yes—unless you would like to make a third.'

He hesitated.

'Suppose she wouldn't agree?'

Helen pulled off her hat and tossed it on to a chair, turning to face him squarely.

'Fergus Oliver, if you throw up any more obstacles in our path, I'll wash my hands of the whole business and let you get on with it yourself!' she declared.

'Don't, Helen!' he implored, thrusting a hand through her arm. 'I should never survive without you!'

'What a child you are—and you came all through the war with a brave record!'

'It's the wearing-down process that gets me,' he confessed. 'You've no idea how often I've tried with Jean.'

'Well, now you can try with Margaret! That would have been the more sensible way in the beginning, I think.'

'She has always been inaccessible. Jean saw to that,' he said bitterly.

Helen turned to where he stood filling his pipe, his broad shoulders propped against the mantelpiece.

'Margaret is six years older now,' she reminded him. 'So are you. Nothing Jean will do can make any difference in the end.'

'I wish I had your confidence,' he said, as Mrs Michie came in with the supper-tray.

'The wee lad's had a grand day, ma'am,' Bessie informed her. 'He's sleepin' like a top now, and he's been no bother at a', though he was loath to go to bed an' leave the pony.'

Helen's questioning eyes sought Fergus's, watching the boyish smile she liked best break in his eyes.

'What have you done?' she asked.

'Murdo Shaw over at Toshiehill had a little beauty for sale—'

'And you bought it?'

'He's perfectly safe, Helen, and Tony rides him like a veteran already.'

Her eyes filled with gratitude even as she protested.

'But—you shouldn't. You can't afford to do things like that.'

'I can afford to give someone a present once in a while,' he said stubbornly. 'You're not angry, really, though, are you?'

'How could I be? I only hope Tony remembered to thank you sufficiently.'

'The pleasure in a kid's eyes is all the thanks you need,' he said. 'Wait till you see him tomorrow!'

'I'm almost as excited as Tony must be!' Helen confessed, and the feeling of warmth that stole into her heart was something she had thought never to know again.

Time healed most wounds, she supposed, time and friendship and kindness, and the warm feeling you got when you were coming home. She looked across the hearth at Fergus Oliver, thinking of Tony in his bed upstairs in the little dressing-room adjoining her own, dreaming of his new possession, and she felt curiously secure and happy all of a sudden, although she knew she could not settle at the Keep indefinitely. But because Tony was happy there she would stay for a little while and perhaps in that time she could repay some of this man's kindness to her and the child who had become the absolute source of her own happiness.

Later that night, as she stood beside Tony's bed looking down at the peaceful face with its slightly smiling mouth, as if even in sleep the child's excitement and pleasure was actually with him, she prayed that nothing might intrude upon that happiness—that she might retain Tony out of the wreckage of a world that had once been hers.

CHAPTER FIVE

'THE days pass so quickly here and yet they are never rushed.'

Helen reined in her mare on the top of a knoll and sat looking down over the rolling grasslands at their feet. Fergus looked, not so much at the broad land of fair promise which he now possessed, as at the woman who, in two short weeks, had led him out of that wilderness of doubt and loneliness, wherein he had wandered so long and so miserably, up on to the high plateau of pride in possession. She had strengthened the desire within him to do everything in his power to keep these lands as they had always been kept, to give back to the soil all it gave so freely. It was Helen who had made him see all that he owed to Oliver's Keep in clear perspective, Helen who had gone out with him in the old battered car over the land that he still felt should have belonged to her and had awakened his sense of obligation and pride; it was Helen who had urged him to put everything he had into the Keep and remain there, and now he was thanking her for her belief in him from the bottom of his heart, although he could not find adequate words in which to express his thanks.

The restlessness which had been mainly occasioned by his unhappiness and disappointment over the Oliver women's attitude towards him had subsided and his original love of the land was again uppermost. The farmer in him saw the vast possibilities of his inheritance and gradually a determination that lack of sufficient money would not hinder him from making a success of the Keep grew strong in him. The land always repaid what you put into it, and Oliver's Keep was to be no exception.

'You don't feel lonely?' he asked. 'Tired of men's company?'

Helen smiled, watching the sun dip down beyond the

hills in a golden veil of mist, and shook her head.

'Who could feel lonely here with so much to do? I'm loving every minute of it, Fergus, and it's all so wonderful for Tony—riding about with you every day and learning about the countryside—about England.'

'Scotland!' he corrected, with a smile. 'That boy of yours is absolutely steeped in Border lore and he's never satisfied. I'll have to be looking up my reference books shortly in case I have no more available material one of these days when he says in that way of his, "Could you tell me just *one more* story, Uncle Fergus—just one!"'

She laughed happily, urging her mount downwards over the new grass. The mare had been her own idea, hired from a neighbouring farmer who had sold Fergus the big, powerful chestnut he was riding, and she was glad now that she had taken the chance when the animal had been offered to her. Apart from the exercise it afforded, it was perhaps the best way of getting about, and Tony was so enraptured with his pony that he rarely went anywhere without it. So the three of them rode out every day, and the fine hill air whipped colour into the boy's cheeks and laid a golden tan upon her own, lending a sparkle to their eyes which began to be reflected in Fergus Oliver's in time. He laughed readily now, and often they could be seen galloping swiftly across a stretch of turf with Helen generally in the lead and Tony a good second, while Fergus would bring up the rear, holding in his horse, much to the old hunter's chagrin, so that the race might go to one or other of his guests.

It was on one of these rides across the foothills that Fergus had first thought of asking his cousin's widow to remain at Oliver's Keep, to make it her permanent home, but Helen had avoided a direct answer and now he approached the subject again, more determinedly this time.

'Helen,' he said, 'you're happy here. You're both happy. You could never find anywhere more suitable for Tony, and you know I want you to stay.'

'I know.' She bent down, laying a hand caressingly on the mare's smooth neck to hide the sudden emotion in her eyes. 'But—later—it would not be fair to you—or to

Margaret.' She looked up, smiling. 'You see, I'm firmly convinced that Margaret's going to come back to the Keep —that it's only a matter of time before you bring her.'

He moved restlessly, pulling in his horse as it slid over some loose stones on the narrow hill road.

'I wish I was half so confident,' he said, 'but I do mean it when I say that I wish you would stay, Helen. The Keep's a big place, big enough for all of us, and you could have your own rooms if you would like it best that way.'

Helen smiled a little sadly. She could not give him her other reason for refusing his offer, the reason that every day she spent at the Keep held its measure of sadness as well as joy, that each stairway and raftered room echoed with a beloved voice which she had never heard there but which rang in her heart as clearly as if her dead husband walked beside her. All these memories of Ken had been with her so vividly during the years of her captivity and she knew they would remain locked in her heart for ever, but she could not live actively with them always. She owed it to Tony to put the past behind her—not to forget, yet not to live entirely with the dead, and she knew that while she remained at Oliver's Keep her task would be doubly hard. Yet she was determined not to leave Fergus Oliver alone again to brood as he had done, and she made up her mind to remain at the Keep until he had substituted Margaret for herself.

'We'll see,' she said lightly. 'One or other of us may change our mind, you know, and I want us both to be free as air to do that if we wish.'

'I won't change mine,' he said doggedly. 'There was going to be room for all the Oliver women here if I had got my way in the first place.'

'You may have to make room for them yet,' she suggested. 'Jean may change her mind.'

'I can't imagine anything causing her to do that short of an earthquake!'

'There are such things, you know!'

'Helen! I believe you can even laugh about Jean Oliver!'

'Why not? She isn't a tragedy, really—except to herself. Pride can be a good or a bad thing, but it generally reverts to oneself in the end and nobody else really feels the sting of it so cruelly.'

'I don't know about that,' he objected. 'She has lashed out with her pride pretty freely in my direction recently.'

'Because you've let her!' She turned in her saddle to look at him in the gathering dusk, seeing him sitting easily on the animal he rode, big and powerful, and found herself wondering again why he had not made a more determined effort to win his heart's desire. 'When are you going to Edinburgh?' she asked quietly.

'I thought you were going to fix that,' he said, watching the chestnut's ears in the dim light. 'I thought you were going to arrange a date.'

She sighed.

'All right, I will, but I really think you should go alone.'

'And have her refuse to see me?'

'I don't think she would do that.'

Firmly she made the statement, willing him to meet her eyes, and finally he looked round and smiled.

'You're a grand sort of person, Helen,' he declared warmly. 'All the same, there are limits, and you must just kick me out when I begin to ask too much of you.'

'Going to Edinburgh isn't asking such a lot,' she returned, 'but after that opening I expect you to do the rest for yourself.'

'Don't worry, I shall—if I once get the opening!' He had shaken off his momentary depression and was brighter now. 'When can we make it a day?'

'When you can most conveniently leave the farm. What about one day next week?'

'Tuesday?'

'That's the day Harper's man is coming from Berwick about the new tractor, isn't it?'

'Yes. Good heavens, Helen, you're even having to keep me right about farm affairs now! What about Thursday then?'

'I'll write to Margaret suggesting Thursday.'

They rode on in silence for a minute or two.

'Will you tell her I'll be with you?' he asked at last.

'I shall tell her I'm bringing someone important with me, and I think she'll know who I mean.'

'I'm as nervous as a kitten about the whole affair already!' he confessed, but he laughed and that seemed good to Helen.

The days passed and the new tractor was bought so that they might make a start on ploughing up the home fields in the autumn to raise roots and feeding stuff again on land that had been more or less neglected for two years, and Tony rode round the yard on its shiny red seat, deciding that it came nowhere near a flesh and blood pony for action, so that Helen picked him up and kissed him impulsively, wondering if she was being selfish in denying him Oliver's Keep as a permanent home.

Early on the Thursday morning, she rose to find that Fergus had been up for over two hours.

'He's like a wee laddie settin' oot on his first Sunday-school trip,' Bessie Michie observed. 'Up at the screich o' day and hardly touchin' a bite o' breakfast for fear he wouldna' get through his work in time to catch the train!'

'He'll manage all right,' Helen said, accepting her bowl of porridge. 'Where's Tony? I heard him racing down the stairs ten minutes ago.'

'He gulped his porridge roastin' hot an' was away oot after Mister Oliver like a young leveret! They're fair attached to each other, these two, ma'am—like father and son almost.'

Helen smiled, knowing how fond Bessie had become of Tony and how eagerly she would have welcomed the news that they had decided to live permanently at the Keep. Fergus had made no secret of his invitation before her and once she had said to Helen in an expansive moment,

'You couldna' do better, ma'am. I wisna' ower fond o' Mister Oliver when I first saw him because o' a' that tittle-tattle that was going on at the time, but now I know that a finer gentleman never walked. It's a true saying that ye never know folk till ye live in the same hoose wi' them, but a body could live wi' Mister Oliver for years and never hae a thought against him.'

Helen had said she was sure of it, but she had not

committed herself about the length of her stay at the Keep. Often the safety and peace that surrounded her here caught at her heart, bidding her stay, but she knew that she must not.

'There they are, ma'am!' Bessie exclaimed, looking down from the long windows over the terrace to the sweep of road beyond, her hands on her ample hips, her eyes twinkling with amusement. 'Down there by the burn—on the brig'—see! My, he's a wee deil that! He's for puttin' the pony to the jump! If Mister Oliver catches him at that—'

Helen crossed quickly to her side just in time to see Tony urging an unwilling MacNab towards the brown water of the swiftly-flowing burn. The staid MacNab had evidently a horror of water for he planted his fore-feet firmly on the ground, laid back his ears, and watched his young rider shoot unceremoniously over his head into mid-stream.

'Oh—!'

The exclamation of horror left Helen's lips as she ran for the door, but before she had reached the open air she was telling herself not to worry. It had not looked a bad spill and, with the exception of the wetting, no very great harm could have come to their intrepid horseman. On the contrary, the incident might very well prove fruitful to serve as a lesson for future, more dangerous occasions. Frequently she had heard Fergus explaining to Tony that he was too young and inexperienced to take jumps . . .

Fergus was carrying him up the rough track towards the Keep when she reached the terrace, the two horses following docilely behind, and she hailed him breathlessly.

'Everything all right? No bones broken?'

'There's not much damage done, but we'll need some hot water and bandages.'

Tony, vacillating between tears and a careless bravado, searched Helen's face anxiously, but one glance at him had convinced her that he was not badly hurt and she turned with Fergus back towards the Keep.

'Well, my lad, we'll never make a horseman out of you at this rate!' she said. 'And poor MacNab looks so sorry, but he thought you understood that he didn't like water jumps.'

'It was only a very little jump,' Tony pointed out, disgruntled.

'But he's not a very big pony.' Fergus had carried him through to the kitchen and deposited him on Bessie's white scrubbed table. 'We're going to make a mess here, Mrs Michie.'

'Never mind the mess, see to the bairn,' Bessie decreed, looking over Helen's shoulder. 'My, but he's cut bad! Jist look at that knee—and his poor hands!'

Tony looked, and the sight of the blood made him turn pale. He was obviously wondering whether he shouldn't have indulged in a few tears, after all, on the strength of all that blood, when Helen intervened.

'We'll soon have it all washed off and a few nice bandages on,' she said practically, 'and then we'll go and let MacNab loose for the day.'

'So that I can come to Edinburgh with you and Uncle Fergus?' Tony queried, brightening.

'No, I think you've had quite enough excitement for one day.' Helen straightened, looking directly at Fergus. 'Uncle Fergus is going to Edinburgh by himself.'

'But, look here, Helen—' Fergus protested, but there was something in Helen's eyes which silenced protest and made him feel ashamed. 'When did you change your mind?' he asked quietly.

'It has been changing gradually since Tuesday and—all this bandaging seems to have settled the argument,' Helen smiled. 'I'd never catch the train now, anyway.'

'Traitor!'

'Not really. I have a feeling that Margaret would appreciate it much more if you sought her out alone.'

'She may consider it a trick.'

Helen wound a bandage with expert skill.

'Some tricks are justified. Besides, there would always be the evidence of all these bandages. If I know Tony, they'll have to be renewed for weeks! I don't know where he picked it up, but he has a positive bandage mania!'

'Can I have just a wee one on my finger, Mummy?' Tony asked. 'It aches something ter'ble.'

'I'm sure it does, my lamb, but a nice quiet hour in bed will soon mend it!'

'Oh no! Mummy, it's really nearly better now. Please can I not go to bed an' just sit in the sun and crayon in my new book?'

'We'll see.' Helen would make no promises, and when she straightened Fergus was still standing looking down at her doubtfully. 'Don't you think I'm right?' she queried. 'Margaret won't want to feel that you've been—taken by the hand.'

'What a poor figure I must cut in your estimation!' he said grimly. 'Sometimes I tell myself that I don't deserve to get Margaret back at all.'

'Of course you do!' Her eyes held his. 'You see, I know just how much you care for her.'

He held out his hand.

'Wish me luck.'

'You know I do.' She pressed his fingers. 'And don't dare to come back without some sort of result!'

'I'll do my best! Chin up, Tony!' he added. 'They're battle scars worthy of a good horseman and we'll make a point-to-point champion of you yet!'

'When will you be coming back?' Tony asked wistfully.

'With the next train—or the last!' Fergus smiled at Helen. 'Be good while I'm away!'

'I shall be doing nothing but writing a few letters,' she returned, securing the final bandage with a few deft stitches. 'I've only written one since I came here—the one to Aunt Anna. It seems strange that I haven't had a reply from her yet, by the way, but perhaps she's just been too busy I don't suppose she can have moved. She's been in that house since she was married, forty years ago.'

'Some folks are like that,' he mused. 'They take root. I wonder if I will strike roots here at the Keep after all. It may all depend on Margaret.'

For a moment Helen felt bitterly disappointed, and then she knew that her fears were groundless. He was just talking. Already he had struck roots deep into the soil of

Oliver's Keep and, with or without Margaret, he would stay there.

'If you mean to catch that train it's time you were changing out of your working clothes,' she reminded him.

'What shall I tell Margaret?' he asked after a moment's hesitation.

'The truth—that Tony had a very slight accident and I decided to stay with him, but as you were coming anyway —well, here you are!'

She heard him whistling in the bathroom and when he came down she saw that he had put on a new tie.

'Good luck!' she said. 'We'll be looking out for you— off the last train!'

He fumbled in his pocket as they walked towards the door.

'You did give me the address of the nurses' home, didn't you? I thought I put it in my wallet—'

'I should have thought you would have known it by heart by this time!' she teased. 'But you'd better make sure. I promised to pick Margaret up there at twelve.'

'I've got it!' He turned in the doorway, looking down at her. 'Keep your fingers crossed for me, Helen.'

'They're already crossed!'

Tony slipped a thin little hand into his.

'I wish I was going with you, Uncle Fergus.'

'You shall next time,' he promised. 'We'll make a proper excursion of it and go to the zoo.'

Syd Willing was waiting with the car at the foot of the steps and as they drove away Fergus Oliver looked over his shoulder for a last view of the Keep. He saw it with the sun striking full upon it, picking out each well-known feature in bold relief and shining down on Helen and the boy standing on the topmost step waving him goodbye. Something hard and emotional stuck in his throat as he thought that so might an Oliver woman out of the past have stood to wave her knightly spouse farewell as he journeyed forth to battle, and suddenly he knew the pride of belonging was strong and fierce in him and that he would never let the Keep go now no matter what happened. He was bound up with it irretrievably, its fate his own. Helen had taught him that, awakening pride of lineage in him so that he acknowledged his debt and was prepared to give all he had to his heritage in his turn. His eyes rested on the child by her side and he wondered if he would ever have a son of his own. It would have to be a son like Tony, he thought, smiling.

How completely the boy had taken possession of his heart! And Helen looked as if she belonged there, too. He could still see her standing at the door in the sunshine, the strong light on her glorious hair, one slim arm raised in final salute, and found himself wondering what would become of her if she persisted in refusing his offer of the Keep as a permanent home.

'What train will I come back for, sir?' Syd asked as they stood waiting on the station platform.

'The last one,' he said firmly.

He was determined not to disappoint Helen, he thought whimsically, as he settled into his corner seat to watch the green land he had come to love slipping away behind him. She was a personality, was Helen, who would not admit defeat!

The journey to Edinburgh went swiftly, paced by his racing thoughts. This was what he had always meant to do —what should have been done years ago! Yet he had tried it all before though not, he was forced to admit, actively. He had let those curt messages which Jean Oliver had sent through their respective lawyers deter him, and now it had taken his cousin's young widow to show him the way. He thought about Helen again and from the very thought of her drew strength. It was now or never, Helen had said, and he meant it to be now.

Strange how timid you were in your early youth, messing things up because you were unsure—not quite confident enough in your own power to handle a situation—and how, as you grew older, you knew that you should have done this or that! A fatalist at heart, he thought that things were measured out that way, that there was a road to travel to a predestined goal and that each mile of it was already marked indelibly to be covered easily or with difficulty as the fates decreed, but what he wanted to see now was

Margaret at the end of the road he was travelling—a glimpse, a sign to sustain him—even though rough country might lie between. Then, he told himself, there would be something to strive for—not just this blind groping in the dark which had tormented him since he had left the Services behind. There had been a goal of sorts there, though danger and death had stalked constantly at his heels. He had been fighting for something—a cause—an ideal—and although indirectly that cause had taken Margaret and his happiness from him he had never regretted nor altered his conviction that he had no right to marry her under the circumstances in which he had lived his daily life. Even now the thought of men he had seen maimed and crippled for life as a result of the war justified his resolution a hundredfold in his own mind. He had come through unscathed, but one of these, his comrades, might have been him.

When the train finally drew into Waverley he jumped up eagerly, cramming on his soft felt hat and racing down the long platform into the sunlit outer world with all the zest of a schoolboy. A tram or bus was out of the question, he felt, hailing a taxi. Margaret would be waiting!

How far was it to the address he had given the driver? And what would he say when he met her? Yes, what would he say? He hadn't even prepared anything in his mind, but Margaret had never cared for pretty speeches and he had never been the one to make them. Shy and inarticulate in youth, he realised that he was not much better now. His pulses were racing madly, his heart beating like a sledge-hammer, and all his brain seemed capable of was repeating 'Margaret! Margaret!' with the joy of such repetition crushing out all other thought.

The taxi slowed up as it turned into a sequestered square where tall elms sprang from a grassy plot in the centre, a reminder of the green countryside from which he had just come and which he knew that Margaret must often long for.

'Here you are, sir.' The driver leaned back in his seat, speaking through the open glass partition between them. 'Number ten it is, sir. A nice bit place for they hard-workin' lasses when they're off duty, an' I'm sure there's nobody deserves it more than they do. I was three months in the Victoria in Glasgow during the last war an' I've always said I owe my life to they cheerful bit lasses as much as I do to the big surgeons.'

'I'm sure you do,' Fergus said earnestly, looking up at the tall Georgian house with its dignified windows and air of spaciousness as he paid his fare. 'Look here,' he added on an impulse, 'could you possibly wait a few minutes? I'll be out in a second. I'm just going to call for someone.'

The taxi driver smiled at him indulgently.

'Right y'are,' he agreed. 'If you'll not be too long.'

'Oh, I won't be long!'

Optimistic, was he? Too optimistic, perhaps? Supposing Margaret was angry or disappointed—or just too disinterested to come when she found Helen wasn't going to be there?

He rang the bell. 'Nonsense!' Helen would have said!

'Can I speak to Miss Margaret Oliver, please—Nurse Oliver?' he asked the hollow-cheeked maid who answered his summons.

'You can step inside,' she said dismally, 'but I don't know if she's in. What name will I say?'

He had not thought of this.

'Will you tell Nurse Oliver her cousin has called. Fergus Oliver is the name.'

Margaret could turn him down now without even seeing him, he thought as the girl disappeared, but he could not have pretended that Helen was there or even hedged so that Margaret would not know who her caller was until she came down.

The girl seemed to be gone an interminable time in which he turned over the pages of two periodicals without even realising that they were essentially feminine, and then there was the sound of returning footsteps on the tiled floor outside and he jumped to his feet.

His eyes were eagerly upon the door when it opened to reveal a tall girl in nurse's uniform; but it was a moment before the full force of disappointment reached him. It wasn't Margaret, but someone she had sent in her stead, a tall, rather plain girl with large grey eyes which looked into his with a mixture of apology and curiosity in their depths.

He moistened his lips to say,

'Nurse Oliver—'

'Margaret asked me to explain when you came—or, at least, when her sister-in-law came, I should say,' the girl broke in. 'She was expecting Mrs Oliver this morning.'

'Mrs Oliver couldn't come, but I was coming with her.' His mind was refusing to take in the situation. Why hadn't Margaret come down? This girl said she had something to explain, but surely Margaret would have seen Helen? 'We —I hoped to take them both out to lunch.'

The tall girl moved towards the table, drawing out a chair for him.

'Won't you sit down, Mr Oliver?' she invited, thinking that he looked suddenly tired. 'Margaret asked me to tell Mrs Oliver that she had gone to Collister and to ask her if she would go out here. You see, we were there yesterday —we had some free time in the afternoon and Margaret thought she'd rather go home than go to the pictures. She has been feeling cold and shivery for a day or two and she thought the Collister air would do her more good than being shut up in a picture theatre, but when we got out as far as Collister she collapsed.'

Fergus jumped to his feet.

'She's ill? But what happened? What was the matter?'

'Well, it was like this,' The speaker was determined that nothing on earth would hurry her or rob her of the dramatic presentation of a very simple incident. 'We've been very busy here—terribly overworked, as a matter of fact—and she's been going about with this Spanish 'flu on her for days and not saying very much. None of us like to complain you know, Mr Oliver, but much as I like and respect Margaret, I think she did wrong. Infection, and all that, you know—'

'Yes, yes, I quite agree.' Fergus could cheerfully have strangled her for her long-windedness, but he realised that only by exercising the utmost patience would he finally hear all there was to know about Margaret. 'That means she's still at home then? Still at Collister?'

'Oh yes, of course. Her eldest sister—such a dignified person, I always think!—has taken complete charge, and when I phoned this morning Mr Hamilton Purdie was there. I don't really think he was there professionally,' she rushed on to confess. 'Margaret and he are rather special friends, if you ask me!' She lowered her voice. 'Of course, I don't really *know*, but I have been putting two and two together lately! By the way, I haven't told you my name, have I? It's Cecelia Ramsay.'

Fergus made a polite murmur of acknowledgment and Cecelia rushed on:

'Now, what will you do? Margaret wanted me to take Mrs Oliver out to Collister, but matron has just asked me to go on duty again—as a special favour. We're so short-staffed, and with Margaret missing the work is positively piling up.' She considered him thoughtfully. 'You are Margaret's cousin, too, aren't you? And I don't suppose you're afraid of Spanish 'flu?'

'Not in the least,' Fergus assured her.

'Then you'll go out to Collister?'

He hesitated.

'You said you weren't afraid of the 'flu!' Cecelia reminded him archly.

He was wondering if he were afraid of Jean Oliver, and then, as plainly as if she had spoken at his elbow, he heard the echo of Helen's voice, 'Nonsense!' It was the way she had of saying it—not scornfully, but refuting the idea of your cowardice and with so much apparent confidence in you that you just couldn't let her down!

'I'll need the address,' he told the waiting Cecelia, who scribbled it on the back of an old envelope, returning it as she remarked confidentially,

'I expect you've come through to Edinburgh for a day or two, and really I should have liked to have taken you to Collister—just to see how Margaret is, you know—but my time off won't be till tomorrow afternoon now. I'll have the evening free, too,' she added hopefully.

Fergus said, 'I'm afraid I'm only here for the day,' and

secured the precious envelope while she was still recovering from her disappointment.

He was quite sure the girl wasn't an intimate friend of Margaret's because it was evident that what she knew about his cousin mainly concerned her hospital life. With the exception of that piece of information about Hamilton Purdie, he reminded himself, standing suddenly abashed before the piece of gossip so lightly passed on, feeling the pain of jealousy in him like a searing flame, and then thinking of Helen again as he said,

'Thanks for all your trouble, Miss Ramsay. Perhaps one day you will have lunch with—Margaret and Mrs Oliver and I when we meet in Edinburgh again?'

Conventional words, but holding so much for him if they ever came true!

Nurse Ramsay saw him to the door regretfully, because, as she confided to the youthful probationer who joined her on her way back upstairs, she was almost sure she had nearly made a conquest. Mr Oliver was so nice and such a gentleman, and although Margaret Oliver was a bit of a dark horse about her private affairs, Cecelia was quite sure that she came of a very good family—'important people, you know, my dear!'

On the pavement outside Fergus stood debating whether to take the taxi out to Collister or go by bus, and then he glanced at his watch and saw that it was almost lunch-time. Of course he couldn't go rushing off and presenting himself on Jean Oliver's doorstep at such an inconvenient hour. Their relationship was far too delicate for that! He smiled wryly as he dismissed the taxi, remembering those far-off days of his youth when they had shared so many meals and he had come and gone as one of the family and always been made welcome.

He shrugged. Oh, well, lunch somewhere in a decent restaurant might help to fortify him for the ordeal of meeting Jean—at last. But the delay irked him, sapping some of his determination, even although he had not the slightest intention of giving up the quest mid-way. He would carry on now to the end. It was now or never, as Helen had said!

Going down Princes Street, he stopped at a florist's window and found himself remembering Margaret's favourite flowers.

'Perhaps it's because of my name, but I love these big pink daisies better than any of your exotic blooms! They're so fresh, and always look as if they've just been dancing in a breeze.'

He could almost hear her saying it as he bought two bunches of pyrethrums and carried them self-consciously out of the shop in the manner of all Scotsmen armed with such a sentimental burden.

The bus to Collister was empty by the time it reached the terminus and he inquired his way as he got out.

'Right up the bank there,' the conductor directed him. 'First house on your left.'

No use getting the wind up about things now, he argued as he reached the gate. You're going in!

Squaring his shoulders, he marched up the gravel drive, mounted the steps before the front door, changed the flowers from his left hand to his right and then back again, and rang the bell.

He had time to take a very deep breath before his summons was answered and at sight of the young maid who opened the door to him he felt amazingly reassured. She smiled at him in quite a friendly way and held the door open when he said.

'I've come to see Miss Oliver. Miss Margaret Oliver.'

'Will you come this way, please?' the girl asked, and behind her he saw a large, empty hall, which gave him further courage.

He was ushered into a room facing out to a pleasant garden at the back of the house and he recognised the furniture as once belonging in the round room at the Keep. There was the big grey chesterfield on to which they had all crowded as kids, and the two easy-chairs, and the mahogany bureau . . .

'Can I say what name, please?'

'Yes. Mr Fergus Oliver.'

He had said it defiantly and stood waiting, but the maid passed out of the room without a moment's hesitation to carry his request upstairs. Not so calmly would Jean receive it, he thought wryly as he waited in the room for ten minutes which gradually began to seem an age. He hadn't exactly expected his visit to be a straightforward affair, of course, he reminded himself, but soon the lapse in time began to strengthen the fear in him that Margaret herself might refuse to see him. There had always been that possibility, although he had tried to crush it back in his mind as he made his way here.

The house remained deathly still, so quiet that the ticking of the small, French clock on the mantelpiece seemed to beat out loudly in the silence, hammering the fact of passing time into his mind. He found himself listening for approaching footsteps, tensed and ready to spring to his feet the moment they reached the door, but when they did come it was without warning, softly, as a cat treads, and when the door opened it was Isobel Oliver, and not Jean, who stood there.

He left the flowers lying on the table and took two paces towards her. After all, they were cousins, and although he had always had the feeling that Isobel had never liked him, it was Jean who ruled the household and make its laws. Perhaps he could deal with Isobel more easily than with Jean, but when he looked down into her eyes he could sense the invisible barrier which her will had raised between them. He remembered Isobel as always being strangely aloof, envious, he had thought, of Jean, grudging her sister the prestige of being recognised as the absolute authority on all things connected with the family, but now he supposed she was here in Jean's stead and that he would be forced to give her his message. And on the instant he felt that he would rather have faced a dozen Jeans than this one Isobel.

'How are you?' he asked awkwardly. 'I came to see Margaret.'

'So I understand.' She crossed the room to stand with the tips of her fingers resting on the polished top of the table where his flowers lay, looking down at them contemptuously. 'I have come down to tell you that you can't see her.'

'Do you mean that she is too ill? I heard at the Nurses' Home—'

She raised her head, her eyes narrowing as she looked at him.

'You went there?'

'Yes. Margaret was to have met Helen to-day, but the boy had a slight accident and I came along instead.' He met her eyes squarely. 'I was coming with Helen—hoping to see Margaret again. I've tried to get into touch with you all so often and—finally—this seemed the only way.'

'We—my sister and I have answered your communications in the only possible way,' she told him, assuming Jean's mantle of authority with such obvious satisfaction that it was almost more than he could do to restrain a smile. 'And we can't really see the need for any further contact.'

'But it's all so ridiculous!' he burst out. 'Surely you see that, Isobel? We're related. It's not as if a complete stranger had taken over the Keep. We were there so much together in the old days—'

'It isn't a question of the Keep,' she answered, her resentful gaze challenging him. 'We do not grudge you what is yours by right.'

'Then—it's Margaret?' He drew in a deep breath. 'That's why I've come to see her. I must see her, Isobel, and you'll help me, won't you?'

He made the appeal desperately, seeing her standing between him and the door leading out to the hall as the symbol of that vague, nameless thing which stood between him and his beloved, and his heart turned suddenly cold in him as a scene out of the past flashed vividly before his eyes. He saw Isobel, at fifteen, flicking a riding-crop against her boots while her angry, dominating eyes surveyed the small group of younger children gathered round the paddock gate—Ken and Hattie and Margaret and himself—listening, wide-eyed, to the unexpected tirade. 'You'll ride where I want you to-day. Jean isn't here, and when she isn't, I'm boss!'

He tried to remember the sequel to that unpleasant ride, but all he could recall was that it had ended disastrously, with Isobel called to book by her father for openly flouting some order he had given and Margaret reduced to tears.

'Help you?' She gave a little, unpleasant laugh. 'Why should I do that when Margaret has absolutely no wish to see you?'

The words hit him with the force of a blow and he knew that she saw him reel under them with fiendish satisfaction, and then anger laid hold of him, anger such as he had never known in all his life before.

'Damn it, Isobel!' he cried, 'you can't take that attitude —no matter what you think you are! I'm dashed if I'll believe Margaret has refused point-blank to see me— unless she is very ill—'

The possibility suddenly quietened him and he looked at her anxiously.

'There's nothing seriously wrong with her,' Isobel said distantly. 'In fact, she's getting up this afternoon, but I am still quite convinced that your visit would be—unwelcome.'

He glared at her with the anger flaming back into his eyes.

'Did she say that?' he challenged.

'No.' She gave him a thin little smile in the pause before she went on with deliberate malice, 'But she has another visitor this afternoon—Mr Hamilton Purdie—and I'm quite sure she'd be—less than pleased if we interrupted them now. You see,' she added with something that was not a smile playing about her hard mouth, 'they are— about to be married.'

'"About to be married?"' He found himself repeating the stilted phrase unbelievingly. 'But Helen said—'

'I'm afraid I am not greatly interested in what my sister-in-law may have told you,' Isobel interrupted in a short, clipped voice. 'The fact remains that you have come here uninvited, knowing that we should resent it, and now I must ask you to leave again as quickly as possible.'

For a moment he fancied that she glanced nervously through the window, as if she might be expecting someone's return—Jean's, no doubt—and then all thought but that of Margaret was driven from his mind and the name of Hamilton Purdie hammered in his ears. It had risen before him ominously even after Helen's reassurance that there was no definite engagement between the celebrated doctor and Margaret, and here it was again, a concrete thing now —Isobel telling him that Hamilton Purdie and Margaret were 'about to be married.'

It was true. He had been given the bare facts and it was no use standing there like a fool staring at Isobel, hating her and refusing to believe her just because her words laid all his hopes in the dust. Margaret belonged to someone else now. It was her own free choice, and Isobel had been quick to let him see that. The family had nothing to do with it—only, they approved. Oh yes, they'd be pleased about anyone like Hamilton Purdie, he thought bitterly, and then he remembered that they had been pleased about him, once, before he had blundered up against an ideal which had run contrary to their pride. But it was no use trying to explain all that now. It was too late. He had lost Margaret.

My God, I've lost her! he thought. It's final now. She's made her own choice—her own free choice, not in the years between when she might have doubted my love, but now—now when she knew that I still wanted her, still loved her as desperately as before! He couldn't believe it.

'Margaret couldn't do this—'

He had uttered the words aloud, a protest from his very heart, and he saw the scorn they provoked lying in Isobel's contemptuous eyes.

'What right have you to blame Margaret, or even to think that she might have one scrap of affection left for you?' she asked wrathfully. 'You almost broke her heart once, and but for her family she might not have got over it, but, thank heavens, she did get over it. And that's why we're not going to stand aside and let you rush in again to do any more damage. I've told you she's going to marry someone else, and this interview is becoming very distasteful to me.'

'I see.'

His lips felt stiff, so that he could hardly utter the words, and he seemed to be seeing her from some vast distance —the severely plain face unredeemed by any softening feature or kindly expression which might have suggested even a fragment of pity for the blow she had dealt; the gaunt, upright figure standing stiffly beside the table, and the large, well-cared-for hands clasped now before her in an attitude of patient endurance as she waited for him to go. They were essentially Isobel. She was taking Jean's place in her absence, but there was nothing about this woman which suggested Jean Oliver's sense of justice and fair play. She was adamant and cruel, glorying in her temporary power—enjoying every minute of it—and striking swiftly and maliciously where she could with no mercy shown, her whole attitude one of justifiable retaliation for a long-past hurt to the Oliver pride which she, at least, was never going to forget.

Swiftly she turned towards the door.

'I don't think there's anything more to be said,' she suggested coldly. 'You know our wish, and you will not try to see my sister again.'

'Margaret?' He stared at her without moving. 'No,' he said, 'I'll not try to see her against her will.'

If she had looked triumphant, he thought, or even satisfied, he would have felt like murder, but her lips only tightened a fraction as she held open the door, saying determinedly,

'I'm afraid I can't spare you any more time. Naturally, with illness in the house, we are kept busy.'

He looked down at the flowers, pushing them across the table towards her—tall daisies especially for Margaret, a slender reminder of the days when love had surrounded them both with happiness!

'Will you take them to her?' he asked unsteadily. 'I — thought she might like them. They were always her favourites.'

She looked at the flowers and away again, saying neither yes nor no, and he passed her to go out into the hall, crossing it as he might have done some barren waste in a haunted dream, noting its every detail while he yet remained aware of its strange, dream-like unreality until the heavy front door closed behind him with a finality which could not be mistaken.

He was out, and it was Margaret who had sent him away. She had sent him away because she no longer cared for him—because she was going to marry someone else!

Well, it was all over now, the hope and striving and the plans for the future—silly, futile plans they seemed now that he knew she was going to marry someone else. He thought of the journey from the Keep and his own buoyancy of spirit, of how sure he had been that Helen must be right and all he needed was just to see Margaret again. He found himself laughing harshly with an inward bitterness he had not known even in those days of fruitless endeavour when he had first tried to get into touch with his cousins to ask them to come back to their old home. It had been hopeless from the beginning. He was seeing that now, and this was the end of it all. There could be nothing more final than this dismissal of Margaret's, even although it had been conveyed to him by proxy.

He tried to tell himself that he was glad she had done it that way, that he could not have endured pity or indifference in her, and yet he knew that he had wanted to see her to satisfy the insatiable longing which ate at his heart. And how to kill that longing? There must be some way—after years, although he could not conceive of any now. A man could not spend the remainder of his life consumed by this burning desire for one woman's presence and live on!

He realised that he was walking rapidly, but in which direction he did not know. Away from civilisation, because there were green hedges on either side of him and low, green hills on the horizon. That had been instinctive, the urge in the animal to hide its hurt, but soon he must force himself to find some other road which would lead him back to Edinburgh and the train that would carry him to the Border—defeated.

The thought brought memories of Helen and a sudden, inexplicable sense of shame rushed through him, yet he had done his best. But he could not think of telling Helen about his failure, although he knew she would have some word for him—pity expressed in a way a man could take it. But he was not ready to go back to Helen yet.

He walked for two hours, following sign-posts along country roads and down into villages steeped in the gentle peace of the everlasting hills, while close at his heels stalked the hounds of memory, driving him on. He thought of the past and of the war years filled with the hope of meeting Margaret again and putting things right, and he reviewed over and over those last brief ten minutes in the austere sitting-room at Collister when all these hopes had been shattered by half a dozen words delivered in the cold, clipped tones of Isobel Oliver's stern disapproval. He wondered why they should loathe him so much—Isobel and Jean, at least—and then told himself grimly that he had succeeded in touching their pride and that, to women like Isobel and Jean, was fatal. Had Margaret, growing up in the years between, inherited such stern pride, he wondered. He could not visualise it, or see her becoming narrow or biased in any way. No, all that concerned him had nothing really to do with pride at all. It was just that Margaret had changed and out of the pity and tenderness of her heart she had found herself unable to tell him so. But what a messenger she had found in Isobel! What a weapon she had delivered, unsheathed, into her sister's willing hands! Even Jean would have wielded it more gently. Isobel had never liked him. He felt sure of that. Isobel had never really liked anyone. She lived remotely, in a world of her own, aping her older sister, but hating her too, with the deep-rooted hatred of intense envy. He had always known about Isobel—vaguely—but today he saw her character clearly, her gloating delight in power, even although she had attained it for only an hour in her sister's absence, the hard, purposeful look in her eyes which had denied him even the promise that Margaret should have his gift of flowers, and that final, brief dismissal as she had closed the door upon him herself. Yes, Isobel Oliver had had her little day and there was no denying that she had made the most of it, obtaining from it the utmost in satisfaction.

He could visualise her return to the room upstairs where Margaret waited, carrying his flowers, but there he was wrong, for as soon as the front door had closed behind him

Isobel Oliver had gone swiftly back into the room they had left and picked the pyrethrums up from the table. She stood with them between her hands for a moment while a procession of violent emotions stormed across her eyes, and then, slowly and deliberately, she crossed to the wide fireplace and crushed the flowers down into the fire. They were burned to a long strip of brown ash long before Jean Oliver returned to Collister at five o'clock.

CHAPTER SIX

IT was after five o'clock when Fergus returned to Edinburgh by bus. He felt deadly tired, drained of all emotion, with that empty feeling which entertains neither further thought nor any concerted plan of action. All he knew was that he would go back to the Keep sometime, and instinctively, it seemed, his thoughts were set upon the last train, recognising that it had something to do with Helen, her laughing reminder before he had left that morning that they wouldn't expect him before then. She had meant that if he didn't return before then she would know that all was well, and his visit to Collister had ended in success. Instead, he thought bitterly, it had fizzled out in abysmal failure—and one shrank from confronting Helen with failure of any sort. He had gone out with high hopes, meaning to conquer—Helen's hopes and his own, and he knew she would be bitterly disappointed on his return. She had liked Margaret on sight. He knew that, because Helen wasn't the sort of person who would back up your opinion unless she really meant it, and she had told him quite candidly that she didn't think Jean Oliver as formidable as he believed her to be. But he hadn't even come up against Jean! It had been Isobel who had administered the rebuff, dealing him the final, crushing blow. Isobel by proxy for Margaret!

Why was he trying to shield Margaret, pretending she could not have done this thing to him? She *had* done it, and in the most unkind manner possible, sending someone else to break the news of her engagement to him like that.

Anger flooded into his heart, anger and despair. He might blame her and try to despise her in an effort to cover up his hurt, but he still loved her, and deep in his heart he knew she had the absolute right of free choice. It was six years since they had parted, six years in which he had never ceased to think of her as the one and only desirable woman, and although he had had no definite proof of her heart's fidelity, she had not married in all that time.

Helen had brought him that news, feeling sure that it must mean something, and he had grasped at her confidence like a drowning man at a floating spar. Well, this was the result! He knew. Better, perhaps, to be sure than to go on enduring the agony of uncertainty which had engulfed him of late when there had seemed no way of ever getting into touch with Margaret again. Helen, with her practical good sense, had seen that the only way was to face the facts boldly, to go out determinedly and grapple with them once and for all. Well, he had grappled, and he had dug this up!

What now? His tired brain could give him no answer, and so he sought the station and Helen.

She was standing on the platform when the train drew in at Burndean, her soft hair blowing in the wind from the hills, her hands thrust deep into the pockets of her tweed suit, dark eyes surveying the carriages one by one, and a feeling he had believed dead in him stirred again as he experienced the true joy of coming home. It was Helen who had taught him what the Keep could mean to him and, but for Helen, he was doubtful if he would ever have returned there after to-day. She had implanted pride of lineage deep in his heart and it seemed he owed it to her —and to Ken—to carry on.

'Hullo!' she greeted him, searching his face. 'This is the first train I've met—honestly! I knew you wouldn't come back by an earlier one.'

He said trying to steady his voice: 'I suppose you've brought the car? Is Syd with you?'

'No, I drove over myself—but don't start scolding! I know the roads about the Keep almost as well as Syd by now.'

Well, he was glad they were going back alone. They could talk in the car, and it might be easier to talk while they drove through the gathering dusk.

'We've had such a day,' she told him. 'You'd almost think things went wrong on purpose just because you had decided to take a few hours off!'

'I could have been back before five,' he said, and saw her look at him sharply and then away again. 'Was it anything serious?'

'No, it was all very trivial and easily enough sorted out.' The laughter had died in her eyes and she got into the seat beside him with a queer little feeling of misgiving at her heart. 'There was nothing that Syd and I couldn't tackle between us.'

She sat silently, waiting for him to speak, her hands clasped tightly in her lap, and he thought it significant that she kept her eyes steadily fixed on the way ahead. She knew. She knew that he had failed, that he had returned empty-handed. Well, he wasn't going to weep on her shoulder about it; that sort of thing would upset Helen, and he had a fair idea that she would secretly despise people who whined over a misfortune. The thing was, though, that nobody had ever been a better listener than Helen; you felt that she understood when there had ceased to be any words to define what was going on inside your brain. Helen found her own words and applied them silently, and what she had to say in return could never be termed preaching. If she wanted to bowl you out she did it straight from the shoulder, and he admired her for that.

'Well, I'm back!' he commented grimly as he started the engine.

'And you're no further forward as far as Margaret is concerned?'

He let the car slide down the gravel approach before he answered.

'We're right at the end of the road, Helen.'

His voice had sounded flat, almost unemotional, but she was quick to realise all the pent-up feelings which lay behind that tone, the frustration and sense of hurt, and the heart's longing that would never grow less, the love which no amount of pride would ever subdue.

She said candidly, 'I'm disappointed. Do you want to tell me what happened?'

'What's the use?' he returned with a flash of angry defiance. 'There can't be any reason why I should go on burdening you with my affairs.'

'I don't feel burdened,' she said quietly. 'It's just as you want, though.'

But he was still half defiant and wholly bitter.

'There's nothing we can make of it,' he declared. 'It has always been the same when I tried anything in their direction. I failed, Helen, failed miserably, "while malignant fate sat by and smiled"!'

'In the shape of Jean Oliver, do you mean?'

'No, curiously enough, I didn't see Jean, although I went out to Collister.'

'With Margaret?' Helen asked in some surprise.

'In search of Margaret. When I got to the Nurses' Home I was told she had gone to Collister the afternoon before with a touch of 'flu—this mild kind that's going around just now—and she had left word for you to go out there.'

Helen turned to look at him, seeing his clear-cut profile etched against the square of the car window and the determined set of his jaw with a little feeling of pride.

'So you bearded all the lions in their den at once!'

'I set out to do it that way,' he answered grimly, 'but eventually I only met one lion. I didn't see Margaret.'

There was a deep silence, at the end of which she asked incredulously,

'They refused to let you see her?'

'Margaret refused me—through her sister.'

'Isobel?'

He nodded, and presently Helen said,

'Isobel was the only one of Ken's family I really disliked.'

She said it with the air of one making a discovery, and he saw that her dark brows were closely drawn together.

'She did her sister act very competently, all the same.' He had steeled his voice to a new hardness. 'And, after all, she was only telling me what Margaret wanted me to know.'

'Which was?'

'That she's going to marry the surgeon fellow—Hamilton Purdie, isn't it?'

'Somehow,' Helen said slowly, 'I don't believe it.'

'But, these are facts, Helen!' He sounded almost impatient. 'She sent down a message.'

'The exact words of which were?'

'There weren't any exact words.' He was frowning now, too. 'Isobel merely told me I had no right to be there, since I had come off my own bat—without a printed card! She added that the family took a pretty poor view of such things and that Margaret was going to be married.'

'When?'

'Helen, don't ask me to cope with details!'

'When, exactly, do they hope Margaret is going to be married?' She pressed the question relentlessly. 'I think it might be rather important to know.'

'Oh, she didn't mention any definite date and I didn't ask her for one. What does it matter, anyway! I believe the phrase Isobel used was that they were "about to be married".'

'And you didn't see anyone else? Not even Hattie?'

'No—nobody else. I got out as quickly as I could after that.'

'Where was Jean?'

'How should I know? Out somewhere, I suppose.'

He raced the engine in the ensuing silence, taking the flat stretch before the Keep at speed.

'I wish you had seen Jean instead of Isobel,' Helen said.

'What difference would it have made? I had to hear the truth some time and it didn't matter a lot who told me in the end as far as I can see.'

He's raw, Helen was thinking, wounded by a cruel stab from Isobel, who would take a fiendish delight in that sort of torture. But Margaret! Why hadn't Margaret made some effort to see him, even if it were only to break it gently to him that the love of all those years ago had died?

Oh, but it couldn't have died! Helen, who had loved so intently herself, repudiated the very thought.

'I'm not going to believe it till I've seen Margaret again,' she declared stoutly. 'And neither must you.'

'It's no use, Helen.' He was sunk in a black mood of despair. 'After all, you met her with this Purdie fellow yourself.'

'And I didn't get the impression that she was in love with him.'

'You were only in their company for a very short time, and he's a splendid catch, isn't he? Margaret's keen on the profession, too—'

'You're building up a case against yourself!'

'I'm trying to face facts.'

'All the unpleasant ones.' She laid an impulsive hand on his knee. 'Forgive me, 'Gus, if I'm raking over the coals, but I feel there's something we must get to the bottom of here. It's all so very—vague.'

' There was nothing vague about Isobel, I can assure you,' he returned grimly, 'and I for one am not going back for any more.'

Anger and hurt pride were predominating now, Helen realised without surprise. It would take him a day or two to get over the anger and perhaps weeks to forget his pride, and they really could not afford to wait for weeks. It looked, therefore, as if it was a job which she must tackle herself in the very near future, and although she wondered why she should interfere at all, she knew she would make one further effort to see Margaret and learn the truth for herself.

Of course, there was the probability that she might be wrong, but she was still convinced that nobody could look like Margaret had done when she had mentioned Fergus and the Keep and then change her mind in a matter of days. She believed that Margaret's affection had been the lasting sort and she was determined to find out in spite of to-day's sorry events.

So, over supper she purposefully dismissed the subject of the Olivers and his disastrous visit to Collister, regaling him with the events of the day at the Keep. Bessie had pulled the gate-legged table close to the fire and they sat long over their coffee talking, but Helen saw that sometimes his eyes were remote, and she guessed that his mind must be slipping back to the room in Edinburgh where all the warmth seemed to have gone out of life for him, never to return. But Fergus's thoughts had gone down even further into the past. He was seeing the round room where they sat as it had been long ago, a big, cheerful room with the lived-in appearance common to the 'house-place' in large families, and he could hear the echo of voices that would ring hollowly in his heart for ever. Yet he would continue to live here, carrying on at the Keep because it was his duty. It was what was expected of him—what Helen expected! He thought that she belonged here as surely as he did and for a wild moment he imagined that he could not do better than ask her to marry him. And then he knew that the idea was fantastic. You couldn't offer anyone as splendid as Helen second best or expect them to mistake pity for love, and suddenly he was face to face with the stark loneliness which had lain at the bottom of the original thought. He had wanted Helen to stand between him and that abysmal loneliness of the soul which he had experienced for six long years while he waited and yearned for Margaret and the chance to find her again. And Helen had understood and offered to help. That was all. Helen was not the kind to fall in love a second time easily, and he had always had the feeling that a good deal of her heart had been left behind in the Far East. Not that it had been buried in Kenneth Oliver's lonely grave—Helen would be wise enough to see the futility of that—but she had lived out there during the impressionable years of her early twenties and all her interests had been centred there. Almost he had sensed a yearning in her to return, a vague wistfulness reaching out to that land where she had first known happiness and love.

Imagination, probably, but there it was, as clean-cut an impression about anyone as he had ever had. He looked across the hearth at her, noticing for the first time that her thoughts appeared to have wandered from the present and that her eyes were troubled.

'Helen, is there anything wrong?' he asked. 'I feel so infernally selfish, thinking only about myself like this—'

'It may be nothing,' she said, rising to take down an envelope from the high mantelpiece where she had laid it after she had opened it and read it through. 'It's a letter from that aunt of mine I told you about who lives in Yorkshire. I wrote to her and I've just had her reply today. She wants me to go down there.'

'You thought of going, of course, didn't you?'

'Yes, I thought of going eventually.' Her eyes looked darker, overshadowed by a deep emotion. 'Now I know I shall have to go at once. Her letter is very short—she's a busy woman.' She slipped the single sheet out of its envelope and handed it to him. 'Would you like to read what she says?'

He took it from her, scanning the handwriting carefully.

'DEAR HELEN,' he read, 'I was right glad to get your letter and hope you really mean it when you say you're going to pay us a visit soon. It was grand news, hearing you had got out of that awful Jap prison, but your letter didn't tell us nearly enough. Our Bill fought in Malaya, you know, but we'll be giving you all the news when you come. This is just to tell you that we'll be right glad to have you and to let you know there's been someone here looking for you. A gentleman from the East, he was, and he said something about a boy you might have with you, but we said we knew nothing about that and he went away.'

Fergus Oliver's eyes were suddenly lifted from the paper to Helen's pale face.

'Do you think it might be—Tony's father?' he asked.

She moistened her dry lips before she answered him.

'I don't know. It may be, and oh, Fergus, I've no right to feel as I do about it! I should be glad—I *am* glad, only there's this other me that wants Tony—that can't bear to part with the little boy who was once the baby I nursed. I don't suppose I should even try to excuse myself—'

Her voice broke suddenly as he bent forward, covering the hand that lay on her knee with strong, protective fingers.

'Helen,' he said, 'maybe a man can't understand as fully as he thinks he does, but I know what you mean, and there's no need to make excuses for the sort of love you've always given Tony. He's the kind of boy who reflects it, too.'

She said in a husky whisper,

'I've been thinking about Tony—about what I should tell him.'

'Do you need to tell him anything at this stage? After all, it may not be his father.'

'I can't think of anyone else who might be looking for me, knowing about Tony—unless it was one of the doctors on the ship coming home. They took a great interest in all the children and Tony was a general favourite.'

She rose abruptly, gripping the edge of the high mantelpiece with strong fingers and laying her forehead against them in a little gesture of weariness which he thought infinitely pathetic. It told him better than any confession could have done how long she had thought around the subject of her ultimate parting with the child, battling with a perfectly natural desire to keep him, yet forcing herself to accept the inevitable and face the fact that the man who was Tony's father and a stranger to her might claim him in a matter of days.

'You won't take Tony with you?' he questioned.

'I don't know.' She spoke with her head still bowed on her hands, gazing into the glowing heart of the fire. 'I wish I knew what was best to do, Fergus. I have spoken to him quite often about his father, trying to build up a sort of word-picture of a man I never really knew, and it will be the most wonderful day in Tony's life if he ever meets him in the flesh. That's why I should be glad,' she repeated. 'Glad—if this is really the man who handed his son into my keeping from that burning ship.'

'If it is,' Fergus reflected, 'it means that they got safely away.'

'But surely it means, too, that they must have been taken prisoner by the Japs, just as we were, because otherwise he would have made some effort to trace Tony before now.'

'Yes, I think that might be the answer,' Fergus agreed. 'Your aunt doesn't mention any name,' he observed, scanning the letter again. 'Would it convey anything to you if she had?'

She shook her head.

'Not a thing. I believe I told you that the papers he gave

me were washed overboard. I hadn't time to look at them. All I knew was that the baby's name was Tony. He told me that as he passed the child down into the lifeboat.' She straightened, her face entirely devoid of colour. 'I'll never forget the look in his eyes for that split second, Fergus—never as long as I live.'

'You'd know him again, of course?'

'Know him! I've thought of him almost constantly during all these years—whenever I looked at Tony, I think! I've thought what it must have meant to him to part with his child like that—handing a baby over to a stranger.'

'He knew you, Helen,' he said quietly. 'I would have done it.'

She turned to him with a little quivering smile.

'Would you? Well, I've done the best I could, and—and if I have to part with Tony now I must tell myself that I always knew it would happen, that—I'm ready and it will be best for Tony. They belong together—'

There was a deep silence and then he said almost vehemently,

'I wish there was some other way out. It seems so unfair.'

'To me? Oh no! I have always known, and I have hoped that he wasn't really dead—for Tony's sake. He seemed the sort of man who would understand a boy, somehow, and Tony's just the age to need him now.' She met his sympathetic eyes across the hearth. 'That was why I was so glad to have him here with you. You could give him so much that I couldn't—a man's outlook on life—something he'll need in after years. I didn't want to make him soft.'

'You wouldn't have done that, Helen, and I must confess that I don't see what Tony is going to do without you.'

'His father—if this is his father—may have married again.'

'Yes,' he said thoughtfully, frowning as he said it, 'that's a possibility.'

'You're thinking that perhaps she might not be the right sort?' Her lips quivered, but she steadied them resolutely. 'I've thought that, too, but it's foolish to meet trouble of that kind half way. If he has married—and whoever she is—how could she possibly fail to love my boy!'

Your boy! he thought compassionately. Yes, Helen, you'll always think of Tony as that!

'Look here,' he said, 'why not leave Tony at the Keep while you go south? He's had enough travelling to last him for quite a bit, and the truth is I'd miss him like the dickens if he went now. If this man does turn out to be his father, why not bring him back here with you and let Tony get acquainted in the surroundings he knows? I think it would be better for him—and easier for you.'

She looked at him for a long moment, her eyes dark with emotion.

'You've been so good about everything,' she said. 'And—yes, I think that would be best for Tony. He loves it here, Fergus, and I think if he were to meet his father here it might make him happier.'

'When will you go?' he asked.

'The day after tomorrow, I think. Can I get a reasonably fast train from Berwick or should I go to Edinburgh?'

'You'd be just about as quick from Berwick in the long run,' he advised. 'Syd will drive you over, and Tony can help me in the fields till you come back.'

'How about Mrs Michie? Won't she think it too much after my jaunt to Edinburgh? Any boy's a handful.'

'Bessie Michie will be in her glory! She's the type who couldn't get on without a bit of a grumble now and then, but it just doesn't mean a thing, and she likes nothing better than being left in full charge!'

'Tomorrow,' she said suddenly, dismissing both their troubles with calm resolution, 'I mean to ride all over the estate. Do you think you might find time to have a picnic lunch with us?'

He knew what she wanted. One last day free as her heart could make it of care, one day to be alone with Tony in the surroundings they had both grown to love in so short a time, one perfect day to treasure against the emptiness of the future.

'I'm going over to Garrielaw to see what Muir's doing about the hill-grazing over on that side,' he said, 'so if you like, we could go as far as Hermitage Castle. That is if you don't think it will be too much for Tony?'

'Nothing would daunt Tony on MacNab! I'm the one who may want to fall out. Remember I'm not a very expert horsewoman yet!' she laughed.

'Would you rather I took the car then?' he asked, knowing what her answer would be even before she spoke.

'Not on your life! I don't think cars can be half so reliable as a good horse on these parts—at least, not cars of the Ford's vintage!'

'I object—on behalf of poor Liz! So far she has proved faithful enough, in spite of numerous wheezes and groans, and if there are some hills she refuses to take except in reverse, it must be the fault of the hills!'

They laughed, and she said through her laughter,

'Let's forget everything tomorrow except the fact that it is one glorious day! I think that's a mistake we all make,' she added more soberly, 'not being able to wall each day in and live it for itself. "And I shall tip my cup to drain the last sweet drop of any joy I may be drinking." Grace Noll Crowell thought that about walled-in days and I mean to drain mine tomorrow, Fergus, whatever may happen in the days that come afterwards.'

He couldn't say anything to that, but as he looked at her standing there on his hearth, where she should have stood by right as the dearly-beloved *châtelaine* of this lovely old house, he vowed that, as far as it might lie within his power, the day she had asked for should be made perfect.

CHAPTER SEVEN

SOME say that in all the dale country Liddesdale of a thousand streams is the fairest of them all, and to Helen Oliver, as she rode through it on that bright May morning with a gentle wind in her hair and the sun caressing her cheeks, it was perfection indeed. She heard the voice of many waters and the singing of the birds; she saw the cloud shadows chasing each other over Larriston Fell and the dappled pattern of leaves on a white-sanded road: she heard the bleating of sheep from a distance and the high call of the peewit echoing plaintively against the silence, and at the bottom of her heart she knew that nothing could ever steal the beauty and the simple joy of this day from her.

They ate their lunch in a glade by the Hermitage Water, and while she gathered up their cups and paper plates to return them to the haversack, Fergus told Tony all he could remember of the castle's history.

'Was it as strong as Oliver's Keep?' the boy demanded at the close of the tale, jealous of their prestige.

'All castles and keeps needed to be strong in those days,' Fergus returned diplomatically, 'but when we get back to the Keep you can compare it with Hermitage and tell me what you think.'

'I think the Keep would be best,' averred Tony stoutly. 'It could see farthest, 'cause it's right in the gap between the hills.'

Helen laughed, pulling him towards her to press a kiss on his serious face.

'Tony, you are a loyal little soul! And now, do we ride back very slowly and get to the Keep in time for tea?'

They were all agreed, and as Fergus helped her to mount he laid a hand on her stirrup strap, saying spontaneously,

'Helen, this day will always remind me that there are

other things in life apart from frustration and disappointment.'

'I'm glad,' she said simply. 'I've enjoyed every minute of it.'

He knew that she was speaking the truth, that she possessed the rare gift of being able to count her blessings and receive the healing in them in full measure, and he marvelled at her resilience, envying her a little. Tomorrow, when she had gone, he knew that he would be cast back into the slough of despond, and he found himself wondering what would be Helen's remedy for that, but would not ask her because he had given her his promise to make this day perfect.

They reached the Keep as the sun hid himself behind a mass of cumulus cloud, and Helen looked up at it as if it were an omen, but she said nothing, smilingly defying it to take from her that which she had.

Bessie Michie was hovering at the kitchen window when they rode into the yard, and Fergus said with a laugh,

'I'll bet she's been watching the road for the last hour and calculating how long it should take the kettle to boil after she had spotted us coming over Highcleugh!'

'I dare say.' Helen moved in her saddle with a groan. 'Oh, Lord! I'm not all in one piece! I'm quite sure of it!'

Fergus grinned unkindly.

'Which piece do you suggest I should move first?'

'Don't laugh—or I'll slay you!' She gave him her hand, lowering herself slowly and painfully out of the saddle. 'If I'm capable of slaying anyone at the moment!'

'Mummy,' Tony laughed, 'you're all folded up!'

'We've gone too far, Helen,' Fergus tried to say seriously.

She straightened with an effort, laughing up at him.

'Not a bit of it. It was worth—even this!'

'A hot bath ought to put you right,' he suggested. 'Better grab it while I delay the tea.'

'I'll do nothing before I have my tea!' She turned as Bessie Michie hurried forward. 'Hullo, Mrs Michie! I know the kettle's on the boil and I'm simply gasping. Never take

'Helen!' Anna Smirthwaite stopped to take breath and look at her. 'Ee, lass, but you 'ave gone thin! Ah all but passed thee by!'

Helen smiled, loving the sound of the rich Yorkshire dialect which swept her back to early youth when this woman with the rough exterior and heart of gold had opened her door to her, welcoming her as one of a family already grown too large for her slender means.

'I'll fatten out soon enough, I expect,' she said. 'Probably when you've had time to get some of your good Yorkshire ham and eggs into me, for I simply refuse to believe that it's not to be had in the dales in spite of rationing and a dozen governments!'

'Maybe ye're reight!' said Anna with her slow smile that was as rich as her broad tongue. 'But we mun get tae bus, lass. It's a bit oot o' toon, is Canderby.'

While they walked to the bus stop Anna gave her details of the family: Bill just back from India; Jose nursing in the south; Gerald and Tom in the Navy; Phyllis taking a special course before being demobilised from the ATS, and the twins still at school.

'What a brood you've had, Aunt Anna!' Helen smiled, 'and how you must have missed them all these past few years.'

'Ay, Ah missed them, but Ah've been real proud of them an' all. Bill 'as done grand, and t'others have been happy in their work, too. Ah've got nowt tae grumble at. Ah've had a full life, an' what more could a woman like me want? Ah've brought up me bairns tae fear God an' tell the truth an' nivver tae do a bad action tae their fellow-man, an' now Ah mun leave t' rest tae theirsels.'

'They'll not let you down,' Helen said. 'I'm sure of that.'

They took their seats in the bus and soon the busy market town was left behind and they were out on a wide white road in a land of broad acres and low, grey stone farmhouses with field upon field of growing crops stretching away in a chequerboard of greens and yellows as far as eye could see, a flat and fertile plain bounded by the high blue ridge of the Cleveland Hills in the north and the distant, smoke-grey Pennines in the west and south.

When she had first gone to Scotland the Border country had reminded Helen strongly of the Yorkshire dales she knew so well and now the similarity seemed even more marked as the bus carried them in among the hills.

'Is Bill at home?' she asked, turning from the window at last.

'Nay, his leave was up last week. He would have liked fine to have seen ye, but Ah doot if ye'd have known him. He's bigger an' broader than ivver!'

'I can always remember the fun we used to have when Bill was at home,' Helen said. 'He was always trying something new.'

'Ay, Bill was a one for an experiment! Allus tryin' summut different, was Bill! D'ye remember when he was just a lad an' Ah said ivverything aboot a hoose should run on oiled wheels?'

'And then the vicar came to tea and sat down on the best chair in the parlour which promptly shot straight across the room, complete with vicar, cup of tea, and bun!'

'Ay, Bill had oiled t'wheels all reight—ivvery wheel in t'hoose! Ah could hae died at the look o' surprise on t'vicar's face when chair hit t'wall!'

'He took it well enough, though,' Helen laughed. 'I always thought he was a very good vicar after that—a very human man! Yes, Aunt Anna, we've had some fun at Canderby in our time, yet when I was first evacuated there I told father I'd probable die of boredom in a week!'

'There's nane o' us dies of havin' too little work tae dae in t'country!' Anna declared. 'An' now, what aboot theesel', lass? We heard you were married, but we nivver got any more letters after that.'

'No, I suppose that was typical of most Jap camps,' Helen observed, her face sobering. 'They just didn't bother to forward our mail, but I did write, Aunt Anna, and sometimes I wondered why you hadn't answered until we became used to unanswered letters and guessed why they had gone astray.'

'They're a bad lot, t' Japs. You should just hear our Bill

on about them, an' that gentleman that was here a week or two back askin' for you had some experience o' them, too, Ah'll be warned.'

Helen's heart seemed to stand still for a moment and then thump on as if she had been running.

'I wanted to ask you about him, Aunt Anna,' she said. 'I must know who he is—all he told you. Did he say anything about Tony—why he had asked about him?'

'He said as how you might have a young lad with you when you came back to England,' Anna explained carefully, 'but Ah could only tell him Ah didn't know anything aboot any boy, an' I nivver knew as how you had a son. "Oh no," says he, "it was not Mrs Oliver's son. You think, then, that your niece returned to England alone?" And I ups and tells him that no niece of Anna Smirthwaite's would leave an unprotected bairn in a foreign land unless she had very good reason for it. And he says "No?" and his mouth was hardlike, as if he thought a' things were possible in a wicked world.'

'But he must have given you his name or left some message,' Helen said urgently.

'His name was Major Grant Pemberton, an' he said as how the boy were his.'

Anna made the statement baldly and subsided into silence, sitting upright on the narrow bus-seat with her woollen gloved hands clasped tightly over her bulging shopping bag and looking straight ahead, as if she sensed the girl by her side might need several minutes to collect her thoughts.

Helen had scarcely felt shock or surprise at the revelation, however. She had known deep within her that this was the news which would be waiting for her at the end of her journey and she tried to accept it calmly.

'Was—Major Pemberton alone?' she asked presently.

'Oh, ay. He had come by car, an' he said as how he were going back to London that neight because he mun go somewhere else in t'mornin'.'

'I see. And—did he leave an address?'

'Nay. He said as how he must try some other way o'

findin' thee, but that he would come back again if he couldn't.'

'And you got my letter soon afterwards?'

'The very next week, but nivver a word has come from him since.'

'You don't know, for instance, if he was living in London or stationed near there?'

'All he said was that he was on leave—same as our Bill—an' that he had been a prisoner of t' Japs, same as you.'

'Then, he did know that much. Oh, Aunt Anna, I seem to have gone all the wrong way about this. I—I've made such a mess of things—'

Helen looked swiftly out of the window, biting her lips to still their sudden trembling.

'What's ter do, lass?' Anna Smirthwaite asked softly. 'What's ter do?'

'I seem to have muddled everything hopelessly,' Helen confessed, finding relief in speech now. 'Tony—the little boy I brought back to England with me—is Major Pemberton's son and it seems dreadful that he should have been forced to search for him like this, not knowing whether he was alive or not. I should have taken more definite steps to trace him long ago, only I didn't even know his name. I knew the name of the ship he was on, of course, but the shipping lines just couldn't help me. There were so many unauthorised people on board every ship in those last few days before the surrender of Singapore that it was impossible to keep any sort of record.'

'Ah warrant you did your best, lass,' was what Anna Smirthwaite said, although she must still have been surprised and puzzled by the situation. 'An' no one can do more nor that.'

'I took care of Tony, that's all I can say,' Helen answered huskily as the bus jerked to a standstill and the half-dozen passengers began to collect their parcels and file out. 'But I don't seem to have done very much else—except tie him round my heartstrings.'

Anna was silent, gazing down the familiar village street with a thoughtful look in her eyes. Canderby stood at the head of the dale, shut in by the hills on either side, the junction of two dale roads where two swift dale rivers met to rush tempestuously beneath a grey stone bridge in the centre of a collection of grey stone dwellings and half a dozen shops. The grey church with its square stone tower stood a little way back on a knoll looking down on the long buildings where a famous dale cheese was made, and the broad, grass-verged road climbed steadily through the village and away to hide itself among the hills.

On all the hills above and around Canderby sheep grazed, filling the air with their bleating, and in the meadows on the low ground the cattle lay in the sun while a lark poured out his heart in song far above in the blue May sky.

'It's—just the same,' Helen said. 'Nothing's changed.'

No, nothing had changed, her thoughts ran on: it was only the people who had gone away who had suffered change, the young people, like Aunt Anna's Bill, and Jose and young Phyllis—and herself! How young and inexperienced had been the Helen Metcalfe who had left Canderby seven years ago with such high hopes to become a nurse and volunteer for service in the East! How young she had been. Yes, how young! Why was it that today she felt a hundred years old? Why was it that all these seven years were seen in retrospect as a lifetime?

It was no use trying to deceive herself. It was because she was going to lose Tony, and she had built her life around Tony. He was the future. He was to have been recompense for all the past.

They climbed the steep main street which so quickly became the moorland road again, and approached the gate of Anna's home. It was one of a short row of grey stone houses with its back garden rising steeply on to the hillside but looking out in front across a green panorama of dale and river and winding road, across acres of rich meadowland to the sheltering hills on the other side. A laburnum tree had spilled a golden carpet of petals on Anna's path and they walked over it to the front door.

'Ah've put thee in Jose's room,' Anna told her. 'Up you go an' Ah'll put on kettle. It's half-day in t'shop.'

The Smirthwaites owned the local hardware store. It

had been in the family for three generations and each generation had raised big families, the eldest son always falling heir to 't'shop,' which yielded no very great profit and demanded quite a lot of hard work. The other members of the family had generally been content to find work in the cheese factory or at local farms, but once or twice a 'scholar' had emerged who had gone on to the Grammar School at Northallerton and from thence into the wider world beyond the dales.

Tom Smirthwaite had been content with his lot in Canderby, had helped to raise his family of seven and passed on, leaving his wife, Anna, to complete the task and see them all to maturity.

Helen had often wondered if Bill, the high-spirited lad who had always looked upon life as one great experiment, would be content to settle down in Canderby and manage 't'shop.' Somehow, she did not think he would, and when she met him again a few days later she was sure that the prospect held no attraction for him. It would be left to Anna Smirthwaite to carry on until one of the twins, who were still at school, was old enough to take some of the responsibility from her stooping shoulders. War had not touched the twins. They knew nothing of the world beyond the dales and an occasional visit to the nearest market town, and they would be content.

Helen put her bag down on the flowered counterpane of Jose's bed and took off her hat and coat. She felt incapable of thought for a moment, and then she crossed to the bay window overlooking the road and the sloping meadows beyond. Beneath her and to the right lay the silent village and before her the field and the river sleeping in the sun, while above and around them rose the quiet hills, shedding their peace and tranquillity over all. She pushed open the window and leaned out, thinking of the man who had been there three weeks ago looking for his son, and seeing his face clearly as if it had been suddenly etched against the patch of blue sky above her head.

What was she to do now? The wind came down from the hills, blowing against her hot cheek and lifting the hair gently from her brow, and it seemed to bring with it a measure of peace. Then from somewhere, and almost as if they had been uttered again in the quiet room behind her, came the echo of Anna Smirthwaite's words. 'Ah warrant ye did your best, lass, an' no one can do more nor that.'

She went downstairs to find Anna infusing the tea.

'You'll be stoppin' with us for a few days till you've made up your mind what to do,' she said.

'I've made up my mind,' Helen said. 'I'm going to London to try to find Major Pemberton.'

There was a silence, and then,

'Ah weel, lass, maybe that's the best way, an' all,' agreed Anna. 'Ah would be thinkin' that it was me duty to spare him even one day's worry aboot his little lad.'

CHAPTER EIGHT

HELEN stayed at Canderby for three days, quiet eventless days in the green dale, full of sunshine and the bleating of lambs. The whole dale resounded with their cries, and the fulfilment of spring was a never-ending wonder to her. Because Anna was busy in 't'shop' she took long walks by herself, thinking mostly of Tony and the man she now knew to be his father. She must do everything in her power to trace him and restore his child to him after these long years of separation which must have been torture to him, and often she would try to visualise the scene of their reunion, hoping that he would fall in with Fergus's suggestion and come to the Keep so that Tony might get to know him in the surroundings he loved so well.

The thought of their inevitable parting was ever with her, and her heart quailed before it. No mother could have felt more deeply for her child than she had done for the small, helpless bundle Major Pemberton had passed to her across a dark gulf of water from a burning ship. She had known the agony of fear when she had listened to his laborious breathing through the crisis of pneumonia; she had experienced joy unutterable at the reassurance in a doctor's voice when he had told her there would be no complications and no further need for anxiety; she had been foolishly worried over possible accidents which had never happened, seeing by the aid of a too vivid imagination a car smash and a child on a tricycle hopelessly trapped; she had laughed and cried and scolded over all the little things that mark the milestones from infancy to seven years old, and now she was going to lose him. It was like facing death, knowing it would come inevitably, seeing the emptiness of what lay ahead, yet being powerless to avert it. It was saying good-bye to something she had foolishly treasured against her own future loneliness, something the very possession of which would double that loneliness and make the thoughts of the past so bitter-sweet.

There was no question of grudging Major Pemberton his child. She was glad that Tony was to know and appreciate his father at last, but there was no denying the ache in her own heart nor the desperate feeling of loss which engulfed her each time she thought of their parting.

'I don't know what to do,' she confessed to Anna, 'but I think the best thing would be to get into touch with the Colonial Office. They may be able to trace him for me from the little I know and, failing that, I suppose I might try the War Office.'

'Ah cannot say as to how you would be going on, lass,' Anna replied, 'but if you've a mind to look up our Bill he might be a help. There's not much he doesn't know about t'war. Ah allus says as how it's aged him, but it's given him a lot of good sense into the bargain.'

'Is he in London?' Helen asked, quite glad of the opportunity of meeting someone she knew in the city who might be able to help her in her search.

'He's near enough. Aldershot t'place is called. You could send him a wire from Northallerton.'

Helen acted on her advice the following day. She spent the night in Northallerton to catch the early morning train to London, and sent her telegram from a small sub-post office near the station. There was no way of getting a reply, so she had to be content to leave it at her request to be met at King's Cross, and hope that Bill Smirthwaite would be there if he could possibly get away.

The five hours' journey left her ample time for thought, and she spent most of it wondering about Major Pemberton—what the war years had done to him, and how he planned to provide for his son. Never once did she give thought to the debt he owed her. It simply did not enter her mind, for to Helen these years had been her own gain. She had loved and cared for a child, the child she had always longed for but which fate had denied her, and she considered herself blessed. That it should end like this had been more or less inevitable right from the start, only she had never let herself think of the consequences of loving so deeply and so utterly. It had been natural to her to give her love unstintedly, and one did not consider reaping where love was sown. It was something poured out liberally from a generous heart with no thought of return, something given spontaneously and gladly that another might benefit—unselfish love, the crown of many a life.

As the train slowed into King's Cross she began to make her plans, plans which she now realised should have been made three days ago when she had first decided to come to London. It would be impossible to travel back to Scotland immediately, and she had nowhere to stay. It was early in the season, however, for holidaymakers, and she hoped to be able to find a room in a quiet, centrally situated hotel. Bill might be able to help her in that respect—if Bill was there to meet her.

She began to look for him, wondering if she would recognise him immediately after all these years, but when she went through the ticket barrier there was nobody answering his description in sight. Disappointed, she turned to call a taxi, but before one had cruised into sight a voice boomed out behind her:

'It is Helen, isn't it? Yes, I was pretty sure of it!' She turned to find his eyes twinkling down into hers. 'What a hectic dash I've made to get here! You and Mum didn't give me much time.'

'My visit was all planned in such a rush and we thought of you at the last moment,' Helen explained, smiling into his pleased eyes. 'Bill, you've grown enormously! I don't think I should have known you if I'd met you in a crowd!'

'You chose a crowded enough place to make a try,' Bill observed, making their way through the swarm of passengers pressing towards the platform she had just left, 'but I'd have known you anywhere. You haven't changed a lot, Helen.'

'Your mother thinks I've gone desperately thin.'

He observed her critically.

'You don't just come up to dale standards, of course, but you'll probably fatten out in time. You've had a nasty experience,' he added more seriously, 'and I expect being on the thin side is the least of it. Where do you suggest we eat?'

'The first step in the fattening process?' Helen laughed. 'Can you make it somewhere quiet? I want to talk.'

'Did you ever know a woman who didn't!' he grinned, halting on the edge of the pavement to signal a taxi. 'I think I know just the sort of place you want.'

When they had settled back against the leather cushioning he turned to look at her more closely.

'Want to begin talking now?' he asked, 'or will you wait till we've eaten?'

'There's quite a lot to be said,' she told him, 'and I'd like to start some enquiries as soon as we've had lunch. You see, Bill, I'm looking for someone I don't know very much about, and it's going to be difficult.'

'It isn't the guy who called at home asking for you, by any chance?' he asked. 'I think Mother got that all wrong, by the way. She said he was looking for his kid and he thought you might have him with you.'

'I have,' Helen explained. 'It's a longish story, Bill, and I'll fill in the details over lunch, but the point is that this Major Pemberton does really seem to be Tony's father, and I've got to find him.'

Bill Smirthwaite gave her a long, straight look.

'It's going to be tough on you, I expect—giving the kid up.'

Helen swallowed hard.

'I can't think of myself in this—I mustn't think, Bill! Self-pity or regret or anything like that would be a poor sort of thing in the face of all this man must have suffered, and I'm glad—yes, I'm glad that I'm on the way to finding him at last.'

'He didn't tell Mother a lot,' Bill said. 'And to be absolutely truthful, I didn't take a great deal of notice of what she said at the time. I thought it was an old admirer seeking you out—the usual sort of thing. A shipboard acquaintance or something like that.'

'No,' Helen said with a little smile, 'it was nothing like that.'

The taxi drew up before the small restaurant he had chosen and they were lucky enough to secure a table in a corner beside one of the net-covered windows overlooking the street. It was a side-street, and to Helen they did not seem to be in the heart of London at all. It was good of Bill to have fallen in with her mood so quickly and she found herself looking across the table at him and remembering what Anna Smirthwaite had said. He had come a long way from the dales.

Over her meal she told him all that had happened as briefly as possible and all she knew about Major Pemberton.

'Which, all boiled down, isn't very much,' he reflected, pushing his empty coffee-cup from him and leaning his arms along the table to look at her reflectively. 'I think our first port of call might be the Colonial Office, as you suggest. That ought to start something, at least.'

He knew his way about London, a fact for which Helen breathed a silent prayer. She had never felt at home there: it was too big, too impersonal for her liking, and now that she was there on a most personal errand she was glad she was not to be forced to find her way alone. It was a strange admission for one who had travelled fearlessly right across the world, and the roots of it were to be found in the turmoil raging in her heart. She was feeling desperately alone of a sudden, facing the loss of the child who had become a very part of her, and London is the last city to alleviate that kind of loneliness. Its size intimidated her, and the people hurrying past on the pavement, bent upon their separate business, all seemed beings from another world. The very friendliness which she had felt on her arrival in the capital from Southampton less than six months ago seemed to have evaporated, leaving her coldly alone, but she could not be daunted in her search for the man whose appearance would inevitably mean the end of her dreams.

Her hand sought Bill's arm as they left the restaurant, stopping him as he would have hailed another taxi.

'Could we walk, please?'

'It will take longer,' he warned, 'and these places are generally as dead as a door nail after about four o'clock. "If you'll come back to-morrow, please . . ." You know the sort of thing.'

'But it's only two-thirty and they've still to have their afternoon tea!' She tried to smile. 'If we could be there by three—'

'All right, we'll step it out. And now you can tell me all about where you're living—this ancestral castle you've struck somewhere in the wilds of Scotland.'

'It isn't at all like that,' she protested, and tried to describe the Keep to him, but the thought of Oliver's Keep brought thoughts of Tony and her heart began to ache with longing again, so that soon she had turned the conversation to Canderby and the dales and he told her that he didn't want to go back to Yorkshire to take up life where he had left it.

'I've been to war, Helen, and it's changed my views about life. You can't say to me now, "Go, bury yourself in the dales and keep shop." I want to do more than that with my life.' He was suddenly confiding. 'I've been working a lot on Radar and it's got me. I couldn't go back to selling egg-whisks and milking-pails and having a drink in the local on Saturday nights. I want to go on experimenting—to be in on the big things that are coming. I've been offered a job after I come out, and the only snag as far as I can see is Mother. Maybe she expects me to go back to the shop.'

'I don't think she does, Bill,' Helen said quietly, knowing what Anna thought. 'She might talk about it, but she wants you to make a success of your life, and if you're not happy in your work how can you make a success of it?'

'I wouldn't be happy in the shop,' he confessed frankly. 'I'm certain of that without even giving it a trial, only I wouldn't hurt her for the world.'

'It would hurt her far more to find out afterwards—as she would be sure to find out. Your mother's pretty shrewd, Bill, and it wouldn't take her long to see that your heart wasn't in the job. Besides,' she added with a whimsical smile, 'I don't really think she wants to give up the shop to anyone—not just yet. If she retired it would take half her interest in life away and she'd feel a useless old woman.'

'I believe you're right,' he reflected. 'And there's the

twins coming on. They're crackers about the dales and there's nothing much for them there except the shop. They'd never want to come south. They're like Mother,' he added with his fond, one-sided smile. 'Yorkshire's the place, and Canderby's the place in Yorkshire!'

'I guess happiness can be found in so many different places,' Helen said almost to herself. 'The same sort of happiness—contentment and peace of mind. Isn't it—the ultimate desire?'

'Yes, I guess so, but it takes some people a lifetime to find it out.' He turned to her abruptly. 'What about you? Are you going to settle down in the old country?'

'I don't know.' A sensation that was almost longing and which she had felt several times in the past few weeks, gripped her, making her voice sound suddenly constrained and husky. 'I can't decide anything definite just yet—not till I've found Tony's father, and then—and then I don't know what I'll do.'

'What about your husband's people? Won't you stay on with them for a while?'

'I don't think I could.' The memories surrounding the Keep and Tony were going to be as poignant as these which lay behind her in the distant land from which she had come, and she would always think of Oliver's Keep as the place where they had known supreme happiness together, where her laughter had answered his so readily and where affection and contentment had surrounded them on all sides. 'There are difficulties there, I'm afraid. My cousin, the new owner, is unmarried and I've really crashed into a bachelor establishment at present.'

'Don't tell me you haven't been good for him!' laughed Bill. 'Man was never made to live alone—or so we are told, probably by a woman!'

'All women can't be designing cats, out for matrimony at any cost!' Helen laughed. 'Surely you're not going to protest that you believe such bunkum?'

'Oh no, I'm no misogynist, and evidently I'm not even very good at making world-shattering utterances!'

'I don't really think you're a man of words!' she said, squeezing his arm affectionately, 'but don't let that daunt you. I expect to hear of you *doing* something world-shattering one of these days!'

'Don't expect too much. I'm a modest sort of bloke, really, but here I've brought you to the portals of the Colonial Office in half the time you would have taken to find it yourself, so you can commend me for efficiency if you like!'

Helen's nervousness was returning, and she said as they mounted the steps,

'Supposing they can't trace him?'

'No use meeting trouble half-way. In spite of all the red tape, they're fairly efficient.'

'But I've so little information for them to go on.'

'That won't matter, I don't think. Anyway, we'll have a try.'

She was being foolishly weak, she thought as she followed him through the glass doors, and she must make one last determined effort to control this sick feeling within her which was the anticipation of catastrophe. It was her duty to find Major Pemberton, to track him down to the end of the earth, if need be, so that Tony might have his father in his life, at last.

Bill was speaking to a clerk over an imposing-looking counter, and she was conscious of letting her cousin take the lead for the moment, resting her burden on his broad and willing shoulders. It was the first time in years that she had been able even to share her responsibilities with someone else who might be interested, and she knew that Bill did not mind.

He was a godsend to her in these first difficult moments when the preliminaries bewildered her, but finally, when they had been passed from one clerk to another and shown into a second office, she gathered the threads into her own hands and explained what she wanted.

There were twenty minutes of suspense and dread and hope all mingled as a brief enquiry was made, and as soon as the clerk came back into the room she knew that he had no news for her.

'If you will leave your address, Mrs Oliver, we will do what we can,' he offered. 'We may even have to pass your enquiry on to the War Office, but we will go further into the matter and let you know as soon as possible.'

It was Bill who thanked him for his helpfulness. She could do nothing but mumble something inarticulate which she felt must only have expressed her disappointment. She must wait. There was nothing definite to be learned to-day —perhaps not even to-morrow or the next day!

'I don't think I can stay in London very long,' she told the clerk, rather as if he might be induced to do something special on her behalf on that account.

'That will be all right,' he assured her, ushering them towards the door. 'We'll communicate with you just as soon as we have anything to report.'

Going down Whitehall Bill stopped suddenly to say,

'Do you think we should have a crack at the War Office on our own? After all, he was in the Army, wasn't he?'

Helen glanced at her watch.

'It's after four,' she said almost wearily. 'Nearly half-past, Bill. I'm an awful coward, but I don't think I could stand another disappointment today.'

So it was that they turned towards Kensington and missed Grant Pemberton by a few minutes. He climbed the stairs of the War Office at exactly twenty-five minutes to five to meet an old friend who was helping to compile the official history of the war, in a room overlooking the busy street along which he had just passed. His mind was busy with the problem of continuing his search for the girl who had been constantly in his mind for the past six years of torment and doubt.

Bill Smirthwaite found Helen a comfortable small hotel in Kensington where she could stay the night, although the proprietor regretted that she must vacate it at noon the following day. They were booked up so far ahead now, he explained, and he had really nothing else to offer her nor could he help her with his knowledge of surrounding hotels. It was the same story everywhere. They just simply hadn't the accommodation, and with the end of the war an increasing number of people seemed to be flocking to London.

'I don't want to "flock" any longer than I can help,' Helen said to Bill, 'although I'm grateful to the little man for all the interest he's taken in us. I feel that I should get back to Tony as soon as ever I can and I think I'll just write in to the War Office and leave the rest to that kind little man we saw this afternoon.'

'I wish I could see you to-morrow,' Bill said, 'even if it were only to see you off to Scotland, but there's a job I simply must attend to and today's leave was a big concession, really.'

'I know it was, and I'm eternally grateful,' Helen responded. 'I'll go back tomorrow, Bill, and hope for the best.'

'It'll come your way,' he assured her. 'And now I must be off. Pity we couldn't have done a show or something.'

Helen felt that she could not have sat through the most entertaining show on earth that evening, but she thanked him nevertheless, and when he had gone she spent the hour before dinner penning her request to the War Office. Perhaps it was the wrong place to apply, she mused, but by doing so she had picked up two threads, and surely one of them would eventually lead Tony to his father.

The journey north on the following day seemed endless and her mind turned this way and that in an agony of suspense and hopelessness. She wanted Major Pemberton to reply, to pick up the threads of her endeavour soon—yes, she wanted that, but each day's delay meant a day longer for her with Tony. Oh! she was frail and human enough to want those days, to cherish those final moments as treasures destined to be lost to her for ever! She would have Tony—her boy!—a little longer—a day, a week, perhaps. Even if Major Pemberton followed her directly to the Keep he might agree to stay there for a day or two. That was the one urgent thought in her mind by the time she had re-crossed the Border, that was all she asked!

When she got down at Burndean she realised that she had not sent word of her return to the Keep. She had come back naturally, as she would have returned home, and her eyes misted over for a moment as they ranged across the familiar outline of the hills to see the sun slanting through cloud across the deep valleys. It was a still day with a mist-like rain sweeping up from the south, more like April weather than May, sunshine and showers chasing each other across the green landscape to make a pattern of light and shade upon the hills, obscuring the high peaks in a pearly grey veil to reveal them again, rain-washed and enchanted, rearing their proud heads against a sudden patch of blue.

How swiftly she had come to love this land! It had given her so much—love and friendship and understanding, and there had been peace of mind here, too, for a little space.

'If there's nobody tae meet ye, ma'am, the carrier's going by the Keep an' he would gie ye a lift.'

She turned to find the stationmaster by her side and smiled, remembering his kindness on the day she had first come to Burndean.

' It was stupid of me, really, but I didn't let them know,' she admitted. 'Do you think the carrier will have room for me?'

'He'll mak' room, ma'am,' said Tom promptly, anxious to be of service to this fine girl even although it was rumoured that she hadn't brought the rightful heir to the Keep, after all. 'Mair was the pity,' Tom reflected inwardly, although he had no grudge against the present owner—none at all!

The carrier covered the distance between the station and Oliver's Keep at a respectful pace, asking if Helen would mind walking the short way from the bridge to the house because 'the road wasna' up to much these days and his tyres were just aboot done.'

She got down and he handed out her bag, waiting until she had crossed the bridge before he drove away.

The sound of the departing car brought a wild shout of delight from the direction of the terrace and Tony came tearing down over the grass towards her, followed at a more dignified pace by Fergus.

'Oh, Mummy! we thought you wasn't ever coming back!' Tony exclaimed breathlessly, hugging her round the waist. 'We've watched and watched every time the post came.'

'I have been thoughtless, darling,' Helen acknowledged, holding him tight and kissing the tawny curls. 'But it's so nice to be back and to see you all again.'

Her eyes met Fergus's on the last words and he stooped to take her bag from her.

'Have you brought me anything?' Tony asked, eyeing the leather grip speculatively. 'And please can I have it *before* tea?'

'I must have a report first to see how good you've been while I've been away!'

His eyes sought Fergus's.

'I have been good, haven't I, Uncle Fergus? An' I've just fed MacNab and all the dogs!'

'Well, I think you deserve something for that, so if you look carefully in the corner of my bag, you might see a parcel tied up in green paper—'

Fergus surrendered the bag, laughing, and Tony ran on ahead with it to investigate the green paper parcel.

'Any luck?' Fergus asked, turning back to Helen.

'It was Tony's father all right,' she said, 'but there was no way of tracing him from Yorkshire, so I went to London.'

'Good heavens! I wish I had known. I would have come with you like a shot. Did you find out anything there?'

'No. We—Bill Smirthwaite met me in London—went to the Colonial Office, and they did all they could for us. At the moment they can't trace anyone of that name—not definitely.'

'What about the War Office?'

'Bill suggested going there, but we didn't even know which records office to apply to. His name is Pemberton —Major Pemberton, but Aunt Anna didn't know which branch of the Army he was in, and apparently there are all sorts of records offices. I wrote a letter, however, explaining things as best I could.' They had reached the hall, and suddenly she sank down on one of the old leather chairs near the fire. 'Heavens, how tired I am! I feel as if I've been travelling for a thousand years!'

He asked no more questions after that, recognising her utter exhaustion of spirit, and over tea he told her what had been happening at the Keep in her absence, trying to steer her mind away from the ever-present thought of losing Tony. In his own heart he knew himself half-resentful of this man who was about to claim his son, because he knew so well what it would mean to Helen. Before they retired for the night he opened the subject briefly to say,

'I hope you will ask Pemberton to come here, Helen. We can't just thrust Tony out with someone who is, after all, a stranger to him in all but name. They must get to know each other gradually.'

'If he writes I can mention it,' Helen answered, and in spite of all her efforts, her voice sounded unutterably weary. 'But tonight I—can't even think any more.'

She climbed the stairs to her room, feeling as if her feet were weighted with lead. Her limbs felt cold and cramped, as cold as the dead weight in her breast which must have been her heart, and she paused at the communicating door leading into the child's room, but would not go in, passing on stiffly, like a sleep-walker. She could not steel herself to take that last good-night peep tonight before she lay down in her own bed because the sight of the sleeping child might be the final arrow which would pierce all her defences and send her resolution crumbling into dust.

The window of her room lay open and she crossed to it in the darkness, guided by the pale wash of starlight. The rain had swept across a track of sky, gradually leaving it clean, and there above her, like a jewel set against dark velvet, burned a single star, so clear and so close that it seemed as if she might stretch up her hand and touch it.

> "And I have seen a star rise in the blackest sky,
> repeatedly:
> It has not failed me yet . . ."

Her pale lips moved, forming the words of hope and faith, but even the beauty of such a thought could bring her little comfort in that moment of her heart's anguish.

CHAPTER NINE

IN the morning she rose resolutely to meet the new day, and while Fergus rode out to a distant farm she spoke to Tony about his father.

'Tony, darling, there's just a chance that we might be going to see your daddy quite soon. You see, while I was away I heard that he had come home—to England, and he's been looking for us. It has all been very difficult. During the war he's been away in another camp where the Japanese kept the soldiers they captured, and he hasn't been able to look for us until now.'

She paused, conscious of the child studying her closely.

'Will he come here?' Tony asked at last.

'Yes, I hope so. Uncle Fergus has asked him to come.'

'So that we'll all be together! He really is a soldier, isn't he?' His great eyes shone with pride. 'Will he wear his uniform when he comes, and will he have a gun?'

'I don't know about the gun, but I think he'll wear his uniform. He'll be very proud that day, Tony.'

'Will you be proud?'

She swallowed something that threatened to choke her.

'Yes,' she managed. 'I'll be—very proud.'

Yes, she would be proud. After all, Tony was something of what she had made him, a gift to the man who had waited so long and endured so much. She was proud that she had been able to keep faith. In Anna Smirthwaite's words, she had done her best 'and no one can do more nor that.'

They rode out together to meet Fergus on his return and had lunch at a nearby farm where Tony had become a firm favourite and MacNab was watered and made welcome to a switch of hay, and at four o'clock they went back to the Keep. While Syd Willing and Fergus stabled the horses Helen helped Tony with MacNab.

'Can I have a pic-a-back into the house, Mummy?' he

demanded as they bolted the stable door. 'Just a wee one!'

She lifted him on to the old mounting stone, and he put soft, warm arms about her neck. Oh, God! she thought, how can I ever let him go!

'Could you be a galloping horse?'

'I'll do my best. Yi'up there!'

She crossed the yard and opened the door leading through the kitchen passage, and as she entered the dim hall under the gallery Bessie followed her through.

'There's a wire for you, ma'am,' she intimated. 'It came half an hour ago, and I put it up on the mantelpiece where you would see it right away.'

Helen let Tony slip down on to a chair, but for a moment she felt powerless to move. It had come. Without opening it she knew that the yellow envelope propped up on the high mantelpiece held the news she wanted yet dreaded. Major Pemberton had been traced and he was coming for his son.

'I'll get it down for you,' Bessie offered, going towards the fire. 'I hope it isn't bad news, ma'am.'

'No, Bessie, I don't think it will be.' She took a step nearer the mantelpiece, but suddenly the room seemed stiflingly hot, and the dark rafters appeared to recede into limitless distance above her head. Her legs felt weak, refusing to bear her weight, and she gripped the edge of the table—something solid, something to hold on to in a world which suddenly seemed to be rocking about her.

'Do you feel all right, ma'am?' Bessie asked anxiously. 'I could call Mr Oliver—'

'No, Bessie, I'm all right now.' She straightened. 'It must have been the change of light—coming in out of the sun to the dim hall. Will you—give me the telegram now, please?'

Bessie Michie handed it to her in silence, not yet convinced that she had wholly recovered from what had looked suspiciously like a 'faint turn.' Helen did not seem to see her. Nothing seemed to matter but the message on the white paper she was trying to steady so that she might read it. It was plain enough, printed clearly on the gummed strips which took up all the available space.

HAVE RECEIVED YOUR MESSAGE AT WAR OFFICE TO-DAY —STOP—WOULD LIKE TO GET INTO TOUCH WITH YOU IMMEDIATELY—STOP—PLEASE WIRE PERMISSION TO VISIT YOU AT ADDRESS YOU GAVE OR FURNISH PARTICULARS OF SOME OTHER MEETING-PLACE—STOP—ALL I CAN HOPE IS THAT TONY WILL BE WITH YOU—STOP—GRANT PEMBERTON AT THE OFFICERS' CLUB ALBEMARLE STREET LONDON.

She read it through again, and then a third time before she turned to the child still standing on the chair beside the door.

'Tony,' she said quietly, 'your daddy will be here the day after tomorrow.'

Her brain was functioning, working out details, but all the rest of her body seemed dead, numbed into immobility by the knowledge of her certain loss, yet her voice had sounded normal and even bright, as if the day after tomorrow would be something for her to look forward to, as it would be for Tony.

She folded the telegram and put it back into its envelope at last, and then she turned to Bessie Michie, who still hovered in the shadows.

'Could we have tea now, Mrs Michie?' she asked. 'We won't have anything cooked. We had a good lunch at Toshiehill, and I'll give Tony his bath earlier to-night. He was rather late last night and he seemed tired this morning.'

The last little services! Well, she had another day in which to perform them—perhaps even two. Two days, unless Fergus could persuade Grant Pemberton to stay at the Keep until Tony and he became better acquainted. And two days can seem a lifetime. She was determined that they would hold a lifetime of happiness, that every minute of every hour would be full of joy for them both, joy untinged by regret or any thought of the darkness of the days to come, and to this end she gave up all her time, wandering hand in hand with Tony down by the riverside or riding out with him across the fields to meet Fergus, and always talking to him about his father.

Although subdued by long experience of confinement,

Tony's excitement was keen enough, and she answered his many questions to the best of her ability—questions about the past, mostly. She could tell him nothing about the future.

'Will my daddy come here to live?'

'For a little while.'

'But surely he will like the Keep. You do, don't you, Mummy?'

The name stirred all the sorrow in Helen's heart, bringing it to the surface again.

'Yes, I like the Keep, but your daddy may not be stay here. Everyone works, Tony, and your daddy's work may take him away again—perhaps abroad—to Singapore, maybe.'

'Do *you* want to go back to Singapore?' His eyes were suddenly wide and distressed. 'The bad Japs have got it, haven't they?'

'They've all gone, Tony. There isn't one left—unless it might be in a prison-camp, so we needn't think of these things any more.'

She knew that Tony thought of the camp and their confinement as nothing more terrifying than an unpleasant dream, one that was swiftly fading into a vague memory, and she was glad that he was young enough to forget entirely in time if the subject were not constantly renewed in his hearing. It was the effects of imprisonment upon the man whom they were so soon to meet upon which her thoughts had dwelt more often in the past few days, and as the hours passed she felt her nervousness mounting, so that when she saw the telegraph messenger from Burndean cycling up the rough track towards the Keep early in the morning of the second day she could not attempt to shorten the boy's journey by hurrying to meet him but stood on the terrace awaiting his arrival with Grant Pemberton's second telegram like a figure carved out of the very stone upon which she leaned for support.

The message said briefly that he would arrive at Burndean at four o'clock and would find his own way to the Keep, but she knew that Fergus would not hear of such an arrangement.

She showed him the telegram when he came in to lunch and he read it through hastily, glancing across the table at her when he had finished.

'Of course, you'll want to meet him, and so will Tony,' he said. 'I'll tell Syd to have the car round at half-past three.'

Nervously she crumbled the bread on her plate without attempting to eat her soup.

'It's going to be strange,' she said with an effort at a smile. 'Just a little—at first.'

'It's not the first stiff hurdle you've taken, Helen,' he reminded her. 'You'll clear it.'

'I hope so.' She met his eyes. 'I'm not really nervous about meeting him. It's—afterwards. He may not think I did all I could to trace him before I brought Tony here.'

'But you know you did, and I can't imagine anyone doubting you for long.' He stretched over to ruffle the boy's tawny head. 'Besides, there's the nipper here. He'll speak for himself—and you!'

Helen smiled at him.

'You have more faith in me than I have in myself,' she said, 'but I dare say I'll perk up before the vital moment. I wonder if I'll recognise Major Pemberton on sight?'

'I shouldn't think there would be much fear of a mistake at a station like Burndean. He'll probably be about the only person getting off the train!' He put down his soup spoon. 'Everything's set for his arrival, and I even saw Mrs Michie slipping up to his room with a "pig" under her apron in case, having come so recently from the East, he might feel our northern beds cold! I don't blame her in a way, either. It's been cold enough for snow these past two mornings after all that fine weather we've had. It's worrying for the crops, and what we really need now is rain.'

Helen said: 'You'll never be anything but a farmer, Fergus! Your mind's set that way now and you couldn't change it even if you would!'

He sat in silence, watching as Bessie changed their plates.

'I guess you're right,' he said when they were alone again. 'I've got over wanting to give it all up. The broad acres have got me.'

'They'll bring you all you want in the end,' she said with conviction. 'It's a grand life—a full, satisfying life, and it's yours—and the Keep's. You can't separate yourself from that fact, Fergus. You couldn't let a stranger come in.'

'No, I suppose not.' The old, bitter twist came back to his mouth, hardening it. 'I'll put all I've got into it, every ounce of endeavour, and then, like the admirable Oliver women of my own generation, I'll stand down and it will pass to some distant relation in the male line, though, heaven knows, I haven't an idea who he will be!'

She put a steady hand over his long fingers where they drummed restlessly on the polished table.

'Long before then,' she said firmly, 'you will have married and have a son of your own.'

He laughed abruptly.

'There's not a chance. I'm cut out for a bachelor, I guess, but I'm learning that the sort of loneliness one finds in a place like the Keep has its compensations. If I work hard enough I can make it pay, and that will give me a lot of satisfaction.'

Helen hesitated and then said something that she had long wanted to say.

'I've often felt that—some of my money should go back into the estate. After all, it would have done if Ken had lived, and I have much more than I need—'

'Don't you believe it! There's the kid—' He broke off, confused by his own stupidity and forgetfulness, remembering that she wouldn't have Tony to plan for in the near future at all. 'I'm sorry, Helen! You must think me a blundering ass, and it's not that I don't appreciate your offer and know why it was made. It's just that—well, that I want to give something to the Keep and all it stands for, too. I'm willing to work like a slave, and the land always repays you in the end. After all, I'm not starting off from scratch. I've inherited something worth while.'

That was all she wanted to hear him say, that and to know he would not throw up his inheritance because love had passed him by.

Not that she considered it had passed him by, finally and irrevocably! She wasn't fool enough to imagine that he had not met his share of charming girls during six years of war but the very fact that he had not made any serious attachment in all that time seemed to prove that he still cared deeply for Margaret and would always remember her as his first and dearest love. Yet, she thought, in every life there is some compensation for love denied, and one day she believed that Fergus Oliver would find it.

Meanwhile, she was not content to suppose that all was lost as far as Margaret was concerned. She still felt sure that Ken's sister retained much of her former affection for her cousin and she could not quite understand the outcome of his visit to Edinburgh. She wished now that she had gone with him, that she had seen Margaret and so found out the truth. The desire to help this man who had been so kind to her and so good to Tony was still very strong in her, and so she decided that she must visit Collister again. She would go, in any case, to say goodbye when she left the Keep.

Immediately after lunch Fergus rode off again in the direction of Toshiehill, where he was arranging for the sale of some lambs, but he promised to return early in the afternoon in time to welcome Grant Pemberton. He had made no offer to accompany them to the station, and Helen knew that it was because he felt she might want to meet Tony's father alone.

She smiled, thinking how thoughtful he was, and how unhappy, and wondered what she could do about the unhappiness. I must do something, she mused, as she waited for Syd Willing to bring round the car, because I feel so strongly that I can!

Tony sat far forward in his seat beside Syd, his eyes eagerly upon the road ahead, laughing heartily as lambs and sheep scattered before the oncoming wheels, leaping back on to the safety of the moor with tails swinging like agitated pendulums. Helen knew he was inwardly excited at the thought of meeting his father at last, knew, too, that he would probably greet him shyly, and she wondered if Grant Pemberton would understand.

She left the car on the station approach, walking on to the platform several minutes before the train was due, every pulse in her body throbbing with her own excitement so that it dulled the ache in her heart a little and she saw the meeting through Tony's eyes.

Would there be many people getting down at Burndean that afternoon, she wondered, and, if so, how would she and Grant Pemberton recognise each other? Farther along the platform she noticed a girl of about her own age standing with a child not much older than Tony, and the two little boys eyed each other speculatively. Would this be confusing to the man coming off the train? Helen wondered where to stand, thinking that the best place might be at the ticket barrier, and took up her position there.

A shrill whistle told her that the train was coming round the curve above the village and her heart began to pound against her breast, while a thousand conflicting thoughts rushed madly round in her brain. This was the beginning of the end. This was everything to Tony. Would the train drawing in towards Burndean bear a man who had been grievously changed by his experiences or the man she thought she had glimpsed in one brief instant of emergency all these years ago? Would he understand how she had tried to find him? If he had married again would Tony be happy in his new home?

That was the most jealous of all the thoughts. A new mother for Tony! The thought seared through her heart like a naked flame, but she tried to suppress it and turned to face the oncoming train.

The girl at the other end of the platform was walking down towards them, scanning the carriages eagerly as they pulled past, and as the train drew to a halt she was standing between Helen and the first-class coach. Helen's eyes sought the row of windows while Tony's fingers fastened over hers in a tight grip of mingled excitement and shyness.

'Is he there, Mummy? Is he?'

'Yes.'

Two soldiers got down from the train, but there was no doubt in Helen Oliver's mind about the one they had come to meet. The tall, upright figure, the lean jaw with the tanned and slightly hollow cheeks had all been etched on her mind during the long years between their meetings, and that swift, keen glance had been the look he had bent on her in the flashing searchlight's gleam. He strode towards her now with never a glance in the other girl's direction, recognising her instantly although she must have presented an entirely different picture in her rough tweeds from the nurse he had last seen leaning over the gunwale of a ship's lifeboat to take his child with her to safety. And in the moment of their meeting it was as if a gentle hand had been placed over Helen's heart, stilling its wild beating, so that she clasped Tony's cold little fingers in both her hands and drew him towards his father.

For a moment no word passed between them. They stood silently looking at each other, these three who had suffered by war and been separated and crossed half the world to meet again, and then Helen Oliver held out her hand, saying without any convention,

'We've been trying to find you for a very long time.'

His fingers fastened over hers in a strong grasp, long, lean fingers on a too thin hand, and his grey-green eyes smiled at her, erasing the lines of suffering on his face and making him look young again. She saw where his hair had turned grey at the temples and there was an old wound scar on the side of his cheek that showed pale against the tanned skin, but all these were instant impressions lost in the real issue as he looked down at his son for the first time.

He laid his case on the platform and stooped to Tony's level, searching the boy's face for all the small pointers of resemblance he remembered—the tawny hair so like his dead wife's, the wide blue eyes and the dimple on the softly rounded chin which Tony still retained from babyhood—and then it seemed to Helen as if he were searching for something else, something less tangible, and instantly she knew what it was. As nervous as they had been at his coming—nervous and eager—this man was nervous, too, and the fear in him had been that he might be met as a stranger, the interloper claiming a child who had nothing to remember him by, a little boy to whom he was not even a name. Into Helen's aching heart there flooded compensation for the love and the truth by which she had lived during those six difficult years, for above all things this man had wanted his son to know about him!

'Well, old man?' Grant Pemberton broke the silence to say in a husky voice that was full of an abounding joy. 'It's been a long time, but here we are, at last!'

'We're glad you've come,' Tony said shyly, and then, with a rush, as if by swiftly acclaiming his desire he might impress it upon the big man who had come so suddenly into their lives, 'and we're all going to live at the Keep!'

Grant Pemberton smiled, his hand not quite steady as he ruffled the tawny curls, and then his eyes were raised suddenly to Helen's, looking at her over the boy's head.

'I have to thank you for this,' he said quietly. 'It might so easily have been—the other way.'

'You've never been a stranger to Tony,' she said. 'It was just that you had never met before.'

He straightened, looking down at her in silence for a moment as if to consolidate his impressions and sweep away the final doubt which had come with him out of the past, and then he said simply,

'This is the end of a very long journey for me, a mental torture which I hope I shall never have to face again.' His eyes went back to the boy preoccupied with the weight of his suitcase. 'He's—everything I would have wished him to be.'

A little tide of warmth and gratitude swept into the barren places of Helen's lonely heart as she smiled back at him.

'You will be much more convinced of that when you've come to know Tony better,' she said. 'And now, shall we go? My cousin has sent the car down and he hopes you will make yourself at home at the Keep for—for as long as you can stay with us.'

The last words came out in a little rush of appeal which did not escape the shrewd grey-green eyes still watching her from under the shading peak of the military cap, but the shadow successfully hid any emotion which might have been in Grant Pemberton's eyes as he said,

'I have no other home to offer Tony at the moment,

although I have several plans for his future. Quite frankly, Mrs Oliver, your offer will be a godsend just now. One can't just dump a child in an hotel and hope that it is going to appear like home, although I suppose Tony has survived sterner experiences than that in the past six years.'

'We have been very lucky,' Helen assured him quickly. 'For your own peace of mind please believe that nothing has happened to us which will seriously affect Tony in the future. He was too young to retain impressions of cruelty or inferiority, and our particular Japs weren't too bad.'

She saw his jaw tighten, as if he could not quite believe that any Japanese official had retained even a scrap of decency during the years when they had seen their national ambition of centuries about to be realised, and then he looked round at Tony again and the hardness left his face as his jaw relaxed a little.

'There's that to be grateful for,' he said. 'It's certainly difficult to imagine anyone being cruel to a child, but that mustn't blind us entirely to the facts of the past six years. Japan is crushed, but the Yellow Peril will rise again if we are not for ever on our guard. I expect you realise that with your experience of the East.'

'Yes, I think I do.' They had reached the car and Tony was already installed in the front beside Syd, glancing shyly at the tall soldier who must surely have a good many adventures to relate and might possibly supplement them to the usual bedtime story if a small boy asked politely enough. 'It's going to be a bit of a squash in the back unless we can get some of your luggage in front.'

Syd, who had relieved the Major of his suitcase as they came through the ticket gate, wedged it successfully between Tony and the door and they set out for the Keep.

'There's lots an' lots of lambs on the road, Daddy!' Tony offered as they neared the moors. 'You'll see them if you look out on my side where they can jump up without going through the fence, Daddy.'

Daddy! He used the word often, lingering over the sound of it in his thoughtful way, recognising it as a thing of actual fact now in place of a vague word out of the past which might or might not materialise into the brave soldier Helen had promised him who would be his own exclusive property in the future. And now he was here in the flesh and in all the magnificence of a fine uniform, sitting in the back of Uncle Fergus Oliver's car, and they were all on their way to the Keep to live happily ever after, like the people in the fairy stories one or other of the mummies used to read aloud every night in the camp before the lamps went out. Tony had liked it best when Helen had read the story aloud. Her voice had never been all shaky, as if she wanted to cry; nor very loud like old Mrs McKenney's, nor too soft so that you couldn't hear very well if anyone whispered or shuffled, and it had laughed when the story wanted you to laugh and whispered when the three little pigs were hiding from the big, bad wolf! Yes, Tony was quite sure that he didn't want to change Helen for anyone else, no matter how nice they might be!

'Your cousin has good land here,' Grant Pemberton remarked as they neared the Keep. 'Is he farming it himself?'

'Some of it. He's going in for sheep mostly, but of course there's a certain amount of ploughing to be done, too. The government insist on that at present and it's sensible enough where the land will yield a good crop. Are you interested in farming?' she asked, suddenly aware that she had no idea what he did apart from his Army service.

'As far as the average man who has chosen the Army as his career can be interested,' he answered with his slow smile. 'I think it's a good life. It's a life in the open, anyway, which is one of the reasons why I chose the Army.'

'You'll be going abroad again?' Helen asked, her heart sinking in spite of all her efforts to control her emotions where the loss of Tony was concerned.

'Undoubtedly, when things get straightened out. At present I'm cooling my heels at the War Office waiting for a posting and not working nearly hard enough in the meantime.'

'But you're due a rest—you need time to recover from your experiences,' she protested.

He smiled grimly.

'You can't erase that sort of thing in a couple of months

or in half a lifetime, and certainly not by sitting around doing nothing but thinking back. It calls for action, but I have been grateful enough for the long leave to help me to trace the boy.'

'I know just how awful that must have been for you,' Helen said gently, 'and I'm so sorry we have not been able to link up before now. I tried the Red Cross and the shipping companies, but there was such utter confusion there at first—everyone trying to trace lost relatives—that I thought it better to bring Tony to England when I had settled my own affairs in Singapore.'

'Then—you don't mean to go back?' he asked, turning to look at her more closely.

'There's—nothing to go back for—nothing personal. My husband was killed in action just before Singapore fell. He was in the rubber business in Malaya before the war and there was quite a lot for me to clear up when I thought about coming home. That was why I was so long getting round to Tony's affairs,' she confessed, 'and, you see, I had no idea whether you were alive or not. We heard that your ship had gone down and there were no known survivors—'

'There were four of us. We drifted fourteen days on a raft and had the infernally bad luck to be picked up by a Jap cruiser. From then on it was one prison-camp after another—some bad, some indifferent, none of them very good.' His mouth hardened again at the memory. 'The last one was about the most notorious camp of the war, I believe. We were as good as dead men in there. Nothing ever got through to us—no mail or parcels, and we never heard what was going on outside. It became a slow, crushing process of trying desperately to hold out against disease and insanity and if my administration days are going to be spent in the Far East, it's going to be difficult to forget these years.'

'Yet you will go back?'

'Oh yes. There's a great deal to be rebuilt out there and we must get down to it right away. Also, I don't think men should go out who know nothing of conditions as they were during the war. I'm not proposing a national policy of revenge, yet it would be folly to forget suffering entirely. Although it will be hard, our aim must be achieving normality now.'

Deep in her heart Helen agreed with him, admiring him for these convictions of his, but she wondered what he was going to do about Tony. If he were sent out to Malaya at once things would be much too unsettled to take a child there, but perhaps there was someone else, some woman who had come into his life since his wife's death upon whom he could rely to look after Tony until he could send back to England for them both.

Again the strange, spear-sharp stab of agony seared through her and she was glad that the Keep came into view at that moment and she could say steadily,

'That is Oliver's Keep on the horizon.'

Tony wriggled round on the front seat to demand,

'Isn't it just like a castle, Daddy? And it has a real moat, only the water isn't in it any more.'

'Bad show, that!' declared their visitor, his tone that of a man who had suddenly rediscovered his youth. 'I have a weakness for moated castles with the water right up to the drawbridge!'

'Do you think Uncle Fergus might fill it sometime?' Tony considered. 'From a tap or something?'

'And drown all his sheep who must have got quite used to grazing in the nice dry moat by this time!' Pemberton laughed. 'No, I think we'd better leave the Keep without its moat.'

'It has turrets,' Tony pointed out, 'and a dungeon where you have to go down with a 'lectric light on a long cord!'

'It sounds terribly exciting!' his father declared. 'I'm half-expecting a knight in armour to meet me at the door!'

'I hope my cousin will be there to meet you,' Helen laughed back, 'although I can't promise he'll be in armour!'

'How long has he lived here?'

'Only a few months. He was my husband's heir.'

'Oh.' He looked down at her, detecting the emotion in her voice, and then his eyes swept back to the turreted fastness of the Keep. 'That sounds tough luck on you,' he observed.

'I've never looked at it like that,' Helen said. 'Fergus has been more than kind ever since we came here and we have become firm friends.'

'I see.' He was still looking up at the Keep, appraising it, his eyes narrowed slightly against the sun which poured over the old stones, mellowing them, and the upward tilt of his head revealed the scar on his cheek to be longer than she had first noticed. She could not remember noticing it at their first meeting, and she shuddered to think how it might have been inflicted, and then Syd had turned the car along the narrow terrace and pulled it up before the front door. Tony got out, clambering over the suitcase, to open the back door for them.

'Please could you come to see MacNab, Daddy?'

'MacNab?' Grant Pemberton looked questioningly back at Helen, his stern mouth suddenly whimsical. 'What a family you have here! Who or what is MacNab?'

'He's my pony,' Tony supplied eagerly, 'an' he's wonderful. He doesn't like jumps, though—not water jumps. Uncle Fergus gave him to me for a s'prise.'

'"Uncle Fergus" appears to be extremely kind,' the tall soldier remarked, his eyes still steadily upon Helen's. 'We must owe him quite a lot which we shall never be able to repay, I'm afraid.'

'He wouldn't want you ever to think of repayment,' Helen said quickly. 'And please believe that he will like having you here.'

She had felt compelled to reassure him for some strange reason which she could not quite define, forced to convince him that Fergus would like the idea of having him there as much as she and Tony would. He understood, of course, about Tony and herself! It was natural, it was what they had waited for all those years, and although it could bring her only heartache in the future there was no denying the fulfilment of the present. She had felt it from the moment he had stepped down from the train and come straight towards her, recognising her across the years as easily as she had remembered him.

Tony escorted his father into the hall where the fire was lit and a table set for tea, and Grant Pemberton looked about him with frank admiration, noting the play of firelight on fine china and the long shafts of sunlight falling between the high stone columns which supported the roof, seeing it all as the perfect complement to Helen Oliver, the girl who should have reigned there by right. It was perhaps then for the first time that he thought he saw the way of the future for Oliver's Keep and the people who lived in it, because Helen Oliver had spoken of her husband's cousin with a light in her eyes which was frankly affection. He was the man who had given her shelter on her return to her homeland, who had shown her kindness, and to Grant Pemberton it seemed but a natural step to the gift of his love.

Without meeting his host, he had already guessed what Fergus Oliver would be like, what manner of man he was, and when Tony accompanied him up the narrow gallery stairs to his room with a great show of importance and they had left Helen in the hall below, he listened to the child's eager chatter about the Keep while he thought that life had a strange way of dealing out compensation to the needy. There could be no question about Helen Oliver belonging there. The Keep was her natural setting, yet he was convinced that it would be by no personal scheming that she would make it her permanent home.

He stood a long time at the high, narrow window overlooking the rolling hills, wondering about life and plans and scarcely-formed desires, and then he turned towards his son with a swift, playful gesture and ruffled the tawny curls which awoke a bitter-sweet memory deep in his heart.

'It's you and me for it, I guess, old man!' he said. 'But it might be worth while to linger a moment here.'

'We must go down for tea,' Tony advised him gravely, taking a child's literal view of time. ''Cos it spoils if it's kept waiting. Mrs Michie says so.'

'And who, would you tell me, is Mrs Michie? Any friend of MacNab's?'

'Oh, she *likes* MacNab, of course, but she's really Uncle Fergus's housekeeper.'

Pemberton's eyebrows went up.

'All right and proper, eh?' he observed, but instantly

he felt ashamed of the thought which had prompted the sarcasm and took the boy's hand in his to go back down the stairs to where Helen waited for them beside the fire.

'We're just going to begin our tea,' she said. 'Fergus hasn't come in yet and he said not to wait for him if he should be late. I expect you're gasping for a cup of tea after that long journey.'

'Travelling doesn't affect me much and I'd much rather travel in England than in Malaya.' He took his cup and sat down in one of the wide leather arm-chairs while Tony joined Helen at the table. 'And now can you tell me something of what happened after your ship drew away that night? The barest details will do for the present,' he added, glancing at Tony, who was blissfully selecting his favourite sandwich from the plate at Helen's elbow. 'Later, perhaps, I can hear those details, if they are not too distressing to you.'

Helen filled her cup, and for the next ten minutes recounted the incidents of these past six years which had almost become like a bad dream to her now, and vividly her listener seemed to see each step of the way, as if he had long imagined it, and with a relief he could not hide.

'I suffered agonies,' he admitted when she had finished, 'wondering what kind of camp you had struck, but praying all the time that you had got clean away. The odds, of course, were all against it.'

'I think everything was against us out there at that time,' she answered. 'In the dark days there seemed nothing but outstanding courage with which to fight back, as witness the Burma campaign.' Suddenly she bent across the table towards him, her eyes full and steady on his. 'I'm glad you are going back,' she said. 'We need men out there who understand.'

And women, he thought, but he said nothing, and presently Fergus Oliver came up the steps to the open door and saw them sitting there talking as if they had known each other all their lives and a swift stab of pain that was half jealousy ran through him at the thought of losing Helen. He had come to regard her as part of the Keep, something standing between him and an utter loneliness of soul which he could not bear to contemplate, and resentment was suddenly strong in him. This man was a stranger to them. What right had he to come and claim all Helen's interest like this? Then Tony turned and saw him, and the tall soldier got to his feet and Helen was introducing them.

'Fergus, this is Tony's father. Major Pemberton—my cousin.'

The two men measured each other with a long, straight look, each wondering about the other's place in Helen's life, and then Fergus's hand shot out and was gripping the lean brown fingers in a genuine grasp of welcome and mutual and instant liking was theirs. Helen saw it and was deeply comforted.

'It's good to have you here,' Fergus said, knowing that Helen thought the same about Pemberton's coming even although his ultimate departure with his son was going to mean the end of a beautiful phase in her life. 'I hope you will make up your mind to stay with us for a while.'

'Mummy said he would, didn't you, Mummy?' Tony put in, and Helen felt Grant Pemberton looking in her direction and flushed.

Did he resent Tony calling her that, she wondered, feeling, perhaps, that she had stolen a name which should have belonged exclusively to his dead wife? Swiftly her eyes found his, searching them for an answer as she explained,

'It was the most natural thing—Tony calling me that.'

'I know.' There was no resentment in him, only a deep appreciation of all she had done for his child, for the way in which she had made the word mother complete for a motherless boy. 'I wasn't thinking of that. I was thinking of how much of your time you must have given up to look after him—your fair share of any fun that was going after you came out of that damnable camp.'

'Tony and I have been happy together in our own way,' she said. 'A very full way, and since we came to the Keep life has been almost perfect.'

She had spoken in an undertone while Fergus asked Tony what it felt like to have a real live daddy home at last, and Grant Pemberton detected the expression of gratitude which brightened her eyes as they rested upon the other man's tall, spare figure and wondered once again if there was some more personal bond between these two apart from that of relationship by marriage. So often kindness had proved the gateway to a deeper emotion, gratitude the stepping-stone to love, and such an arrangement would certainly be compensation for the extraordinary raw deal which fate had meted out to Helen Oliver. Only—and he didn't have to stop to consider this—he was quite sure that Helen wasn't the type who would expect compensation from life, who would whine and protest against her lot. She'd be the sort who'd take life in both hands and hang on, and in the end she'd make the most of it. She was the sort of woman his mother had been, the pioneer type, and the only fitting mate for the man who saw his life's work in the far corners of the earth, however remote or unpleasant they might be.

So while they drank another cup of tea and Fergus satisfied a hearty appetite, he studied Helen under cover of the light flow of conversation, feeling that he was getting to know his son through her. It was all so natural that he might have been just any ordinary soldier coming home to his family to meet the son whom he had only seen at brief intervals during six years of war. Thousands of men had been in the same position and thousands more had been faced by the terrible tragedy of meeting their wives again as strangers. The odd thing about it was that, even although he had never known Helen Oliver, he could not consider her now as a stranger. He remembered those nights in the prison camp when he had lain, his body wracked with pain, his mind torn asunder by anxiety, thinking of her, seeing her face clearly in the bright gleam of eastern starlight—the steady dependability of her fearless eyes, the determination of her small, set chin, and the compassion of her generous mouth. Her face had floated before him in the wildest dreams, gently reassuring, because he knew that he had rarely been wrong in his estimate of his fellow-men. And you judged women like Helen Oliver largely by a man's standard. He was no judge of women, but one knew about people like Helen. There was nothing complex in their nature: they were simple and straightforward—and rare.

So he summed her up, the woman who had been in his constant thoughts for six long years and whom he was seeing for the first time in an utterly unexpected setting, realising that it was the first sight of Oliver's Keep which had upset his calculations about her, yet glad that he had come there to find her and Tony.

He had dreaded a meeting in London, in the lounge of some fashionable hotel, or even in Blair Bartholomew's room at the War Office. He had pictured such meeting places, rejecting them fastidiously, although he would have swept Tony up and carried him off in the midst of traffic-jammed Piccadilly if the need had arisen. The surroundings in which he now found himself, however, were all that he could have wished for, and when finally Tony was persuaded to go off to bed and Helen led him away to mount the gallery stairs he tried to express his sense of obligation to the man who owned it all.

'I'm going to owe you much more than I can ever repay in the way of hospitality,' he said, passing over his tobacco pouch as they strolled leisurely outside to saunter along the shelf of rock which formed the terrace on the western side of the Keep. 'This is the sort of experience that can be invaluable to a boy.'

'It was only natural that he should come with Helen,' Fergus said, 'and natural that Helen should be here. It is her home by right. I inherited it after her husband was killed in Malaya.'

'Yes, she told me. She had never been here before, then?'

'No. This is her first visit, but Ken—her husband— must have told her so much about his home. He loved the old place.'

'Yet he went abroad?'

'There was work to be done out there and his father was still a vigorous old man when Ken left Scotland in 'thirty-seven. They had rubber interests in Malaya and my uncle always believed in the personal touch, so he sent Ken out to be there for a year or two to learn the business.

Then the war came along and Ken joined up there, so that there was very little hope of his return until it was all over.'

'I suppose he met Mrs Oliver in Malaya.'

'Yes. Helen was nursing in Singapore during the first phase of the war and then, when the Japs came in, she went up-country. I know they had a very short honeymoon and next to no married life, but Helen seems to think it was all worth while.'

In her innermost heart, thought Grant Pemberton, she must know how short it has been—as short as the love Nina and I shared in that same warm, bright, heartbreaking land!

'I don't suppose she'll go back,' he said, making a statement of the words rather than a question.

'I don't want her to go back,' Fergus confessed. 'I want her to make her home here.'

His guest glanced at him sharply, and then his eyes roved over the green foothills before them, letting the peace of the long gloaming hour, which he had missed more than anything else when he had first taken up his appointment in the Straits Settlement, fall gently upon his spirit.

'And what does she say?' he asked at last, leaning his arms along the balustrade of rough sandstone which edged the terrace where the rock fell sheer away to the moat below.

Fergus hesitated.

'Well, quite frankly, I suppose things are different now,' he confessed. 'Before, she had the boy to consider and Helen planned most things around Tony. It may have been madness, but it was a magnificent sort of madness—'

'And I've just been suggesting that she may have lost a lot of "fun" by sacrificing all her time to my son!'

The last word had come haltingly, yet with a gentle pride, as a word not often used but cherished in the secret places of a strong man's heart, and Fergus Oliver, who had not been quite sure whether he was going to like this man or not, who had been more than half prepared to consider him an interloper, knew that all these impressions had been swept aside in the first half hour after their meeting, and that he was now considering Grant Pemberton as a friend rather than a passing acquaintance. Perhaps it all hinged on Tony, on their mutual interest in the boy, but he was quite certain that they were destined to get on well together.

This fact alone, early recognised, helped Fergus to forget that streak of self-effacement which was so nearly an inferiority complex, allowing him to blossom out into the perfect host and a most agreeable companion.

'Helen,' he said, 'doesn't use the word sacrifice in any way connected with Tony. Taking care of him is all so much part of her life now, as it has been for the past six years.'

He paused, conscious that the other man had stiffened and was now gazing out across the valley with his pipe clasped between hands on which the knuckles showed white from pressure. His lean jaw was tight-drawn and a small, insistent pulse beat visibly high on his cheek as the minutes slipped away in silence.

'I've thought of all these things,' he said at last in a voice that was suddenly constrained. 'I've had years to think of all the complications that I am likely to meet at the end of —all this.'

But for the sudden tremor in his deep voice, his words might have sounded callous, yet Fergus knew there was no streak of selfishness in this man which would rob Helen of all that accumulated love without giving a thought to what it would cost her. He had thought over all these things and had apparently not been able to arrive at any satisfactory solution. Or had he? Fergus could not quite be sure, and in the uncertain light of dusk which now wrapped them round there was little to be learned from the expression on his guest's face. His profile was almost granite-like as he saw it etched against the grey sky, and he did not turn as Fergus said,

'There won't be many—not complications of Helen's making. You needn't be afraid of that.'

Pemberton made no answer to that piece of assurance, only turning from his rather grim contemplation of the westering sun when Helen herself came briskly along the terrace to intimate that Tony was safely in bed and already asleep.

They turned then, walking round the Keep together, three people whose accumulated problems in life might have daunted a lesser spirit than Helen's, but not once until she had reached the seclusion of her own room and Grant Pemberton had retired to his did she relax the stern discipline which she had imposed upon herself. Then, as she stood looking in upon the sleeping child in the room adjoining her own, she let all the floodtide of loss and loneliness sweep over her unrestrained.

'Oh, Tony,' she whispered brokenly into the shadows, 'how can I ever let you go? And what will I do with all my life when you are gone!'

There seemed no answer anywhere to such a heart-cry, there in the quiet room or anywhere else in the world. Even the hills beyond the lancet windows seemed to draw back, stern and coldly indifferent to her plea, reflecting the greyness of her despair with all the sunshine gone from them. There was no hope left, nothing she could stretch out to touch that would bring her comfort. And then she began to remember—a man's quiet voice, kindly eyes holding a measure of suffering which could yet reflect compassion, a stern mouth relaxing over a child's name, and that sense of latent strength and purposefulness which she had recognised in Grant Pemberton long before she had even known his name. Everything she had asked, all she had hoped for in Tony's father, was summed up in the person of the man who had come to claim him, and she knew a mounting sense of gratitude to a Higher Being for that fact alone.

'Tomorrow,' she said aloud as she turned back to her own room, 'I must begin to face our parting. At least that has been granted to me. There will be no swift, searing break—'

She stood before the long, narrow window like a figure carved in stone, seeing the last shadows falling across the hills, and in a room facing hers on the far, turreted corner of the grey, baronial pile that was Oliver's Keep a man looked out towards these same hills and saw the shadows on them like the reflection of the problems lying thick and dark across the pathway of his future.

Grant Pemberton was no weakling, but at that point in his life he confessed himself to be without sign or hope. He had made plans—wild, mad plans dreamed behind prison bars, and his release from captivity had filled him with as wild and as mad a hope. Only now, at this moment when he believed he had reached journey's end, had he been forced to come down to earth and see things in their true perspective, and only now was he able to tell himself dispassionately that he had been a fool. Wasn't the fact that he had his child at last compensation for many a dream? The thought brought the fact of Helen's inevitable loss sharply to mind, and he saw her without compensation, with a yearning in her that no man could fully understand, the deep, searing grief of mother-love turned away empty-handed.

The thought reached down into the very depths of him, shaking him physically and mentally, so that when he turned away from the window and stood in the full circle of lamp-light his face looked drawn and grey, and all the marks of the years of suffering behind him were pencilled strongly about his mouth and eyes, making him look years older than his actual age and stamping the shadow of unhappiness clearly across his brow.

'God,' he murmured, 'if there is a solution to all this, let me see it—in Thy time!'

CHAPTER TEN

GRANT PEMBERTON had been at the Keep for two weeks before he spoke again of his intention of returning to Malaya, and in these days he had seemed happy and contented enough, falling into their routine as if it had been part of his life for years.

Much to Helen's relief, Fergus and he had become fast friends, and there was absolutely no doubt about Tony's affection for his father. Although she had patiently laid the foundations of that affection throughout the years, she gave herself very little credit for the happiness it was bringing now, and was content just to see them together and to watch their love ripening day by day into complete understanding of each other.

They rode often with Fergus over the estate to the outlying farms, Tony on MacNab and Grant on Helen's mare while she busied herself with the household tasks she had taken over from Mrs Michie, but often she found time to stop beside a window high up in the Keep which commanded a view of the valley beyond the ridge to watch them riding away or coming home, with her heart full of a gentle pride in the boy whose first years of life had been her sacred trust. He was a child to be proud of, with his small, steady hands gripping the reins with a sure, light touch and his laughing, healthy face turned to the man's who rode beside him. And then she would look at Grant and think how alike they were and feel confident in the future for them both.

Consideration of her own future she had thrust aside for the moment, thinking that there would be plenty of time to spare for that later. She would find some work to do somewhere, and considered herself lucky to have no financial difficulties in the meantime.

Quite often she would find herself thinking back to the first months of the war and life as it had been in Singapore before she had been moved north to the base hospital. She had never envied the women parasites of that era; she had been a worker, loving her profession and the sense of usefulness it afforded her, and once or twice she found herself considering nursing as a future sanctuary.

When she thought of her profession she invariably thought of Margaret Oliver and, conscience stricken, would accuse herself of having done very little to help Fergus in that direction since Grant Pemberton's arrival. Of course, it had only been a fortnight, but it seemed that he had been there a lifetime. One day quite soon, she decided, she would go to Edinburgh again and while she was there she would make a point of seeing Margaret alone!

When she had first landed in England she had made tentative inquiries about adopting Tony legally and before Grant's appearance Fergus had taken the matter up with his solicitor in Edinburgh, but now that the whole matter would naturally be dropped she felt that she owed Mr Fairbairn a personal explanation and decided to visit the capital again at the beginning of the following week.

'I shall go out to Collister,' she told Fergus quite frankly the day before, 'and try to see Margaret.'

He averted his eyes, saying harshly,

'What's the use? You'll just be wasting your time.'

'I don't think so,' she answered firmly. 'Besides, Margaret's been ill and I could hardly go to Edinburgh without visiting her. This time I hope Jean will be at home.'

'You'll be running your head up against a stone wall there too,' he assured her, 'just as much as I did with Isobel.'

'Have you ever heard of Faintheart?' she accused. 'I'm not going to be all that easily discouraged and please don't say a word to deter me before Major Pemberton. I'm going to ask him to come with me and take Tony to the zoo while I go out to Collister.'

'I shall envy you your day—apart from Collister,' he said. 'Are you coming with us this afternoon? You've been effacing yourself far too much these past few days.'

'There was quite a lot to do, and you realise, of course,

that there's a shortage of hacks! However, if you're not riding over, I'll come with you.'

'As a matter of fact, the Shaws are cutting hay down in the dale fields. They're sheltered there and it's always early, so I've promised to turn out and give them a hand. Tony's crazy about the idea of riding round with the reaper, but the rest of us could be a lot of help.'

'I'd love it!' Helen declared, her eyes shining. 'What does Major Pemberton think of the idea?'

'Grant? Oh, he's eager enough. Hasn't had a chance of haymaking since he was a laddie at school. That's settled, then? Tony and I will ride over and Syd can take you and Grant in the car.'

It was evidently settled most satisfactorily as far as Fergus was concerned, and Helen could not account for the sudden restlessness which made her almost averse to going alone with Grant Pemberton even on such a short journey. Toshiehill was less than four miles away—a ten-minute ride at most—yet her heart beat strongly against her breast at the thought of it and the little Cockney's presence seemed a strange relief.

A senseless reaction of frayed nerves, she considered it, but could not wholly dismiss it, and during the drive to Toshiehill was more quiet than usual in consequence.

'I should have offered to let you ride your own mare on such a warm day,' Pemberton remarked as Syd negotiated the winding dale road. 'I've confiscated her completely since my arrival, I'm afraid, but I wish you would say quite frankly if you need her.'

'I would have told you if I had needed her,' Helen assured him. 'I didn't go out with Tony and Fergus every day even before you came.'

'But you haven't been out at all since, and I feel guilty.' He looked down at her. 'But perhaps you're taking over the reins indoors?'

His meaning eluded her, and she said almost awkwardly,

'I'm trying to help Fergus all I can just now. He's finding it difficult to settle down, but I think things will come straight for him before long. Oliver's Keep is a big place for him to attempt to manage single-handed.'

'He seems determined to do it, though.' There was admiration in the deep voice and a liking for his host which sent a thrill of warmth all through Helen. 'He's the sort who'll get on just by sheer grit and determination to win through and things are not looking so bad. I suppose the main trouble in a place like this is lack of capital.'

'Mainly,' Helen agreed, but she knew that Fergus would never be really happy at the Keep if he failed to win Margaret Oliver for his wife.

They had reached Toshiehill, a red-roofed cluster of white-washed buildings sheltering behind a screen of young beeches, and as they got out of the car they could hear the whirr of the reaper in the field down the lane and the warm, sweet smell of cut hay filled the air all about them.

Jessie Shaw came down the lane to meet them, a stout, rosy-cheeked woman in a big printed apron with her greying hair pinned at the back of her head in a tight bun from which tendrils of it had escaped in the wind to curl round her neck and stray across her cheek. She thrust them back with a freckled forearm and smiled at Helen.

'They're a' doon at the big field wi' the reapers,' she intimated. 'The wee laddie an' Mr Oliver, too. Would you put your car round behind the dyke so that the men can get by when they come up wi' the machine? Just through that gate will do fine,' she directed Syd.

'You're getting a grand day for the hay, Mrs Shaw,' Helen said as she got down to watch Grant directing Syd through the narrow gateway where he could park the car along the side of the byres, and when he came back she introduced him to the farmer's wife.

'I've heard o' ye,' Jessie Shaw said, her bright eyes taking in every detail of his bronzed face and tall, striking figure. 'The wee laddie is fair full of excitement about you coming, and he's just as excited, too, about the idea o' drivin' the reaper!'

'As long as he's not in the way or making himself a nuisance,' Grant said, 'it's wonderful for him.'

'He's no nuisance at a',' declared Jessie. 'We can do wi' a' the help we can get these days and even a sma' pair o' hands can work wonders when they're directed in the right way. Apart from a' that, though, it's grand fun for the bairn, an' I like fine to see him enjoyin' himsel'.' She turned back to Helen. 'Will ye tak' a cup o' tea before ye mak' for the field, Mistress Oliver?'

'I'd much rather wait for milk and new scones later on, thanks all the same,' Helen said. 'I've brought you a gooseberry tart and a slab of cake from Mrs Michie. She's been baking all morning.'

'She said maybe she'd come down later and lend a hand wi' the tea,' Jessie explained. 'I saw her yesterday in the village. Well, off ye go if you're no' for a drink o' tea, and I'll follow ye up!'

Syd had already ambled off at a leisurely pace towards the sound of the reaper and Helen and Grant followed him down the lane to where another gate led into the field where the workers were busy in the sun. The reaper was in the far corner and they could see Tony's grey shirt and old panama hat where he sat perched up beside the driver, but he appeared far too fully occupied to notice them at that distance. The field was more than half cut and Fergus was raking near the hedge. He saw them immediately and came across to where they stood.

'No loitering permitted!' he challenged. 'Get your coats off to it and I'll guarantee you'll work up the best appetite you've ever had long before Mrs Shaw appears with the tea!'

'We should have brought our rations with us,' Helen smiled, shading her eyes against the sun to watch the reaper. 'Tony looks in his element, doesn't he? Has he been sitting up there all the time?'

'Every minute since he came.' Fergus took Grant's jacket from him to fold it in a corner with some others. 'Better take off your shirt, too,' he advised, 'unless you're allergic to insect bites?'

Grant appeared to hesitate before he said briefly:

'I'm not, but I think I'll stick to the shirt, if you don't mind. The heat doesn't particularly affect me.'

'It just about kills me coming on so suddenly,' Fergus confessed. 'A week or two ago we were freezing up here, and all I could get out of anybody in the way of sympathy was that it was a "snell" wind but "seasonable." I'm quite prepared to admit this is an improvement, and I'm also prepared to argue that you'll not want that shirt on once you've started tossing this hay around!'

'I'll take a chance,' Grant laughed, but there was something restrained in his laughter which linked it in Helen's mind with his first hesitation over discarding the open-necked bush shirt he wore.

All through the warm June afternoon they worked side by side, while Tony passed and re-passed them on the reaper as it made its ever-narrowing square in the centre of the field, waving his panama hat madly to attract attention when his voice would not carry above the sound of the machine.

At last there was only a patch of waving grass left, and Mrs Shaw brought down the tea. The farmer had evidently promised Tony that he should cut this last stretch by himself, and the child's delight knew no bounds. He could scarcely eat his tea, although Bessie Michie had appeared with his favourite chocolate cake, and after one small wedge had been hastily disposed of, he obtained Bessie's promise of another if he cut what remained of the hay in record time, and flew off down the field with a whoop of delight.

'That laddie's got every labourer of my farm fair daft about him!' Dan Shaw declared with a smile which suggested that his employees were not alone in their admiration of the young gentleman from the Keep. 'I'd make a farmer of him if I were you, sir.'

'It's early days to decide yet,' Grant Pemberton returned, 'but I've always considered it a grand life, and it's a pretty dependable way of earning your living.'

'Ay, world conditions don't affect you an awful lot—apart frae being told by the Ministry to plant corn where corn would never grow in a thousand years!' agreed the old man. 'But I'm no' complaining. I just let them have their wee bit say an' carry on in my own way!'

'When all this is in, what will you do next?' Helen asked.

'Oh, the sheep'll be needin' a bit dip and then there'll

be the main harvestin' to come on and the threshing. The wee fellow will enjoy the threshing when he can sit up on the big machine a' day!'

But long before threshing time Tony would be gone, Helen thought, and some of the magic went out of the day for her, so that she fell silent as they went back to their work in the field and Mrs Shaw and Bessie collected the tea baskets to carry them back to the farm.

It was seven o'clock before the last stook was in place and Tony got down from his seat to claim the reward of his labours.

'He's tired,' Helen said, 'though I'm quite sure he won't admit it. I think we should take him back by car, Fergus. The Shaws will keep MacNab till to-morrow.'

'Will he be all right?' Tony wanted to know. 'Will he get enough hay?'

'He'll get far more hay here than he'd ever get at the Keep,' Fergus assured him, 'and you can come for him tomorrow by yourself.'

'Tomorrow,' Helen said, 'we are going to Edinburgh.'

Grant Pemberton had flung himself down on the pile of loose hay they had used at tea time and he looked up at Helen with a questioning expression in his eyes.

'Need we?' he asked.

'You needn't if you don't want to come, but I thought Tony might like a day at the zoo while I visit my relations. There's—something else I must do, too—'

Tony flung himself down beside his father.

'I would like to see the zoo,' he said, ''cos they're not going to lead the hay till the day after tomorrow.'

'And by such things are great decisions made!' Pemberton ruffled his son's hair. 'All right, you old scoundrel, the zoo it is, and I escort you both to Edinburgh in the morning!'

He rose, stooping to pull Tony to his feet, but the child's eyes were fixed in a fascinated stare on the brown skin covering his chest where the open-necked shirt had fallen apart to reveal it ridged by a line of ugly scars.

'Daddy, what are these marks?'

'They're scratches, and they take a time to heal.'

But Helen knew they were weals inflicted by some camp despot while he had been powerless to defend himself, just another victim of the baser side of war when the habits of civilisation are abandoned and she shuddered at the thought of all his proud spirit must have endured so that he might one day claim his son again. Then, suddenly, their eyes met over Tony's head and he smiled, telling her without words that this was compensation greater than he had ever dreamed about, and her heart lifted and was glad for his sake.

On the way home Tony sat between them in the back of the car while Mrs Michie shared the front seat with Syd Willing.

'Is it like this in Malaya?' Tony asked sleepily. 'Hay-making n'everything?'

'Not quite the same,' his father explained. 'You see, it's a very long way away from Scotland and much nearer the equator, so that it's nearly always sunny and bright there. But you remember how quickly the night comes, don't you?'

Tony nodded.

'Not like here,' he agreed. 'I like it here, and I'll like when we go to the zoo tomorrow. Are there zoos in Malaya, too, Daddy?'

'There's not so much need for them, because there are plenty of animals roaming about in their natural state—tigers, leopards and elephants, to say nothing of a cunning old fellow called the tapir, which is a kind of rhinoceros, only smaller,' Pemberton explained.

'And there are deer, too,' Helen put in. 'Funny barking deer that make you jump when you first hear them, and little mouse-deer no bigger than a hare. And once I saw a honey-bear stealing pineapples right under an old Chinese storekeeper's nose!'

Tony laughed, a sleepy chuckle, although he was quite prepared for more.

'Are there birds—robins an' larks an' things?'

'There's a little fellow called the Straits robin, although he bears no resemblance to Mrs Michie's tame gentleman with the red breast who calls at the kitchen door for crumbs,' his father told him. 'Our robin is black and white, but he's very tame and friendly, too, he sings as sweetly as any nightingale. There's a Malayan sparrow which is called a munia, by the way, and he has a white head and flies around in a huge flock, usually in the padi fields.'

'Padi's rice, isn't it? We got a lot of it in the camp. I don't like rice,' said Tony decisively. 'I'd rather have rhubarb and custard the way Mrs Michie makes it.'

'But rice is good for you, all the same,' Bessie turned from the front seat to remind him, 'and we could be doing with some of it here again, only we'll have to wait till others that need it more than we do are served.'

The car came to a standstill before the Keep and she got out, while Grant helped Tony down. When he turned back to give his hand to Helen he found her still seated in the car gazing out through her side-window towards the low green hills against the western horizon, but he knew that she was not seeing them and said quietly,

'I'm sorry. Have I been reviving too many memories?'

'You've taken me back,' she admitted, her voice not quite steady. 'There's something about it that grips you.'

'It will never let you go,' he said with conviction. 'You will always remember.'

But that was not all, Helen thought as she followed Bessie Michie up the steps to the door of Oliver's Keep. It wasn't just the memory of cool hill-stations set against a background of jungle-clad mountain or the long white roads winding away through the rubber plantations to the little *kampong* in the clearing with its collection of thatched huts built high off the ground; it wasn't the vivid green of padi fields under a cloudless sky or the waving arecanut palms beside the shore—it was something bigger and deeper than all these, something she sensed yet could not quite define, something savouring of recompense for past sorrows, promising a fulfilment in life for which she longed. To go back! Did she really want to go back? Was the East calling her as once this land where she had no real home had called?

Again and again during the evening after Tony had been put to bed her mind fled back to the old familiar scenes and she remembered the brilliant sunshine and the warmth, and the kindly friendships, and the little bungalows on the high-lands with the colourful natives calling out a cheerful *tabek* as they passed. She could close her eyes and see again the almost breathtaking beauty of kingfishers flying low over some clear stream, all their brilliant plumage reflected in the mirrorlike surface of the water—blues and greens and reds that defied description—and in her ears sounded the shrill whistle of the cicada echoing through the hush of a Malayan garden. She could see the little lizards flashing up the sun-warmed walls and hear their familiar harsh clucking as they stalked the unsuspecting moths and brought them to their doom.

It was all so clear—so desperately clear—yet more clear and more dominating than the sharpest memory came the echo of a man's quiet voice.

'It will never let you go,' it said. 'You will always remember.'

Across the room Grant Pemberton sat in the worn leather arm-chair beside his host. They were both smoking last pipes and she looked at him in the lamplight casting its yellow pool down upon their heads, and suddenly knew why she would always remember. It was because he had brought back to her that which she had lost. Not because with him had come memories of blue lagoons and bluer skies against which the tall palms tossed their glittering fronds in the breeze from the sea, but simply because she loved him.

She had known it for a very long time, perhaps even from the day they had first met down there on the draughty little platform at Burndean junction, which was far enough away from coconut groves and little flashing lizards darting in the sun. Malaya and Grant Pemberton were bound up together, just as that warm, lovely, heartbreaking country would always remain bound up with the happiest memories of her life—and Grant was going back!

He was going back, and he would take Tony back with him, and that would be all. She pressed her hand suddenly close against her lips to stifle the cry of protest which almost escaped them, knowing that with his departure the light of life itself would go out for her.

CHAPTER ELEVEN

THE journey to Edinburgh on the following day was, for Helen, a strange mixture of pleasure and pain. To be with Grant and have Tony by her side was unutterable joy, yet again and again her thoughts would swerve with a little, twisting pain to the knowledge that such happiness could only be short-lived, that soon they would both be gone out of her life—the child she had cherished for so long and the man she had come to love.

She knew that she had found this second love of hers gradually through the years of trial and captivity when the memory of that swift meeting on the high seas had been ever with her, lending her courage and giving her a hope for the future. There had been nothing swift or cataclysmic about it, really. Only the recognition of it had come suddenly.

It was difficult to reason out why she had fallen in love with Grant Pemberton. She only knew that it was true, that the joy and the pain of it were filling her heart, and that every moment left to her was infinitely precious.

Acknowledging this, she was tempted to abandon the plans she had already made and take this day with all its promise of perfection for herself, but then she remembered Fergus and her promise to him, and the way he had looked when they had set out from the Keep. She could not go back on that promise to go to Collister even although it had been her own suggestion and not his expressed wish, and she felt, too, that she owed it to Margaret Oliver, who was Ken's sister.

Sitting in her corner of the carriage facing Grant and Tony, she thought about her dead husband, knowing that Ken would not grudge her this second chance of happiness if he knew. Her throat contracted painfully and tears stung at the back of her eyes as she thought that it was all going to be as short-lived as that former happiness she had known in her first marriage. Perhaps she wasn't destined for lifelong happiness, but if that were so, why was she permitted these brief glimpses of all it could mean?

There seemed no adequate answer to such a question, and she put it away from her, resolving not to trammel the joy of to-day with the bitterness of to-morrow.

'I wish you were coming to the zoo with us,' Tony said, slipping a small, warm hand into hers as they walked along the platform. 'We would have such fun!'

Helen laughed as her eyes met Grant's.

'Couldn't you?' he asked her. 'Visiting relations always seems such a waste of time on a sunny day!'

'There's a special reason for this visit, though,' Helen returned, 'and I really must see the family lawyer. I told you I had wanted to adopt Tony and that Fergus spoke to Mr Fairbairn about it, so I feel I owe him an explanation.'

There was a deeply penetrating look in his eyes as they held hers.

'I've changed all that, haven't I?' he said. 'Do you want me to come with you to the solicitor's?'

'I don't think it's really necessary, but if you would like to come we could all have lunch together afterwards.'

'O-oh! that would be lovely!' exclaimed Tony, and Grant smiled.

'You know Edinburgh better than I do, so I'll leave the choice of the restaurant to you,' he said.

Fairbairn, Betts and Fairbairn had been the Olivers' solicitors for three generations and George Fairbairn, the senior partner, was well aware of the differences which existed between the present owner of the Keep and the remaining Miss Olivers. He thought it a pity that they did not wish to hold any sort of communication one with the other, but was forced to respect the wishes of his clients. It was with a deep, personal interest, however, that he agreed to see Mrs Kenneth Oliver when she sent in her name that morning. His eldest son and Kenneth Oliver had been firm friends all their lives and both had been killed in action in the Far East, forging a bond between the two families which went deeper than a mere business allegiance, and now that he was about to meet the girl

Kenneth Oliver had married so far away from his home he felt that he was forging another link with his dead son.

When they were ushered into his private room, Helen saw his eyes go swiftly to the tall soldier accompanying her and then to the child. He knew about Tony, of course, but not about Grant, so very swiftly she introduced the two men, explaining the situation and her errand in a low voice while Tony wandered to the far window to inspect Mr Fairbairn's case of butterflies.

'I must congratulate you both,' George Fairbairn said when she had finished. 'I'm glad you both got through, and we'll just drop the adoption queries right away, Mrs Oliver. There's been no harm done.'

And it appears, he mused, as if there might be a much more satisfactory solution in the offing—if he were any judge of human nature and the way a woman looked at a man! A good thing, he thought, if they did marry. Good for the boy and the man, too.

They spoke of Malaya, and although Helen had never met his son, she was able to tell him quite a lot about him and the gallant way in which he had died. Ken had always wanted her to meet Donald Fairbairn, but it had been fated otherwise. They had been but a name to one another, although Helen had often felt that she had known her husband's greatest friend.

Reluctantly, therefore, George Fairbairn told them he had another appointment and Tony was parted from the engrossing case by the window, with the firm promise that some of the butterflies would be sent to the Keep at a later date to start him with a collection of his own.

'You'll be able to gather quite a lot of different species when you go back to Malaya,' the old man suggested. 'Some of these came from there.'

He patted the child on the head as they walked together to the door, thinking how much he would have given for a grandson of his own, and when he left them he said to Helen, clasping her hand warmly,

'I wish you all the happiness in the world, my dear, for you so richly deserve it.'

He had looked at Grant as he spoke and Helen's heart

contracted at the suggestion in his words which coupled their lives together. He had seen her love for Grant even in that short time, and he had thought that life had given her back her lost happiness in abundant measure! George Fairbairn was glad that she seemed to have found compensation in a second love as strong and tender as the first, recognising instantly all the qualities about Grant which would make him an ideal husband, and he had long ago guessed from Fergus Oliver's letters relating to the adoption of the boy how deeply she cared for the child, so that the old man went back to his desk with a kindly smile playing about his mouth while at the back of his mind he reviewed the case of the remaining Olivers, wishing from an entirely friendly viewpoint that they would settle their differences amicably. Trifling difficulties, he called them in his own mind, quite sure that a solution was possible there, also.

'And if there is one,' he murmured, sitting down at his desk again, 'I've a feeling that young woman will find it sooner than anyone else.'

Helen, however, had abandoned the problem of Fergus and her in-laws for at least an hour, and during that time she knew the meaning of perfect happiness. Even although it was over an austerity luncheon in a crowded restaurant it was her hour with the man she loved and no word or thought could adequately express all it meant to her.

'I feel like Tony and wish you were coming to the zoo with us,' Grant said. 'It would complete our day.'

Her heart raced painfully as she hesitated, tempted to throw every other responsibility to the winds but what she owed to love, and in the end she made a concession.

'I must go out to Collister to see Margaret, but I'll leave early, if you like, and come to the zoo. Unless'—she hesitated—'you would like to come to Collister with me?'

'We'll leave it at a meeting at the zoo,' Grant decided. 'Your relations aren't expecting us.'

'They're not even expecting me!' Helen confessed. 'I suppose I should have written or telephoned this morning, but—well, I just wanted to drop in on them unexpectedly.

I feel ashamed that I haven't been to see Margaret before this, really.'

'It rather sounds as if I've been partly to blame for your neglect,' Grant said. 'Margaret is your sister-in-law, isn't she?'

'Yes.'

She felt half inclined to tell him why she was making this unexpected call, that it was because she so firmly believed Margaret and Fergus to be essential to each other, and then she remembered that the fact was more or less in the nature of a confidence between Fergus and herself and said nothing further.

They parted when he had found her a taxi to take her out to Collister and she leaned forward to wave from the window to Tony until they were out of sight. Then she sat back against the leather cushioning trying to concentrate upon what might be the events of the next two hours only to find her mind reverting to the hour just past, to the little commonplace things which had made up her happiness—to a word or a look or a smile which had branded itself on her memory for all time. It had passed so quickly—too quickly—but she had garnered the joy of it and held it close against the barrenness of the days to come. She wondered if it was inevitable that she should have fallen in love with Tony's father. Had it been part of a natural sequence of events beyond her control? They had been thrown together abruptly by fate and parted, but Tony had been the link between them all these years, so that it seemed she had known Grant Pemberton all that time.

'Here you are, miss,' the taxi driver announced as he pulled his car up on the brae before a pair of closed iron gates. 'The gentleman paid me the fare before you left Edinburgh so that will be all right. Would you be needin' me to wait?'

'No—no, thank you. I'll be able to get a bus back, and I'm quite sure there will be someone at home.'

She was thinking of Grant's generosity and thoughtfulness, wishing that such care for her might colour all the future, and with a little pang of longing knew the futility of such wishes. What was the use of longing or wishing either, and such thoughts led inevitably to self-pity, which she abhorred. The future might lie bleakly before her, but she must endeavour to make the best of it, yet sometimes it shook her to remember that she must face it without Grant, even without the instinctive feeling that he was there somewhere in the background which was the sustaining thought that had comforted her during the past six years when she had hoped against hope that one day he would come for Tony. Yes, she had hoped that, even although behind it all had lain the dread of loss which his coming would inflict. It had lain dormant in her mind, but now it was alive and she must accept it, schooling herself not to grudge Grant the happiness which was his by right. She knew that she could not bear him any grudge—because she loved him.

She stood at the gate while the taxi reversed and went chugging down the hill again, and it was several minutes before she bent forward and turned the handle. The loud squeak of the rusty hinges made her look up at the quiet house almost guiltily, but immediately she wondered why she should care what any of the Olivers thought of her unexpected call and marched up the short drive to ring the front-door bell.

Several minutes elapsed before her summons was answered and the maid opened the door.

'Do you remember me, Millie?' Helen asked. 'I'm Mrs Oliver—Mrs Kenneth Oliver.'

'Oh yes, ma'am! Will you come in? It'll be Miss Jean you'll be wanting to see.'

Helen accepted the suggestion with a smile. Probably she would have to see Jean first, no matter for whom she asked!

The girl disappeared, leaving her standing in the hall, but soon there was a murmur of voices and Jean Oliver came through the baize-covered door which evidently led to the kitchen premises. She held out her hand, although Helen fancied that she could detect the old restraint in her manner as she said,

'This is most unexpected, Helen. You've caught us in the midst of jam making.'

'I hope you don't mind me coming like this,' Helen said. 'I was in Edinburgh on business and wanted to call. I came to see Mr Fairbairn about Tony—about adopting him. His father has turned up now so all that had to be cancelled.'

'My dear child, how worrying for you.' Jean led the way into a small sitting-room at the side of the house overlooking a sunken garden where roses grew in colourful profusion and their scent was wafted in at the open window. 'But perhaps it is just as well when you knew so little about the boy's background.'

'I never had any fear about Tony's background,' Helen answered firmly. 'You see, I knew what his father would be like—if he ever came back.'

'But how could you, my dear? You told us that you had merely glimpsed the man from a lifeboat or something.'

'Yes, that was all,' Helen admitted, 'but so often a glimpse in an emergency can tell you all you need to know—more than you ever find out about other people in years.'

'I don't agree with first impressions being right,' Jean said briskly. 'Quite often a person is acting a part for sheer effect. Are you still staying at the Keep?'

She fired the question as Helen sat down in the chair she had indicated beside the window.

'Yes, we're all at the Keep at the moment—Tony and his father, too. Fergus asked Major Pemberton to stay and he seemed glad of the opportunity to get to know Tony really well before he—before they go away together.'

Jean considered her searchingly.

'You're letting this make you unhappy,' she declared not unkindly. 'It will be a big mistake, Helen, to fret too much over the child.'

'How can I help it!' Helen said chokingly. 'He has been my whole life for so long.'

'Yes, it's a great pity; but I don't suppose you really feel that this Major Pemberton has no right to his son.'

'Oh no—no!' The cry came straight from Helen's heart. 'I didn't mean to suggest such a thing. He has every right, and I'm glad he's come back—for Tony's sake. He's so fine and decent—the sort of man who'd go through fire and water for the people he loved.'

'How long have you known Major Pemberton?' Jean asked.

'He has been at the Keep for two weeks.'

'Long enough for you to have fallen in love with him?'

Helen flushed and sprang to her feet.

'What makes you say that?'

'My dear girl, when a woman talks in the way you have just done about a man and under such circumstances there is only one conclusion to be drawn. Are you going to marry him?'

'No.'

Jean nodded her head with a little smile of satisfaction.

'I am glad you have taken the sensible view of things and see that you owe it to Kenneth's memory to wait,' she approved.

'Wait! I've waited for six years, Jean—if it was a question of waiting! But it isn't. We—there is nothing between Major Pemberton and me—not any question of marrying—but if there was I would feel that I had a right to my happiness and I would take it.'

Challenged, Jean Oliver stood in the centre of the room looking across it at her young sister-in-law incredulously before she said distantly,

'Of course, it is not my place to tell you what you should do. I felt sorry for you, Helen; that was all.'

Helen moved slowly round the table to stand beside her, a small, tremulous smile breaking at the corners of her mouth.

'I know you felt sorry,' she said. 'It was kind of you. And now I'll tell you why I've come. It was to see Margaret.'

Instantly Jean Oliver stiffened, even drawing herself away a little as their eyes met and held.

'Meg has gone out,' she said. 'Mr Purdie came to take her for a run into the country. It's the first day she's been out—apart from sitting in the garden and I don't really know when they'll be back.'

'Oh!' Helen could not help showing her keen disappointment. 'I thought I might have seen her. I meant to write, but I have been to London and in Yorkshire since I was here last time. Major Pemberton was trying to trace us and when I knew that, I had to make an effort to find him.'

Jean Oliver was evidently not disposed to enter into any further discussion about Major Pemberton and she switched the conversation by asking conventionally,

'You'll take a cup of tea, of course? I can't promise you that Margaret will have returned before you go. She has been ill and at home for about three weeks now.'

'Yes—'

Helen paused, realising that Jean had spoken as if she was breaking the news of Margaret's illness for the first time, yet Jean must have known that Fergus would carry the news back to the Keep. Unless—sudden thought!—Jean Oliver knew nothing about her cousin's recent visit to Collister. Helen's pulses quickened. Could it be possible? Fergus had seen Isobel, but not Jean. Yes, she was quite sure of that because she remembered Fergus saying bitterly that he had 'only bearded one lion in its den' and then explaining vaguely that Jean had been out for the afternoon when he had called. It had been Isobel who had carried Margaret's message to him, and it had been a cruel message, the sort of thing Helen could not imagine any girl sending to a man she had once loved so passionately. The small fact was enough to sow the first seed of doubt in her quick brain and make her wonder just how much Jean Oliver really knew about her cousin's visit to Collister.

She had little time to pursue the subject, however, as Hattie and Isobel appeared at the door together, Hattie coming forward to kiss her impulsively while Isobel stood transfixed in the doorway, her face white and set, her small mouth twisted into something that may have been meant for a smile but which held no welcome and no kindness.

'This is a lovely surprise,' Hattie declared. 'When did you come, Helen, and why didn't you let us know so that one of us could have met you at the station?'

'Helen is in Edinburgh on business, Hattie,' her eldest sister told her briskly. 'She has been seeing Mr Fairbairn.'

'About adopting Tony? He told me when I was in about some bonds,' Hattie rushed on to explain. 'Has it all gone through successfully?'

'Tony's father has turned up,' Helen explained, 'so I

have been putting everything right. Of course, I can't adopt Tony now.'

'Oh, Helen!' Hattie said, and that was all, because she knew that her sister was waiting to give an order about tea and her sphere was in the kitchen, but Helen caught the sympathy in her tone, seeing the understanding in her eyes, and felt again that little rush of warmth towards Kenneth's third sister which she had experienced at their first meeting.

'We'll have tea early, Hattie,' Jean said. 'Unless we can persuade Helen to stay the night with us?'

'I'm sorry,' Helen thanked her, 'but I couldn't, though it's kind of you to ask. I came up with Major Pemberton and Tony and I've promised to meet them later. Tony wanted to go to the zoo and we thought this was a good opportunity.'

'I had no idea Major Pemberton was with you,' Jean said, mildly interested. 'Couldn't you have brought him to Collister?'

'I could have done,' Helen admitted, 'but three people arriving unexpectedly is rather a tall order in these days of rationing, especially when one of them is a small boy with a large appetite!'

'Yes, perhaps it is,' Jean admitted in her candid way, 'but we could have managed, I dare say.'

It was at this point, or possibly a little before it, that Helen first noticed how strangely silent Isobel was. At their first meeting she could scarcely have been termed gushing, but so far she had not spoken at all and there seemed something almost furtive about her silence. Helen could feel Isobel's eyes upon her when she was occupied in conversation with Hattie or Jean, but as soon as she turned her head in her direction the narrow eyes were averted and Isobel was seen to be gazing abstractedly out of the window.

When the tea was brought in she made no effort to help Hattie with it but sat listening to all her sisters had to say to their visitor as if keeping the closest check upon every word. Nothing further was said about Margaret, and that fact alone seemed to satisfy Isobel.

Helen pondered over this conviction as she drank her

second cup of tea and presently she saw Isobel stiffen and sit up in her chair as if listening alertly to some sound outside.

'Will that be Mr Purdie's car?' Jean asked, turning her head towards the window to listen. 'We must ask him to stay for tea, Isobel. He has been so kind about taking Margaret out. Possibly she didn't feel inclined to go into an hotel for tea.'

Isobel rose, but before she had reached the door leading into the hall Hattie had opened it, announcing with a note in her voice that sounded like relief,

'Here's Margaret and Mr Purdie. I think he's coming in with her so I've brought the extra cups and saucers and I'll put the kettle on again.'

'Don't flap, Hattie,' Isobel said so sharply that Helen looked up at her in amazement. 'He's coming to tea all right and he'll probably praise your wretched scones and hint that you're the best housekeeper he's ever laid eyes on—'

'Isobel—please!' Hattie implored, her tortured eyes on the cruelly-smiling lips, as if she fought dumbly against a further revelation of her love from such a bitter source. 'You know I don't want anyone to praise my work.'

Isobel laughed unpleasantly, sitting down in her chair again as Hamilton Purdie and Margaret came into the room.

'Helen!' Margaret exclaimed, 'how glad I am to see you! I thought you would have come before—or even phoned the Home and they would have told you I was here.'

'I should have done,' Helen said, ashamed, 'but I've had such a lot to do. I've been in Yorkshire since I was here that last time and in London, but I hope you're going to forgive me.'

'You know I shall!' Margaret's voice was suddenly wistful. 'How were you to know I was ill?'

The words struck Helen with the force of a blow and without thought she looked instantly in Isobel's direction, meeting narrowed eyes which held a deliberate challenge. Yes, she thought, only Isobel Oliver knew of Fergus's visit to Collister! And for some reason best known to herself, Isobel had kept it secret.

Was it possible? Was she quite mad to think such a thing? Helen's mind spun round amid the hum of conversation until she realised that she was taking her part in the small talk without really hearing what was being said. All that she seemed to hear was Margaret's voice, sounding a little weary now, with much of its gaiety gone, and Hamilton Purdie's deep tones, while the conviction was driven into her mind with mounting certainty that these two were not engaged to be married, nor ever had been. Isobel, without telling Fergus a deliberate lie, had quite deliberately created a false impression, assuring herself with child-like smugness that the two things were poles apart, so that to Helen's first instinctive dislike of Isobel Oliver was added a definite contempt. Nothing could excuse such an act in her eyes, for to tamper with another's chance of happiness for any reason at all seemed to Helen the most contemptible action in the world. She could not see how she could possibly interfere, however, without creating a most unpleasant scene. Definitely to accuse Isobel on so flimsy evidence would be madness, yet she felt that something must be done.

'I'm afraid I've tired Margaret a little,' Hamilton Purdie was apologising. 'We got out of the car and walked a little way in the sunshine.'

'I enjoyed that,' Margaret declared. 'I—I liked being out again—'

She passed a hand uncertainly across her brow, swaying suddenly towards a chair, and Purdie caught her as she would have fallen.

'It's nothing,' he assured them. 'She's overtaxed her strength, that's all. I should have known better than to let her walk so far.'

'I'll take her up to her room,' Jean suggested briskly. 'I thought the run in the sunshine would have done her good.'

She led Margaret towards the door and Purdie followed them, but as they passed Helen Margaret stopped and held out her hand.

'Don't go without saying goodbye to me, will you?' she begged.

'Of course not.' Helen folded the cold fingers in her own warm grasp. 'I'll come up presently.'

She turned back towards the fire to find Isobel standing at the far side of the hearth gazing at her maliciously.

'Well,' she said, 'don't you think you've done enough damage for one afternoon? Margaret is easily distressed just now, and anyone coming from the Keep is sure to upset her?'

'Can you tell me why?' Helen asked, her eyes hard and level on the flashing grey ones. 'I wouldn't do Margaret any harm for the world.'

'Then, stop coming here.' Isobel's lips were pale and shaken. 'You belong at the Keep—you're a link with it, and Margaret wants to forget all that. We all want to forget that there is someone else there, someone who has no right to be there at all! Perhaps you don't know that he was engaged to my sister at one time and broke it off? Perhaps he doesn't want you to know that, though, when he is interested enough to have you staying at the Keep all this time.'

The sneer in her voice stung Helen.

'That's not true,' she flashed. 'Fergus and I are not "interested" in each other in the way you mean.'

Isobel answered her with a faintly mocking smile.

'At first I thought you were a go-between, but now I wonder why you come here at all,' she said. 'Even a blind person could see what it would mean to you to marry Fergus Oliver.'

'How could you *say* such a thing! How could you even think it?' Helen cried, but Isobel had gone from the room, and she was left confronting a closed door which opened presently to admit Hattie again.

'Hattie, when Margaret was first taken ill,' Helen asked, 'did you know that Fergus came from the Keep to see her?'

Hattie gave a small start, like a sleep-walker awakening from some unpleasant dream.

'Fergus? Do you mean that he came here—to Collister?'

'Yes—one day when Jean was away from home for the

afternoon. He came to see Margaret, but when he came back to the Keep he said Margaret had refused to see him.'

'But, Helen, when could all this have happened?' Hattie protested. 'There's been no word of it, and Jean would have mentioned his visit—'

'If Jean had known about it.'

'Do you mean,' Hattie asked slowly, 'that Isobel saw Fergus?'

'Yes.'

'But—she wouldn't dare!' Hattie could not quite grasp the full significance of the situation. 'She must have told someone.'

'Do you think she told Margaret?' Helen asked grimly.

'No, because I don't think Margaret would have refused to see Fergus.'

'You mean that, really? You are convinced of it, Hattie?' Helen's eyes gleamed with suppressed excitement. 'If it's true it means so much!'

She paused, hearing quick footsteps on the tiled floor of the hall, and then the door opened and Isobel came back into the room. She glanced at them both suspiciously before she addressed Helen as she would have done a stranger.

'Margaret insists that you go up to see her before you leave, and Mr Purdie thinks she should rest for an hour now, so will you go up right away?'

Hattie stooped to switch off the electric kettle, and Helen turned towards the hall feeling curiously defeated and most bitterly disappointed. Much might have come of that conversation alone with Hattie, she thought, if only they could have discussed this thing for five minutes longer.

Mounting the stairs, she knew that she could not approach Margaret directly, that perhaps her own unexpected visit, the shock of seeing someone from the Keep, had contributed in part to Margaret's collapse. All she could do was to wait, but her heartbeats increased excitedly when she thought that she would be waiting with some sort of hope now, the conviction that she had always been right about Margaret's love for Fergus.

Hamilton Purdie was standing at the foot of the bed

reading a thermometer when she reached the room and he crossed to her side to say quickly,

'Five minutes. I know you will understand.'

'Yes—of course.'

Jean was sitting on a chair beside her sister's bed, looking concerned, but Margaret smiled as Helen came forward.

'I'm an awful fraud, really,' she accused herself, 'because now I feel perfectly all right!'

'You've overdone things,' Jean said sternly. 'But you must get an hour's sleep now and take things easier next time you go out. I certainly would never have let you go if I hadn't thought it would do you a world of good, and Mr Purdie seemed to think so, too.'

'Mr Purdie,' Helen thought. Would even Jean Oliver call her prospective brother-in-law 'Mr Purdie'? Surely she would descend to Hamilton, at least! Oh, didn't it all prove that there was no engagement between Margaret and the doctor! Helen's pulses beat more quickly as she bent to kiss Margaret's pale cheek, although she felt curiously guilty as she passed Purdie in the doorway five minutes later. She liked him, and she was very well aware that she was coming between him and his heart's desire, but it was one of these things that happened, she told herself—people being hurt who didn't deserve to be—yet somehow she felt that Hamilton Purdie had never seemed entirely convinced that Margaret was for him.

Jean followed her down the stairs.

'You seem to have been thrust into the midst of a family mêlée,' she observed, 'but I must confess to feeling rather anxious about Margaret. She has not picked up nearly as quickly as she should after this illness, and it's really most worrying.'

'Doctor Purdie seems to think it is just the natural reaction from over-tiredness,' Helen said. 'I hope she will soon be well again and, if I may, I'll phone in the morning to see how she is.'

'That's most thoughtful of you,' Jean answered warmly enough, and then Helen saw her eyes harden as they travelled to where Hattie stood at the far end of the hall in hat and coat, obviously ready to go out.

'Where are you going, Hattie?' she asked sharply. 'I didn't expect you to go out this afternoon.'

Hattie drew in a deep breath, saying quite firmly,

'I'll see Helen back to Edinburgh before I go on to Sybil's for the evening.'

'But you visit Sybil on a Thursday,' her sister reminded her. 'You always have done.'

'Things can change,' Hattie returned with a surprising show of spirit. 'Even visiting days, and Sybil won't mind.'

'Suppose she is out when you reach there,' Jean suggested, the slow colour of anger rising steadily on her cheeks.

'Then I must just come home again,' Hattie returned mildly.

Rebellion! Helen thought. What could it mean?—for it seemed that Hattie was not so much concerned with paying an unexpected call as with continuing that interrupted conversation with Helen alone!

'Very well,' Jean said frigidly. 'You are certainly old enough to please yourself in these matters, Hattie, but I should have thought that when your sister was ill in bed, you would have reconsidered any idea you may have had of going out for the evening.'

'I don't think Margaret is seriously ill,' Hattie affirmed, 'and she has you and Isobel to look after her till I get back.'

'She certainly won't want for anything,' her sister assured her frigidly, although her eyes held a decidedly curious expression in their frosty depths and it appeared that she was both annoyed and baffled by this sudden change in Hattie's attitude.

But Hattie stood her ground more determinedly than Helen would have given her credit for and presently they went out together and down the brae to the bus stop at the foot.

The rising excitement in Helen made her ask as soon as they were seated well forward in the bus with no fear of anyone overhearing their conversation,

'Margaret isn't engaged to Doctor Purdie, is she, Hattie? Not even unofficially?'

'No.' There was a pause in which Hattie Oliver examined

the fingertips of her doeskin gloves with the utmost attention. 'No, they are not engaged to be married, but I think they very soon will be.'

'Which means you think Margaret may come to care for him?'

'How could she when she already cares so deeply for someone else!'

The vehemence behind the soft voice surprised Helen for a moment.

'It's Fergus, isn't it?' she asked.

Hattie nodded.

'It has always been Fergus for Meg right from the beginning—ever since they were children, in fact. I know that so definitely, even though Meg has passed beyond confiding in anyone these days. It shows how deeply she has been hurt by his attitude and that is why I believe she is on the border line of not caring very much what happens—why she might quite suddenly decide to marry Hamilton.'

And you couldn't bear that, Helen thought. You couldn't bear to live in that quiet house seeing your love of so many years coming and going as your sister's husband! Oh, quietly selfish Hattie, is that all?

'It wouldn't be fair to him,' Hattie's small, measured voice went on. 'He has so much to give and Meg is the type who must give all to love or nothing. There just wouldn't be any hope of a compromise being successful. She might be happy for a while in his companionship, but even companionship is no substitute for love.' She turned swiftly in her seat and Helen thought that no one could possibly have called Hattie Oliver colourless at that moment. Her eyes were aglow with deep feeling and a bright flush burned in her cheeks. 'I know this so definitely, Helen,' she said, 'and in these past few weeks I seem to have seen Hamilton and Meg rushing towards a precipice—blindly. He is so much in love with her that reason would finally go by the board and he would discount the difference in their ages and hope that one day Meg's youth would give him back his own lost youth. But it's never like that, Helen. The years would become an ever-widening chasm between them and one day he would see her fretting to be free.'

'But, Hattie, I know Fergus is still in love with Margaret.'

Hattie's fingers fastened on her arm.

'You're sure of that—quite sure?'

Helen smiled.

'My dear, I've been living in the same house for weeks past and—we've talked.'

'Then—what does he say about the war years—the years when all Margaret's letters remained unanswered?'

'He wrote. He tried to get into touch with all of you, but he came up against a blank wall. Everything, apparently, was done through your solicitors.'

Hattie flushed.

'Yes, Jean insisted it should be done that way after their engagement was broken off. We could never understand that—Margaret would never explain why they had quarrelled—and, of course, it was an injury to Jean's—to our pride. The Olivers have always been sure of their betrothals before they were publicly announced and Jean could not bear the thought of the gossip here in Edinburgh and among the people we knew round about the Keep.'

'But it was Margaret's affair—Margaret's hurt!'

'As a family, we share all these things,' Hattie said proudly.

Helen longed to tell her that such things couldn't be shared, not fundamentally, but she contented herself with the observation,

'People can interfere for the best of motives, I suppose, but that doesn't get us any nearer a solution of the missing letters. They couldn't all have gone astray. Fergus said he wrote more than once and I do know he called here with some flowers when Margaret was first taken ill.'

Hattie was frowning, for through her mind had suddenly flashed the memory of some charred embers she had found in the sitting-room grate one afternoon when she had gone to replenish the fire just before tea. They had been the burned stalks of flowers and she had been puzzled to know where they had come from. All the vases had been freshly filled that morning and the old flowers burned in the kitchen range in her usual tidy way, but she had forgotten to mention the matter to Jean and later it had entirely slipped her memory. Now she remembered that Isobel had been in the room when she had gone in, gazing sullenly out of the window, and that she had got to her feet stiffly, as if she had been sitting in the same position for a very long time.

Isobel!

Her mind turned from the thought of treachery and she would not discuss her sister even with Helen. Family loyalty was too strong in her for that, but she thought of Margaret, who was also her sister, and was determined that this thing should not lie another day in abeyance.

The determination gave her a new confidence. She felt her own individuality for the first time in years, felt free and unshackled, with her own convictions clearly before her—not Jean's nor Isobel's, nor even the family's. An injury had been done and she thought she knew the truth about it—or some of the truth—and even she had never been in love with Hamilton Purdie she assured herself that she would have probed it to the bottom for Margaret's sake.

She felt as if she were breaking fetters all round, shedding that dreadful sense of inferiority which had overshadowed her life for years, and facing an issue courageously at last. What, she wondered, had occasioned such a change in her? Perhaps it all dated back to those conversations with Hamilton when he had first started coming to the house and she had gone to tell him that Margaret would not keep him waiting any more than five minutes. They had sat on opposite sides of the sitting-room hearth talking chiefly about his mother, a wonderful old lady whom Hattie had known well and respected deeply, but once or twice they had discussed books and the Keep and what she was going to do with the future. It was then she had fully awakened to what a useless thing her life really was. And empty! She had known about the emptiness ever since he had come back into it, but he had come back with Margaret and she had tried to accept the fact that he was not for her. Then, gradually, the knowledge of Margaret's apathy had crept across her consciousness like an insidious shadow and she saw how little Purdie would get out of such a union. It seemed no form of conceit to contrast it with what she knew she could offer him. She loved him and Margaret did not, and there was an end to argument. And now that she had stumbled upon the truth about Fergus Oliver she knew that matters could not be allowed to rest there, for she was firmly convinced that Margaret had always remained in love with Fergus, whatever she might have said to the contrary. Wilful and headstrong Margaret had been in those days—reckless, Jean had called her, but Hattie had seen her sober down, had seen a look in her eyes sometimes that was heartbreak and, if ever the Keep had to be mentioned, a tremor of the lips that was longing unutterable.

They both felt that way about the Keep. They loved it —not as Jean and Isobel loved it, with a fierce pride, but with a tender passion that seemed a deeper thing in so many ways. None of them would ever forget it, but perhaps only Margaret and herself longed to return there under any circumstances. Hattie could feel no grudge against her cousin for possessing it, but her heart warmed within her at the thought of Margaret returning there one day as its mistress. It was all so fitting, she thought and—secretly—romantic!

'Helen,' she asked abruptly, 'do you know why they quarrelled?'

'There was no quarrel,' Helen returned firmly. 'Fergus would not bind Meg to a man who might return from the war a hopeless cripple—that was all.'

There was a long silence and then Hattie said,

'We've misjudged him so. We've all been such blind fools.'

She left Helen in Princes Street, bestowing a warm kiss upon her cheek and hoping that they would meet again soon, and then she made her way to her friend's small villa for tea. Whatever course she had set herself since leaving Collister, she must now vindicate her reason for accompanying Helen from the house.

Sybil had just come in from her afternoon walk with her

small daughter, and as Hattie watched her friend settling the chubby baby in her play-pen she experienced a well-known pang of envy. Not for her the joys of a home and children of her own. She had let her life pass, always subservient to Jean's will, and for a moment she knew unutterable bitterness at the thought of her sister's domination. Then she was telling herself severely that her own weakness had brought about the situation as surely as Jean's amazing will. If she had stood out for freedom—if she had insisted upon living her own life as once Sybil had urged her to do . . .

'What price the family?' Sybil asked gaily. 'Jean still on top of the world?'

'She's worried about Meg,' Hattie confided, and went on to tell her about Margaret's collapse, but would not mention her conversation with Helen until she was sure that she and Helen were on the right track.

Helen and she! Yes, they were in a sort of partnership, but she did not wonder why Helen was doing it or what she was going to get out of it, as a smaller nature might have done, and certainly she did not believe for one moment that there was anything in it for herself. Even if she had believed that Hamilton Purdie was going to be irretrievably miserable at the loss of Margaret she would have done all in her power to ensure her sister's happiness, but as it was she believed Purdie already realised what a risk their marriage would be.

Such risks were taken daily. She was well aware of the fact, but that was beside the point. There was still a chance of happiness for Margaret, at least, such happiness as Sybil now possessed.

'I must leave early,' she told her friend. 'I—I have quite a lot to discuss with Jean and Isobel.'

'But you spend your life discussing things with Jean and Isobel!' Sybil pointed out, her merry eyes sobering as she spoke. 'Don't you ever want to escape, Hattie?'

Hattie's lips parted in a strange little smile.

'Perhaps I've left it too late for complete escape,' she mused. 'Perhaps.'

Sybil did not try to detain her. She had never pressed

her friend for confidences: they had all come in Hattie's own good time so that perhaps Sybil Dykes knew more about Hattie Oliver than any other living creature. Long ago she had recognised the ardent spirit beneath her friend's placid exterior, hoping that one day she would see Hattie break through the stranglehold of her older sisters' domination and emerge into the sun, but the months had passed into years, with Hattie growing older and, apparently, resigned to her lot, and Sybil had felt baffled and disappointed even while she knew there was very little anyone could do about it but Hattie herself.

Lately, it had seemed to Sybil that Hattie had grown apathetic and a little dull, and once or twice when she had spoken about Hamilton Purdie there had been a look of hopelessness in her eyes which had not been good to see. Today, however, her eyes were gleaming and there was a look of stern resolution about her, a purpose which brought out all the latent determination in her, making her an individual once more. Sybil Dykes was not a curious woman, but as she watched her friend depart for Collister that afternoon a lively speculation burned in her grey eyes. It might be fun to be an unseen witness of Hattie's meeting with her family, thought she.

The bus which took Hattie to Collister seemed to crawl one minute and fly the next. She was nervous and impatient by turn as she sat in the seat facing the door thinking what she was going to say when she got home, first to Isobel and then to Jean. Certainly she must tackle Isobel about Fergus's visit and the charred flowers in the sitting-room grate. Had she the courage? She must *find* the courage! Then she would go to Margaret, telling her the simple truth, and after that she could do nothing but wait and let events take their own course. But at least she would have satisfied her own uneasy conscience.

More than once she had aligned herself against Margaret because she had considered Fergus's attitude over the broken engagement deplorable, but now she was touched by his thought for her sister and her romantic mind fastened upon the poignancy of the situation to the exclusion of all else.

Isobel was at the sitting-room window when she hurried up the drive and she stood fumbling for her key under her sister's eye. Supposing Isobel and Jean were together? She had planned to tackle Isobel alone and then Jean, if need be, appealing to her to see justice done, but she had not considered them together. It had always seemed too formidable a combination for her in the past, and so she decided to await her opportunity of speaking to Isobel alone, although she had the uneasy feeling that much of her new-found resolution might evaporate with the passing of time.

Isobel, however, proved to be the sole occupant of the room when she reached it, asking almost guiltily,

'Is Jean downstairs?'

'No, she's up in Margaret's room. Your hero has gone and Jean decided to sit with Margaret for a while.' Isobel had picked up the embroidery she was busy with, but her eyes were still suspiciously upon her sister's flushed face. 'Are you staying?' she asked sarcastically, seeing that Hattie had discarded neither hat nor coat and still clutched her handbag firmly in one gloved hand. 'You appear to have returned earlier than usual.'

'I wanted to see you, Isa,' Hattie began in a choked tone. 'There's something—something I have to ask you.'

Isobel's eyes sharpened.

'It sounds as if it must be something momentous,' she observed dryly. 'But if it isn't really important why don't you take off your coat?'

'It is important.' Both hands were clenched over Hattie's bag now. 'It's important to Meg and—and to all of us.'

'Really, Hattie, you make me tired!' Isobel expostulated. 'What is the trouble now and why must you be so melodramatic about it? Has it something to do with Helen?' sharply.

'No—although Helen knows about it. You see, Isobel, she told me Fergus came here some time ago with flowers for Meg.'

Isobel jumped to her feet.

'What of it?' she demanded.

'You didn't tell Meg, and you burned the flowers so that no one else would know!'

Hattie's indignation burned in two red spots high up on either cheek as the accusation fell into a silence fraught with anger and distrust on one side and cold fury on the other.

'What business is this of yours?' Isobel demanded. 'I was here alone—in charge during Jean's absence. What I did was on her behalf and I am quite sure she would have approved my actions.'

'Then why didn't you tell her afterwards?' Hattie demanded, her flagging courage suddenly renewed. 'Shall I tell you, Isobel? It was because you knew she *wouldn't* approve, because such underhand methods are not Jean's way. She would not have stooped to the thing you have done. She's proud and jealous of the family honour, but she's fair and loyal, too. Fergus has written to Meg, but his letters have gone astray, and more than once it was you who went to Mr Fairbairn's office to collect our mail. Jean wouldn't tamper with anyone's correspondence, no matter how strongly she felt.'

'But I would! Is that what you mean, Hattie?' Isobel's lips were a thin, compressed line. 'Well, supposing I admit that I destroyed those letters—what of it? Margaret had given him up. Their engagement was broken off. Was that any fault of mine? Did I part them? Did I discover that freedom during war meant more to me than my given promise to an Oliver?'

'Fergus didn't want freedom—not that sort of freedom, but you made sure their parting would be for ever!'

'I made sure that no tardy apology on his part would soften Meg after all these years.'

'You made sure of that on your own, without consulting anyone? Not even Jean!'

'Why should I always consult Jean? I have enough intelligence of my own!'

Then, you rebelled, too, Hattie thought, but would not follow up the thought at that point because of her concern about Margaret.

'But why—afterwards—did you refuse to take his message up to Meg? The day he brought the flowers, I mean.'

'Because I have always disliked Fergus Oliver, and because Jean and I both consider Hamilton Purdie an acquisition to the family. Left alone, Meg will marry him one day.'

'Left alone she would have been married to Fergus by now and be back at the Keep!' flashed Hattie.

'And you with her? Was that the idea, Hattie? Now I think I can see the real reason for your interest, because I don't think even you would be stupid enough to imagine that Hamilton Purdie would as much as look at you if he lost Meg.'

Hattie flushed to the roots of her hair.

'I'm not doing this because—because I hope to step into Meg's shoes,' she said with a quiet dignity. 'I'm probing for the truth because I think we should be just and because I know Meg is still in love with Fergus.'

'She hasn't told you that. Meg confides in none of us these days.'

'Probably because we have all gone the wrong way about looking for her confidences. You can't force anyone to tell you the secret feelings of their heart, Isobel, just as you can't force them to love the person *you* consider most suitable for them. Love isn't like that.'

'You seem to know a great deal about love of a sudden, Hattie, for one with so little experience!'

'I know that it should be fearless and brave and not afraid of expressing itself, and I know that it should fight for its right to survive.'

Isobel laughed unpleasantly.

'Such eloquence, my dear! Are you prepared to tell all this to Jean?'

'No, but I mean to go to Meg—'

'Prepared to tell me what?'

Isobel swung round to confront Jean in the doorway and a sullen expression darkened her face.

'Hattie's come home with a bee in her bonnet,' she observed with seeming carelessness. 'She'll want to tell you all about it, I've no doubt.'

Her eyes said that Hattie would be too much afraid, but

Jean looked across the room at her younger sister to ask firmly,

'What is it, Hattie? I could hear your voices raised in argument from the top of the staircase and I thought something must be amiss. Has anything gone wrong?'

'Everything seems to have gone wrong.' Hattie sought rather desperately for the courage to continue. She was weakening, and Isobel was standing at the far side of the fireplace with the old, derisive smile on her lips, silently mocking her and conscious of her desire to turn and fly from the room. But she wasn't going to run! She had started this thing and, for Margaret's sake, she must go through with it. 'Isobel has just admitted that Fergus Oliver came here to see Meg and that she sent him away again without even telling Meg he had come, and years ago there were letters which she destroyed—Meg's letters.'

It had all come out in a rush, and in the silence which followed on the heels of her impassioned accusation the ticking of the clock on the mantelpiece above her head seemed to hammer out the passing seconds, beating her words back into her own brain. There were letters which she destroyed . . .

'Is this true, Isobel?'

Jean's voice was like ice and she drew herself up to her full height to face Isobel across the room.

'I kept the letters back—yes, but I did not destroy them. They are still in my keeping.'

Isobel had spoken calmly, righteously, and her eyes did not waver as they met her sister's.

'You *kept* them?'

'I considered it a service to the family.'

'A service, Isobel? A despicable act like that done stealthily without my knowledge!' Jean was finding it hard to control her temper. 'What right had you to take the law into your own hands in this way when you knew what I think about such things?'

'When I knew what you thought! That's just it! I've had to know what you thought about everything all my life—I've had to bow to your decisions and be the second, unimportant Miss Oliver ever since father died! I've had to listen to all you've planned and say "yes" and be pleased because you *knew* what was good for Oliver's Keep and the family! I've been a nonentity for years, with no say and no rights—the second Miss Oliver—something negligible, in the background all the time, waiting to agree to everything you did! Well, I got tired of it, so I did something on my own initiative at last, but if you think I did wrong, Meg can have her letters. There are three of them—two from the Keep and one from London, but they are all from Fergus Oliver.'

Jean moved decisively towards the door, flinging it open.

'Get them, get them at once, Isobel!'

Isobel passed her, her head held high, an angry defiance lighting her eyes, while Hattie drew off her gloves and fumbled in her bag for a handkerchief.

'For heavens sake, Hattie, don't start sniffling!' Jean exploded irritably. 'We've got something to settle here and, since you brought it to the light of day, you'd better be prepared to see it through to the end without going completely to pieces and weeping all over the place. There's nothing despicable about what you have done. That all remains with Isobel.'

'Don't be too hard on her, Jean,' Hattie pleaded. 'I suppose she thought she was doing it for the best.'

'For the best! Tampering with someone else's correspondence—stooping so low as that! It amazes me in an Oliver woman—in Isobel! Oh, I don't know what to say! I'm at a loss—frankly at a loss! Such a thing has never happened in the family before—such duplicity! I simply can't understand Isobel's mentality. She must have been mad—quite mad!'

But Hattie thought that she could understand Isobel. Desiring power and thwarted at every turn, Isobel had seized her opportunity to wield a little power. Isobel had rebelled, just as this afternoon she, also, had rebelled against Jean's everlasting authority. Of course, Isobel had taken the wrong way of going about things; she had been secretive and vindictive and in the process she had hurt Margaret. That was the unforgivable thing, Hattie thought, as she stood apprehensively watching the doorway for her sister's return. That was what she would never be able to understand.

Isobel returned at last, carrying the letters, her lips pursed, her eyes hard as steel, and Jean took them from her without a word.

'What are you going to do?' Isobel asked.

'Give them to Margaret, to whom they belong.'

'In spite of all you've said? In spite of how you've always felt about Fergus Oliver and the Keep!'

'I feel nothing about the Keep—no resentment,' Jean told her with dignity. 'I only hope that he is running it as it should be run.'

'How can he do that when he has so little money?' Isobel gloated maliciously. 'The place must be going to pigs and whistles, and I can't see that he'll care very much. If he had married Meg instead of making a fool of her, we might all have been there now.'

'I don't think that would have worked,' said Jean dryly. 'Young people are best left alone.'

'You've changed your tune somewhat, haven't you?' Isobel sneered. 'Weren't you the one who first tried to influence Meg?'

'Their engagement was broken off and I simply did not encourage a friendship after that,' Jean agreed. 'It was a blow to our pride, and I'm not attempting to deny the fact, Isobel, but I could never, *never* have stooped to any underhand method to achieve my end, as you have done. And why you have done it defeats me. You could not have imagined for one minute that I should have approved.'

'No, perhaps not,' Isobel agreed stonily. 'Perhaps I thought I'd take the law into my own hands for once to accomplish something that might have evaded you! Perhaps that seemed real power to me. I don't know. Anyway, I prevented him from seeing Margaret and that was what you wanted, too, wasn't it?—on your higher plane! Even though you wouldn't "stoop" to my methods you wanted the same thing—you wanted to separate them, to make quite sure that there would be no more foolishness and that Meg would marry Hamilton Purdie and settle down admirably in Edinburgh. The funny thing is,' Isobel added with a serpent's glance in Hattie's direction, 'that someone else had the idea of bringing your dear Mr Purdie into the family circle if it hadn't been for Margaret!'

'Be quiet, Isobel!' Jean commanded. 'You have always had much too bitter a tongue and this is no time for such pleasantries. I expect you to make Margaret a full apology in the morning after she has seen these letters and heard my explanation.'

'By the morning,' Isobel returned defiantly, 'I won't be here.'

'Oh, yes you will,' Jean contradicted firmly. 'This is your home, Isobel, and the door will always remain open to you. Scenes like these blow past, although we may not be able to forget them in a hurry, but we are Olivers and we will remain together as long as we continue unmarried.'

'You can make anything sound like an ultimatum!' Isobel told her, 'but I have made up my mind to take a holiday—a long holiday on the south coast. Millie Hunt is at Worthing just now and she has invited me to go there more than once. Perhaps I can be more use to an invalid than I am here in what you choose to call "my own home".'

'Collister will always remain your home as long as I am alive,' Jean answered, 'but a wrong has been done and it must be put right before you leave. We shall see Margaret in the morning.'

'Please, Jean,' Hattie asked when Isobel had flounced from the room, 'will you give Meg her letters tonight?'

Jean turned to gaze at her thoughtfully.

'How much do you know about this, Hattie,' she questioned. 'What part have you taken? As a go-between?'

'Not between Fergus and Meg, but I have spoken to Helen. It was she who told me Fergus had been here,' Hattie explained, 'and after that I put two and two together. That was all.'

'Your two and two seems to have added up to quite a pretty sum-total of treachery,' her sister observed grimly, 'and as usual I suppose I shall be left to clear it all up.'

'I think Fergus's letters might do that,' Hattie suggested eagerly. 'Do give them to Meg right away, Jean!'

'She's asleep just now—or should be.' Jean appeared

to hesitate. 'Perhaps the excitement wouldn't be good for her.'

'Oh, why not? That sort of excitement never killed anyone, Jean. It would be untold happiness—release from all these doubting years when they were parted by war and a stupid misunderstanding!'

'The misunderstanding was of their own making!'

'I know that. Yes—yes, it was partly of their own making, but we sealed the issues, didn't we? We influenced Meg so firmly. She was very young at the time, Jean—barely twenty, and we must blame ourselves for bringing too great a pressure to bear against her love, for binding it up with family ties—'

'You are being far too dramatic, Hattie,' her sister reproved. 'It has always been a fault of yours, I'm afraid. Some of what you say is true, I'll admit, but we are far from entirely to blame. Margaret herself was headstrong and self-willed, you know, and whatever their quarrel was about, it can hardly be laid at our door.'

'They didn't quarrel,' Hattie said in a slow, measured tone which suddenly carried weight. 'Fergus thought he shouldn't marry, that was all. He didn't want to tie Meg—even by engagement—to someone who might come back maimed for life, and she saw his point in a way, though she thought it foolish and promised to wait. But he told her she must be free—completely free. Perhaps he thought he wouldn't come back—perhaps he had that feeling—and so he wanted her to have every chance of happiness—a second love.'

Jean was gazing at her intently, most of the hardness gone out of her face, which was very pale.

'Why wasn't I told this long ago?' she asked at last. 'It would have made a great deal of difference to my attitude.'

'Nobody knew but Meg, and maybe she thought that none of us would understand. You—we've always been hard with her, Jean—far too hard, and we're paying for it now in the shame of never having had her complete confidence.'

'Perhaps you're right,' Jean Oliver said slowly. 'You've

made me feel—a useless old busybody with no decent feeling in me.'

'We can try to put things right,' Hattie answered eagerly, 'and please tell Margaret now.'

It was a strange thing to be setting her will against Jean's, she thought, but a necessary thing. She wanted Margaret to have her letters without delay—to have her chance of happiness before it was too late.

'Very well,' Jean said, 'I'll go up to her now.'

Margaret was sitting up in bed when her sister reached her room and at sight of Jean she frowned.

'I wish you wouldn't upset yourself about me, Jean,' she said. 'I'm all right, really.' She pushed a hand through the heavy mass of hair falling over her brow in a little gesture of weariness which made her look the small girl Jean Oliver still considered her. 'I don't know why I had to act so stupidly—making an exhibition of myself like that. Hammy and I didn't really walk very far—'

'I'm not so sure now that it was the walk that did it,' Jean said, her pursed mouth closing in an even sterner line as she advanced with the letters in her hand. 'Perhaps it was the sight of someone from the Keep when you were least expecting them.'

Margaret's eyes leapt to hers, dark and burning and full of accusation.

'Why do you say that? Why should I care about—the Keep any more than you do?'

'I don't know, Meg, and if that's going to be your attitude we'll leave the matter there. I've often wondered why we haven't had your complete confidence all these years, but I'm not asking for it unless you want to give it.' Jean drew in a deep breath. 'What I'm here to do is to try to right a wrong that has been done. These are your letters.' She laid them down on the coverlet near her sister's hand. 'They are letters you should have had years ago.'

Margaret was gazing at her now in utter bewilderment.

'What happened to them, Jean?'

'They were taken from Mr Fairbairn's office and—kept back.'

Margaret leaned forward, her eyes suddenly alert.

'Kept back?' she repeated. 'But who would keep them? If they were mine why weren't they given to me?'

'Because someone thought—mistakenly—that it was the best thing to do. Why, I shall never know.'

Margaret's hand went out to cover the letters, yet her eyes did not leave her sister's face.

'They were from Fergus,' she said slowly and bitterly. 'That's why they were kept back. You knew they were from him!'

'I knew nothing about them until I saw them for the first time this afternoon.'

'Then—it was Isobel!' Margaret flung the bedclothes aside and struggled to her feet. 'Isobel did this. She always hated Fergus—she would do it because she hated him and hoped it would make him leave the Keep!'

She was trembling, her hands clenched at her sides, the letters clutched in one of them while the pent-up anger and thwarted love of years struggled for some kind of expression which would ease the pain in her heart.

'Hush!' Jean pressed her back towards the bed. 'You mustn't excite yourself like this, Meg. You've been ill—'

'Ill! I've been ill with worry, wondering what I should do to find some sort of happiness in life. I've been weary and tired and horribly depressed and there hasn't seemed much use going on, and now you tell me that it all might not have happened and ask me not to excite myself! Do you never get excited, Jean? Have you never felt angry and bitter and thwarted—have you never felt hopeless because something has largely been your own fault—because you've lost something that you might have had by being stronger?'

'My dear, if you're talking about Fergus Oliver and the Keep I can't see how you can possibly blame yourself.'

'I'm not even thinking about the Keep!' Margaret cried. 'If he had been a beggar, Jean, I would still have loved him. He didn't own Oliver's Keep when I first knew him and—and our love was something very beautiful then. Now—now . . .'

'I'm sorry,' Jean Oliver said almost humbly. 'I am entirely to blame. These letters which Isobel kept are not the real issue. It was my attitude in the first place which made Isobel feel that she should act in this way, I expect.'

'You're not *excusing* her?'

'No, not for one moment. What she did was despicable and utterly beyond my conception of human nature. She acted without my advice for once in her life and it has been disastrous.' The old, dominant note was uppermost again. 'I shall see that you have the apology which is due to you, Meg, you can be quite sure of that.'

'Apology! What good will that do? It won't bring Fergus back again or undo all these weeks of torture and doubt. Isobel may apologise but she's done what she set out to do, hasn't she? And everyone in this house has helped her—indirectly, maybe, but helped her all the same!' Margaret's voice rose on a sob. 'Do you think I want her tardy apology? Do you think it will help—now?'

'Meg,' Jean said with surprising gentleness, 'don't you think you had better read your letters and see what they say?'

Margaret's taut young figure seemed to slump on the edge of the bed as she opened her hand and looked at the crushed envelopes.

'What's the use? They're months old—perhaps even years old.'

'I'm going downstairs,' Jean said definitely. 'I'll send Hattie up with your tea-tray in a few minutes' time.'

There was an inarticulate sound from the bed which might have been protest or assent, but she did not turn to discover which. Instead she went briskly down the wide staircase to set her side of the house of Oliver in order.

Margaret sat on the edge of the bed for more than ten minutes after she had gone, sat without moving with the heavy look of a sleep-walker stamped upon her face, her eyes dull and glassy, her red mouth drooping at the corners. What was the use? What was the use? Her own words rang in her ears like a knell. The damage was done. The letters she held were months old and in all that time Fergus had never tried to contact her again. He had given up trying. That was what had happened. It was all so banal. He had just ceased to care—he who had cared so much. There was nothing left. It had all fizzled out, extinguished by Isobel's perfidy and her own foolishness. Oh no, she couldn't blame it all on Isobel! There was her own part in it—her stupid pride and childish petulance and her desperate lack of faith. Yes, that above all—her lack of faith! Deep in her heart she had trusted him as much as she had wanted him, but she hadn't been strong enough to stand by his decisions with him. She had let herself be influenced—by Jean and Isobel, and by Hattie in a lesser degree—but if her love hadn't been little and cowardly and weak it would have surmounted all that.

She had written and he had not answered, but his answer was here, lying between her shaking hands. She looked down at the letters and her eyes clouded with tears. Oh, why should it be too late now? Why had fate done this to her? She could not even open them lest the pain of what he had written would crush her heart for ever.

Then, suddenly, she was thinking of Helen, seeing her steady eyes with that look of purpose in them that was so reassuring, and hearing Helen's voice with the knowledge that her sister-in-law had been trying to tell her something, even on that first day of their meeting when there had been no way of saying very much to each other because they were not alone. They had never been alone. Someone had always been there, standing between them and the truth!

What was the truth? She felt her heart swelling as if it must burst its bounds and break out into the light of that truth—the only truth she wanted to believe in! 'I've never known a man more lonely,' Helen had said. 'Lonely of heart, Margaret—missing everything.' Helen had been trying to tell her in the only way possible that she believed Fergus still loved her! Oh, *could* she believe it? Could she really believe it!

Her nervous hands fumbled for the letters and she sat staring down at her name written in the old, familiar handwriting for a moment before she opened the first one. It was short; two pages written in a sprawling, schoolboy style, and the second one was shorter still. The third was nothing more than a note, but they told her what she wanted to know and when she folded them up again the tears were streaming down her cheeks.

'Oh, Fergus,' she whispered brokenly, 'all these years—'

Then, resolutely and with a strength of purpose in her eyes which made her look very much Jean Oliver's sister, she got up from the bed and began to dress, and when Hattie appeared with her tray she found her standing at the dressing-table in a red woollen suit doing her hair.

'Put it down, Hattie,' she said, 'and don't go. I want to speak to you.'

Hattie glanced at her nervously.

'You shouldn't be up, Meg. Jean said—'

'As if I cared what Jean said, or anyone else! Hattie, why don't you shake the shackles off and be free—be yourself—an individual, not just a shadow of Jean and Isobel!'

'I've tried to. Perhaps I can even yet.' Hattie looked about her uncertainly. 'The letters? Did Jean give them to you?'

'Yes.' Margaret turned from the mirror, her eyes shining. 'Oh, Hattie, if it isn't too late they might mean all the difference between living and—and just existing!'

'You mean that you—couldn't have been happy—really happy—with Hamilton—ever?'

Hattie, you're giving yourself away, thought Margaret, but all she said very decisively was,

'He would make anyone happy, Hattie—he's so fine and decent—but I had no right even to dream of offering him so little in return. And I've got to tell him that—tonight if possible.'

'Because of the letters—because of what you found in them?'

Hattie's eagerness was almost pathetic and there was a far-away look in Margaret's eyes as she answered her.

'No, not because of that. They were written so long ago that I can't even tell if Fergus still feels the same way now, but they have convinced me that I have no right to offer anyone else second best—not anyone like Hammy.'

'What are you going to do?' Hattie asked dully, because

there was no very great elation in her heart now at the thought of Hamilton Purdie's freedom. Because he had lost Meg was no reason why he should turn to Meg's sister, even for sympathy and understanding. 'Jean will never hear of you going out again this evening.'

'Hattie,' Margaret exclaimed, 'let's get rid of this Jean complex and do something we really want to do for a change! You can't let anyone rule your life completely—not even anyone like Jean. I've known it for a long time and I've tried to break out gradually, but maybe it has to come to a complete upheaval in the end—the final show-down. Well, this is it for me. I'm going to Oliver's Keep.'

'Meg—!'

'Why not?' Margaret lifted her head proudly. 'Fergus wrote to me and I didn't answer his letters—because of what Isobel did.' Her hands clenched spasmodically on her lap. 'I'll never forgive her for that,' she declared. 'Never, as long as I live! But Fergus doesn't know what became of his letters and I've got to tell him. I'm not going asking for his love. That may be dead.' Her voice all but quivered. 'But I owe him an explanation and, as I see it, it's got to be a personal one.'

'Meg—he loves you. Helen told me that, and she knows. She's lived at the Keep and she's not the sort of person to say such a thing unless she was sure.'

Margaret flushed.

'I believe you've made it more difficult for me to go now,' she said slowly.

'Oh, why should it be difficult!' Hattie cried. 'If you love him nothing should keep you back now.'

'If I love him! If! I've loved him every moment of every stricken day since I lost him! I've always loved him, but since I've thought I had lost him my love has been an agony inside me, Hattie. I can't tell you what it's been like—nobody could imagine.'

She stopped abruptly, gazing at her sister with eyes which suddenly saw beneath the surface, realising that she had no need to tell Hattie about love and loss and the utter conflict of the soul when hope has died, and she continued to look at Hattie, awed and bewildered and suddenly angry with herself. Hattie had loved Hamilton Purdie all these years and then she had calmly stepped in and taken his friendship—and his love—because she was lonely! Oh, could how Hattie ever have spoken to her again—ever have done anything for her!

'Hattie,' she confessed, 'I've been an utter fool. Try to forgive me and—and get something out of life if you can. Don't just sit down under Jean's thumb and waste all the years that are left. There must be something you've wanted to do—something somewhere.'

'All I have ever done,' said Hattie with a smile, 'is be a good housekeeper.'

'But Jean is the housekeeper here, really. It's not even housekeeping, Hattie, it's just—'

'Obeying orders? Perhaps I've got too used to that,' Hattie mused. 'I enjoyed my work at the canteen during the war, but that's over now. I'm thirty-five, Meg, and perhaps I should be grateful at the thought of having a home like Collister instead of kicking against the pricks.'

'But you're not grateful, Hattie! Deep in your heart you're not!'

'Oh, well—'

'Please make a stand! Please *do* something. We'll do it together!'

Hattie smiled.

'We'll see,' she said.

'And now,' Margaret observed grimly, 'I'm going downstairs to find Isobel.'

To Hattie the next quarter of an hour was a nightmare as she stood in the kitchen listening to the angry voices in the sitting-room at the end of the passage—Meg's and Isobel's voice, and then Jean's. She was not asked to take any part in the conflict, although she had already played a part, and when it was all over she felt shaken and unhappy. Nothing like this had ever happened before—nothing with such finality about it, and she wondered where it would end, although she was still quite convinced that it had been her duty to reveal the truth when she had discovered it.

At the end of fifteen minutes she heard Margaret run up

the stairs again and Jean's voice in the room she had left, low and insistent, continuing the conversation with Isobel alone, and then footsteps on the stairs once more and the front door slamming.

Margaret had gone out! In a panic of indecision Hattie wondered if she should follow, and then she recognised the futility of an attempt to overtake her sister when Margaret had obtained such a start. She was evidently bound for Edinburgh and would be on the bus before she could even collect her hat and coat.

Margaret caught the bus by a hairsbreadth, running down the brae to board it flushed and breathless, but triumphant, and as it carried her citywards she made her plans.

Hamilton Purdie was coming out of his consulting room when she was admitted to the house in Brinkmere Crescent, and at sight her of he strode across the hall with a look of utter amazement in his eyes.

'Meg, what is this? What are you doing here?'

'I've got to see you.' She tried to smile. 'I'm really all right, so don't think of doping me! I promise you I'm not going to faint again.'

He led her back into the consulting room and closed the door.

'You didn't come here to tell me that. What *is* the trouble?'

Her eyes misted over before the look of anxiety in his.

'Oh, Hammy, I'm not worth the care everyone takes of me!' she burst out. 'I'm a fool and I haven't even the strength—or is it the courage?—to tell you what I've come to say!'

'Need you tell me?' His hands were suddenly strong and vital on hers. 'I think I know, Meg. You've made up your mind to go back to the Keep.'

'In a way—yes, but it isn't because I know he loves me. I don't. It's because—because anything else would be such a poor second best, Hammy. Oh, can you ever understand me? Can you ever forgive me?'

'For offering me your friendship? Meg, my dear, you're surely not proposing to take that away?'

She clung to his hands.

'No—oh, no!' Her lips quivered. 'How good you are!'

'Because we've both suddenly seen what should have been so evident to me long ago?' He smiled whimsically. 'It wouldn't have worked, Meg—not when we looked at it sanely.'

'I wonder if I've ever been sane,' she said unevenly, 'throwing away all I had, but even if—if it's never going to be the same again, Hammy, I had to tell you first. I—I'd never be able to make you happy. Not in the way you deserve. I'd always be thinking of Fergus and what might have been.'

And might still be, Hamilton Purdie thought, envying the man who held the priceless gift of Margaret Oliver's love, yet not grudging him that love because his acceptance of it would make Margaret ideally happy. He admired her, too, for coming to him like this, for not waiting until she had made sure of her old love before she finally rejected him. Somehow, that was Margaret—valiant and young and true—and one expected such things from her. He had thought to capture her gay spirit, but he knew now that it would have been imprisonment without the free gift of her love. That love had been given irretrievably to someone else, someone she had met in the first flush of youth when his own youth had almost been behind him, and he could not blame her for the gap of years which separated them nor for loving still where once her heart had been given.

'I'm going out to Greydykes,' he said. 'Will you come with me, Meg?'

'Is it ready, at last?' Her eyes flashed with excitement at thought of the project which had been very near his heart all through the war years. 'Your own nursing home! Oh, Hammy, I can see you doing such wonders there—after-care and all the rest of it. I'll want to come quite often to look on, even though I'm not qualified to take part.'

'You'll always be welcome, Meg.' He had turned to a cabinet against the wall and began to mix something in a glass. 'And now I want you to drink this up before we go. I'm not taking any chances of returning you to Collister ready to pass out again!'

'I won't! Not this time.' Margaret took the glass obediently. 'What is the beastly stuff, anyway?'

'Nothing very deadly, so drink it up and we'll go.' He seemed eager to get away; perhaps eager to leave the scene of his disappointment behind him and look to the future and the shaping of an ideal. 'They've made a grand job of the house, and I'll soon have the grounds put in order. There are still some Army huts to move, but if the house is all right I'll not worry too much about the gardens at present. hope to get my first patients out there by the end of next month, but the big snag at present is domestic staff. I can't even lay hands on a housekeeper.'

Margaret said 'No?' vaguely, thinking of something she and Hattie had been talking about before she left Collister, and when the car drew up before the stone-pillared doorway of Greydykes she did not immediately follow her companion up the steps. He had opened the door and moved into the cool, marble-floored hall before she joined him, standing by his side to gaze up at the superbly painted panels on the ceiling with a look in her eyes which suggested that her thoughts were far away. They had reached the kitchen regions, however, before she attempted to put them into words.

'These are the domestic offices,' he said, as proud of the new paint and shining tiles as he had been of the bedrooms upstairs and the small, beautifully appointed operating theatre on the first floor. 'All my worries would be over if I saw them occupied.'

'Have you—ever thought of Hattie?' Margaret asked in a firm, measured voice. 'She knows all about this sort of thing, and I think it would be good for her to get away from Collister for a while—into some interesting job.'

He looked at her intently.

'You think they could spare her?'

'At Collister?' She laughed abruptly. 'The trouble with Collister is that there are too many of us there— Jean and Hattie and Isobel and me all falling over each other and getting in each other's way. We're due for a change all round. It will do everyone a lot of good.'

'But Hattie?' he said. 'How could one approach her?'

'Tell her that you need her, Hammy—if you do need her.'

'Need her! She'd be the answer to everything—the sort of person I need here—capable and sympathetic and kindly, yet it never struck me to ask her. I always thought Jean needed her about the house.'

'Jean doesn't *need* anyone, not in any real sense of needing people, and in the end I suppose she'll feel quite pleased that Hattie is—necessary to you.'

'Why do you say "in the end"? Do you expect Hattie to meet some sort of opposition?'

'Undoubtedly,' Margaret smiled. 'But with your backing I don't think it will be too stiff!'

'I often wondered if Jean approved of me.'

'You know she does—tremendously! Oh, Hammy, make this all right for Hattie, and I'll bless you to the end of my days!'

'It's very much a case of Hattie making things all right for me, if she is willing to tackle the job,' he returned quietly as he led her out into the twilight and helped her into his car.

CHAPTER TWELVE

WHEN she had parted with Hattie in Princes Street, Helen remembered her promise to join Tony and his father at the zoo, and with a smile she boarded a tram and made her way there, only to realise at the entrance gate how gigantic a task she had set herself attempting to find a man and a small boy in that warren of paths, to say nothing of the crowd of human beings wandering leisurely from one enclosure to another, but Helen was young enough to enjoy a visit to the zoo on her own account, and presently made her way to the monkey house where she believed she had as good a chance of catching up with Tony and Grant as anywhere. Tony invariably gravitated to the monkeys, and there she found them, laughing together like a couple of schoolboys over the antics of an old chimpanzee who had caught hold of a piece of wire and was poking it through the bars of his cage at the spectators, withdrawing it cunningly whenever anyone made a catch, much as it must have been done in reverse many times. The knowing gleam in the little beady eyes and the dance of victory which followed every successful tug-of-war convulsed Tony, and Helen came up behind them unseen.

'How long have you been doing this for the benefit of the whole zoo?'

'Oh, Mummy! it's been such fun! Daddy poked the wire through and the chimp caught it and pulled and pulled an' we couldn't hold on! He was too strong, and when he got it he made a wireless aerial all across his cage and then sat back and scratched his head just like an old man who didn't think it was quite right! Then he took it down and tried it another way—'

'Don't you think you've caused quite enough commotion for one afternoon?' Helen asked, her laughing eyes meeting Grant's over his son's head. 'Let the chimp have the wire and we'll have some tea!'

He glanced at his watch, surrendering the fragment of wire he had just caught to an eager small boy on Tony's far side.

'Heavens! is it really that time? I meant to come to the main gate round about four o'clock. How did you manage to find us?'

'By instinct, I should think—or knowing how fond Tony was of the monkey house at Regent's Park!'

'And your visit to your in-laws?' he asked. 'Was it successful?'

'In some ways, although not quite so successful as I should have wished.'

She was frowning and almost abruptly he changed the subject.

'This has been a wonderful two weeks. I'm going to miss the freedom I've enjoyed here when I go back to London.'

'But—there's no question of you having to go back just yet?' Her heart seemed to be standing still, waiting for his answer. 'I mean, you have indefinite leave—until they send for you.'

'I had a letter yesterday,' he said. 'I must be in London before the week-end.'

'Oh!' They were in the rose garden adjoining the restaurant and to Helen it seemed as if every bird had suddenly stopped singing and the whole bright world around her had gone dark. 'When must you go?' she asked flatly as they walked into the shade of the building.

'I should go to-morrow, but all my inclinations are to put it off until Thursday or Friday.'

He had spoken lightly, but behind the lightness she could detect something deeper, a worried note which suggested that his mind was not at rest and beyond that a sudden, strange reserve which she had glimpsed vaguely once or twice before.

'My appointment must have come through,' he added when they were seated at a table in the dining hall and he had given his order to the waitress. 'That could be their only reason for sending for me at such short notice.'

Tony was at the window, gazing through it at the inquisitive sparrows hopping on the stone flags outside and Grant

Pemberton's eyes rested upon him with a definite look of worry. Helen saw that look and in spite of the restraint which had risen like a barrier between them, knew that she must offer to help.

'You're worried,' she said. 'Is it about Tony?'

'Yes—partly.' He looked up, meeting her concerned eyes. 'Could I leave him with you for another week—till I've had time to look around?'

'Who else would you leave him with?'

Her heart soared and the day was suddenly fair again. What did it matter that her respite was only for a week, that the agony of parting was only postponed for an hour or two longer? She would have Tony and she had the prospect of seeing Grant again!

'You mustn't worry. I'll take care of him,' she promised.

He said suddenly and abruptly,

'We have no right to force ourselves upon you any longer than you expected. You have done so much for us already—more than I shall ever be able to repay.'

'Please,' Helen said, 'don't talk of repayment or anything like that. One doesn't think of repayment when something is done for love.'

She saw him look at her sharply and then away again, as if he put a desire or an impulse from him, and Tony came back to the table with the advent of sandwiches and lemonade and the conversation reverted to polar bears and sea-lions and the difference between a dingo and a wolf.

They caught the five-thirty train for Burndean, where Fergus met them with the car, and for the remainder of the evening there was no further opportunity for conversation of a personal kind. Helen would have liked to have given Fergus some message from Margaret, but there was none to give and she could only content herself with reporting that his cousin was well again and hope that waiting would eventually achieve the results she had set out to achieve.

In the morning Grant refused an invitation to ride to Toshiehill with Fergus, saying that he would write some letters and post them in the village when he went down to send off his wire to London. Tony, torn between a ride to

Toshiehill and a visit to the village sweet-shop, finally decided on Toshiehill, reminding his father that sweets could always be bought and carried up from the village in a paper bag!

'He's going to miss all this, and MacNab in particular,' Grant said to Helen as they stood watching the riders' departure. 'It's going to be a problem wondering what I can give him in return.'

'I think—just being with you will make up to Tony for quite a lot. Besides,'—she tried to keep her voice steady—'there's the thought of going back to Malaya and seeing all these tigers and things you promised him!'

'*We* promised,' he reminded her. 'You took your share in the story-telling, remember?'

Behind the lightness in his voice she could still detect that strange, disturbing note of uncertainty which proclaimed the troubled mind, and as he filled his pipe and lit it she wondered if she should ask him if he needed any further help.

'You've no idea where you'll be going—which part of Malaya?' she asked.

'None at all.' He drew at his pipe, a deep frown between his dark brows. 'There are some parts, of course, where it would be definitely unwise to take a child for a year or so until they are properly rebuilt, but if I were reasonably near one of the hill stations or a town where I could be sure of his education I'd take him back with me and chance everything.'

'You'll know, of course, when you come back from London.'

'Yes, quite definitely, I should think.'

There was an odd silence between them, the silence of mounting, unsaid things. What could be wrong? Helen wondered. He seemed changed, drawn away by that strange reserve, yet curiously in need of her. But how could she break through his unapproachableness? Suddenly she felt that her own heart was barren of words, that nothing she could say would ever help. There was nothing in her but that ache of longing which she knew would only increase with the passing years, and the way ahead was suddenly more than she could contemplate.

'I must go in,' she said abruptly, to cover the tremor in her voice. 'There's stacks of work to do—'

'Helen,' he said quietly, 'is Tony going to be in the way?'

'In the way?' She turned to him, meeting something hard in his eyes which she could not understand. 'Why do you say that? Why do you even think such a thing!'

'I'm sorry.' His mouth softened a little. 'You've been very patient.'

'I've wanted to do it. Patience just doesn't come into it.' Her hands were suddenly clenched at her side. 'Can't you understand that Tony's been my whole life these past six years? There's no question about being "patient" or "kind" or anything like that.'

'Yes, I understand,' he said slowly, 'but you are building a new life now and it would be madness to let Tony or I stand in your way when we will have so little part in it.'

What was he trying to say? What was he trying to do to her? She knew they had no part in her life from now on, nor she in theirs—she had accepted that—but it was cruelty to put it into words. She could not look at him: there had been a bitterness in his tone that she could not understand and she wondered if she could have failed him in any way. But she could not ask. Words were denied her lest words should rush from her innermost heart, betraying her love for him.

'I must go now,' she repeated. 'You must want to get your letters written.'

He stood watching her, his pipe between his hands, and long after she had gone he was still leaning there against the stone rail of the terrace, his eyes shadowed and his mouth twisted wryly as he contemplated a future in which he had no great faith.

It was there that the girl in the blue tweed coat saw him when she came over the familiar hump-backed bridge and looked up at Oliver's Keep for the first time in six years, and her heart bounded madly as she mistook him for the Keep's owner and then settled back to its steady, though slightly quickened beating as she saw him to be a stranger.

Margaret Oliver knew who he was, and because Helen had spoken about him with a certain look in her eyes, she went up the road to meet him with an interest which helped her to forget for a moment the almost paralysing nervousness which had possessed her ever since she had come off the train at Burndean.

'I'm Margaret Oliver,' she said with that frank smile of hers when she finally reached the terrace. 'And you're Tony's father. Helen has told us all about you.'

She held out her hand and Grant Pemberton found himself clasping the slim fingers warmly, liking this girl who seemed at home here yet strangely uneasy. Of course, she would be one of the displaced Olivers, and he had already gathered from a remark dropped here and there by Helen and young Oliver himself that none of the original family had set foot in the Keep since the harsh rule of male succession had forced them to leave it.

This, then, might be in the nature of an epoch-making incident! He studied Margaret—the proud lift of her head, the steady eyes and small, determined chin and liked what he saw.

'I'll tell Helen you're here,' he said, stuffing his pipe into his jacket pocket. 'Or will you come with me?'

He saw her hesitate for a fraction of a second and then her head went up.

'Of course,' she said. 'I know my way about quite well. I lived here till I was eighteen. Sometimes it seems a lifetime and sometimes just a day in an endless age of living away from it!' She ran her hand along the sun-warmed stone of the terrace with a small, caressing movement, looking down over the deep vale at their feet where the river ran like a strip of silver. 'I didn't know that any place could be so binding—possessing one half of you no matter how you tried to forget,' she added huskily.

'There is always some place like that,' he answered, and she thought that his eyes had a remote look all of a sudden, seeing some distant scene.

'I suppose so. You were out East, weren't you? I suppose you are keen to go back.'

'My work is there,' he told her. 'I must go back.'

They had turned towards the door to find it open, the hall beyond bathed in the dusty light of slanting sunshine which came pouring in through the high arrow-slits above the gallery, and he stepped back to let her pass, noting the almost imperceptible hesitation before she walked through the doorway to stand as if arrested by some spell within the pathway of rich, warm light.

'I've always remembered it like this—so magically lovely on a summer morning—'

He felt that she was hardly speaking to him and followed her silently while she walked slowly across the flagstones worn by the feet of her ancestors for over three hundred years. He felt a sense of pilgrimage and of his own intrusion, and left her in search of Helen.

When they came back into the hall together Margaret was standing in the shadows beside the gallery stairs, her eyes lifted towards the line of portraits on the wall above along which the sun had travelled, making them look warm and lifelike. She turned and saw them, coming slowly back across the flags to meet them.

'Hullo, Helen,' she said. 'I've come to see Fergus.'

'He will be back soon,' Helen said, bending to kiss her and to whisper, 'oh, Margaret, I'm so glad!'

'There's so much I must explain. I thought—he wouldn't take it as an intrusion—me coming like this—'

'How could he when he's wanted you to come for so long!' Helen led her towards the leather settee beside the fireplace. 'You'll stay? He may not be back until after lunch.'

'I don't know. I came away without letting them know when I'd be back, but they knew where I was going.' Small lights of defiance kindled in the blue eyes. 'I made no secret of it, nor why I thought I should come.'

'Let me get you some cocoa,' Helen offered, 'and then I think I'll telephone to Fergus at Toshiehill.'

'Oh, no—please! Don't bring him back specially for me,' Margaret begged. 'I can wait.'

I've waited all these years, she thought, but now when the time has come I'm cowardly enough to want to put our meeting off for an hour or two because I am afraid of what

I might see in his eyes when we do meet!

Helen looks confident—sure that Fergus will be glad I've come, but perhaps he'll just be glad in a cousinly way, glad that the old prejudices have been broken down at last and the Olivers are gathering under one roof. The Olivers! But I don't really represent them, for I haven't a scrap of courage left!

While she drank the cocoa Helen made for her and they spoke about nursing and the future, she found herself studying Grant Pemberton and wondering if Helen would ever marry again. The man and the question seemed closely linked, yet she had no grounds for believing that Helen was in love with Tony's father. The man himself appeared an enigma, shutting away any emotions he might have felt in his innermost heart, yet she found him charming and courteous and very interesting to talk to when Helen went to help Mrs Michie and see to the extra place for lunch.

In that half hour while they were alone she thought that Grant Pemberton unbent a little, as if a constraining element had been lifted when Helen left the room, but no very clear impression could rise above the mounting excitement of her own thoughts as she realised that any moment now might bring Fergus Oliver through the doorway behind them to find her there.

When he did come she sensed his presence even before she saw his tall figure in the shapeless jacket and ancient riding breeches blocking the doorway, and she got unsteadily to her feet as their eyes met across the room.

'Margaret—!'

It was a choked, incredulous utterance, but it conveyed something which neither of the two people who heard it could doubt. Margaret took two steps across the hall to find her hands imprisoned in a hard grasp while Fergus's love for her shone in his eyes like a beacon.

'You've come,' he said. 'Margaret—you've come! I can hardly believe it!'

He did not ask her if she still loved him: the fact that she was there seemed to make all other explanations unnecessary because there could only be one reason for her coming. She loved him, and when he looked at her again he saw it shining in her eyes.

Later there were explanations, but that one moment of mutual recognition had cancelled any need for them. Their hearts had spoken and words were poor and needless things after that.

Grant Pemberton stood for several seconds looking from one to the other in utter bewilderment before, finally, he left them alone to go in search of Tony.

At the luncheon table, after Fergus had asked them to drink a toast to his renewed engagement, Grant intimated his intention of returning to London the following day. He did not look at Helen as he said it and she felt the old chill of misgiving creeping over her as she contemplated the empty future. What was she to do with it—all these years stretching barrenly away before her? Fergus and Margaret were planning an early wedding and Grant was rushing off to London two days sooner than he need have gone! Her eyes fell on Tony's bright head and her food threatened to choke her, but soon she was catechising herself, trying to marshal her errant thoughts to some semblance of order. It's self-pity and where will that ever get you? You've known all this had to happen and now you're crying out against it like a weak fool instead of facing it in the way you should—the only way you can! Oh, don't let him see, don't let any of them see what a coward you are at heart, how you shrink from the hurt of it and cry out against the inevitable. You've had your happiness in this world—once. It wasn't long, but it was incredibly sweet and lovely, and so you should be content. But you know it could be repeated—if only . . . These words have broken people's hearts before now, and broken their spirit, too. Don't let them break yours, Helen!

She held up her head, taking her part in the conversation, even forgetting a little as she listened to Margaret's plans.

'It would be wonderful to be married from the Keep!' Margaret's eyes were shining with mingled love for the man by her side and her old home. 'We always planned a wedding in Burndean kirk, Fergus—remember?'

'I'm thinking ahead—not back!' Fergus told her, his strong fingers locked tightly in hers. 'There's going to be nothing we ever planned that won't come true!'

Margaret's bright face sobered a little.

'We thought to have—the whole family at the wedding,' she said. 'Jean and Isobel won't come, but I'll have to get over my disappointment about Jean. But Hattie will come!' Her eyes brightened. 'Hattie was always more gentle and —kind. I'd like Hattie to be my bridesmaid. And you, Helen!' She turned impulsively towards her sister-in-law. 'You won't go until after the wedding, will you? I could have Tony, too—as a page.'

She saw the colour go out of Helen's face, but in a moment Helen said warmly,

'I won't let you down, and—couldn't you ask Jean to come to your wedding—very specially?'

'I want everybody to come!' Margaret said, getting up and stretching out her arms as if to embrace the whole world. 'I want it to be the happiest day the Keep has ever seen!'

'Meg!' Fergus laughed, 'you'd make it a bright day in a thunderstorm!'

'Which seems to be rapidly approaching!' observed Grant from his viewpoint at the window. 'These clouds have been gathering for the past hour.'

'Which means I must get back to Edinburgh by the five train,' Margaret said. 'I know our dales when a thunderstorm sets in. Besides'—she looked confidently back at Fergus—'I must break our news to what remains of the family. Isobel left for the south coast early this morning,' she added coldly, 'but there's Jean and Hattie.'

'If you wait till the morning you can go as far as Burndean with Grant,' Fergus suggested. 'We can phone Collister and break the glad news that way in the meantime. What do you say, Meg?'

'Well—perhaps I shall, if this storm doesn't blow over.' She crossed to the window to stand beside Grant, small and diminutive beside his towering six feet. 'Will you come to my wedding, too, Major Pemberton?' she asked.

He looked down at her, smiling into her eager eyes.

'If I'm not on my way to the other side of the world by then,' he promised.

Neither question nor answer had reached Helen, but she sensed a tension about Grant which had been most noticeable during the meal. He seemed to be restraining even his thoughts and, in consequence, his speech appeared brisk and almost impatient, as if he stood aloof—slightly bored, perhaps, by all these plans in which he would not take any part, for before Margaret and Fergus were married he and Tony would be gone! What delight Tony would have taken in being Margaret's page, she thought, for Margaret had spoken of a little herald's costume hidden away in an old trunk at Collister which had been used at a children's fancy-dress ball when they had all been young. She had not added that her brother had worn it, but Helen knew by the look in her eyes that it must have been Ken's.

Well, Tony would never wear it and she would stay at the Keep till the wedding was over, but after that—after that? . . . Where would she go? What would she do? The world was a big place in which to forget, but, oh! not big enough!

Perhaps she would go abroad for a while when travelling arrangements were easier to make—to the Swiss Alps or the South of France where she could lie in the sun—and think? No, that was no way out. Perhaps work was—filling all her days with work—hard and strenuous work—so that she might be too tired at the end of them even to think.

'We're going out,' Margaret intimated, 'in spite of the rain. We're going over to the manse to see the minister about banns and things.'

'It's no use wasting time!' Fergus added with a grin, and then, more seriously, 'we've wasted enough.'

They went out half an hour later, taking Tony with them to sit in front with Syd Willing, and Helen turned back into the darkening hall, closing the door against the first flash of lightning as the storm broke.

'I suppose they'll be all right,' she said, and was surprised at the nervousness of her own voice which had nothing to do with the storm. 'Syd knows the roads pretty well by now.'

'Yes.' Grant was standing in the shadow of the velvet hangings at the window beside the door and he did not turn as she came up behind him to look out. 'They've got the car. It's not as if they were riding.'

There was a silence and then she said over a clap of thunder,

'The storm has come on so suddenly, and it was such a bright morning when Margaret came.'

'Can you doubt that it is still bright for her?'

'No. They will share it all now—the shadows and the brightness. I hope life will be kind to them.'

'Has it been kind to you, Helen?' His voice was suddenly rough, all the constraint gone out of it. 'I thought you had found compensation here.'

'At the Keep? You—did you think that Fergus and I would marry?'

'Yes.' She could see a muscle working in his tensed jaw in the flash of lightning which cleaved the room with its cold, blue flame. 'It seemed obvious and wholly desirable.'

'But—I was never in love with Fergus.'

The room had leapt into darkness again, but before the thunderclap wrenched the silence apart she heard his swift movement towards her, felt his hands unsteadily on her arms, turning her round to face him in what light there was.

'Helen—what right have I to tell you that I love you? I have nothing to offer you—no decent home like the Keep—perhaps nothing more than a problematical bungalow in the wilds. I'd be asking you to give up the luxuries you deserve now after all these years of captivity to live my life—perhaps even to rough it somewhere up-country—' Suddenly his hands tightened on her arms and his breath was warm on her cheek. 'But I am asking you that,' he ended in a low, determined voice. 'Helen, will you marry me?'

She stood for a moment, not believing, while the thunder rolled among the hills and the swift, deep stabs of lightning cut across the darkness that held them close like an encircling arm, and then she buried her head against the rough tweed of his jacket while all the unhappiness of the past drained away from her.

'Grant,' she whispered. 'Oh, Grant!'

'Is that my answer?' She heard the suppressed elation in his voice and could imagine the whimsical smile curving his mouth. 'Helen, have you nothing more to say to me?'

'So much more! Oh, my darling, so much more! But it takes time—'

'How long?' His lips were close against her hair. 'I'm going away in the morning.'

'But to come back! To come back for Tony and me!'

She raised her head and their lips met as his arms went round her, holding her close.

'I could never imagine you two apart,' he said. 'Even long before I came to the Keep, Helen, I spent my life thinking of you and Tony together, building my mad dreams about you and the future—praying that they would one day come true. I remembered you as you looked that night in the lifeboat—calm and reliable in an emergency, but tender as you took the child, and I remembered you that way for six years. When I found you at the Keep I thought I had reached journey's end, and then I came face to face with reality.'

'You thought that I was going to marry Fergus?' She looked up at him in the strengthening light, amazed at his blindness. 'But there was never any question of our marriage.'

'I didn't know about Margaret then, and you were so happy here that it seemed the inevitable sequel to all you had gone through—recompense for all you had lost.'

'If there is any recompense it is here—beside you,' she said softly. 'Always to be with you, Grant, wherever you go!'

'That's another thing.' His arms relaxed and he held her from him a little way, looking down at her and searching her eyes intently. 'Going back. Can you bear to go back to Malaya, Helen? My work is there and I must go, but it may revive so many memories for you.'

'It's not just—going somewhere that brings back memories,' she said huskily. 'They are in your heart wherever you go, but I want to go back to Malaya, Grant. I knew it that day we told Tony about the Straits robin and the barking deer. I could see the padi fields lying green in the sun and smell the scent of ripe pineapples piled under the palms, and I knew that part of me had been left behind there and that one day I should have to go back.'

'Helen!' His arms encircled her again and he kissed her tenderly. 'You have given me so much—hope and a belief in the future!'

'You always had that belief,' she said with tender pride in him, her eyes shining as she looked up at his strong profile outlined against the grey square of window. 'You knew that there was something for you to do out there—something to rebuild. And I may be doing that, too,' she added softly. 'Helping to rebuild something Ken gave his life for. Not just rubber plantations and a right-of-way for the English—I don't mean that—it's what you know you're going out to do—establishing justice, setting up a fair administration so that no man can be a down-trodden serf in his own land.' Her hands slid into his. 'There's so much to do,' she said. 'So much to do—together.'

CHAPTER THIRTEEN

'IT'S not being rushed and it's not going to be a "hole-in-corner" affair!' Margaret Oliver protested proudly, confronting her sister across the breakfast table a week later. 'I'm going to be married in Burndean kirk, but both Fergus and I want it to be before Helen goes abroad so that she can be there.'

Jean frowned.

'Helen has made an equally hasty decision about this Major Pemberton,' she observed, 'but perhaps it is the way things are done these days and I am merely being old-fashioned in my judgment. They are to be married in Edinburgh by special licence, I believe.'

'Not in Edinburgh,' Margaret corrected her. 'Fergus persuaded them to be married from the Keep. They met there and it has been Helen's home since she returned to England. Jean,'—she rose impulsively, coming round behind her sister's chair—'would nothing induce you to come to the Keep—not even to be at my wedding?'

The tears were very near the surface of her clear eyes and all the hardness and determination with which she had met her sister's opposition in the past few days had evaporated before her desire to see Jean at her wedding.

'Couldn't you? Couldn't you?' she pleaded. 'Oh, Jean, it would mean so much to us both!'

Jean Oliver folded her table-napkin and inserted it tidily into its silver ring.

'I intend to be at both ceremonies,' she said mildly. 'What is Helen going to do with the child?'

'Tony? Oh, he's old enough to sit quietly—with you, Jean, in the Oliver pew!'

'Very well, then. Tut, tut, Meg, don't let us weep about it or be unduly sentimental! As head of the family it is my duty to see you safely married and—well, I liked Helen as soon as I met her, and she had written me a very charming letter about Kenneth. I can hardly think she has entirely forgotten him, and this second marriage of hers may be quite successful, especially as she is so very much attached to the boy.'

'What about Hattie?' Margaret asked. 'She thinks someone younger should be my bridesmaid, but I do want her to. Couldn't you persuade her, Jean?'

'My powers of persuasion where Hattie is concerned have evidently become quite negative,' Jean returned dryly, but without malice. 'She has accepted this job Hamilton Purdie has offered her as housekeeper in his new nursing home and calmly announced before she went out this morning that she will be starting work there at the beginning of next month.'

'I'm so glad!' Margaret exclaimed. 'It's what she needed, Jean—a useful job to do. Don't grudge her her freedom.'

'She'll find she has far less freedom at Greydykes than she had here,' Jean returned tartly. 'But that is no concern of mine. Hattie is old enough to know what she is doing. You'll wear your grandmother's wedding dress, of course, Meg—suitably altered—and the Honiton lace veil.' She rose and crossed to the door. 'If you are not going out this morning you can come upstairs with me and I'll unpack them.'

'Oh, Jean! this is wonderful of you!' Margaret cried. 'You're making it all perfect for me!'

'Nonsense! I'm doing no more than my duty. Run and fetch the key to the front-attic door.'

Margaret followed her upstairs with the keys to find her standing on the top landing with a strange, far-away look in her eyes, but she came out of her reverie immediately and opened the door to precede Margaret into the room.

'Here we are! Everything should be in here.' But for a moment she stood without opening the big basket trunk with its steel rod and black padlocks which Margaret remembered so well from childhood days. Her tall body was very erect, her face paler than usual, but her eyes held a softer light than Margaret had ever seen in them before. 'I thought this would never be used again—because it could only be used from Oliver's Keep,' she said quietly.

Bending down, she inserted one of her keys in the padlocks, drew out the bar, and raised the lid. Inside a foam of tissue paper met Margaret's excited gaze and carefully, almost reverently, Jean Oliver lifted up sheet after sheet to reveal, at last, the long, soft folds of pure Honiton lace which had been made into a bridal veil a hundred years ago. Her strong hands trembled as she lifted it, and suddenly Margaret realised with what loving care it had all been laid away. Jean had done that—Jean getting it ready for a wedding at the Keep which had never come off, and perhaps forcing herself to look at it again in silent bitterness in the after years so that it might be preserved without damage—an heirloom from the Keep which would never be used again.

They turned and looked at each other, the veil between them, and Margaret wondered if Jean had ever thought of wearing it herself. She had been young once, but early she had resumed all the responsibilities of a mother's part in that large household, and perhaps her own dreams had been folded away as carefully as her grandmother's wedding gown.

'Jean,' she said, 'I'm sorry. I've said so many things that were cruel and bitter—'

'You were young, Meg, and an injustice was done you, but perhaps it can all be forgotten in the happiness of your wedding day. Will you try on the dress?'

'Oh yes, please! Oh, Jean, it's—it's unbelievably lovely! I don't want it changed—not a lot. It would spoil it.'

She slipped out of her house-coat, standing slim and upright before the long mirror propped up against the attic wall while her sister slipped the wedding dress over her head.

'An eighteen-inch waist!' Jean observed. 'That will have to be altered, my lady! You can't come near your grandmother for a trim waist-line!'

'I don't want to!' Margaret laughed. 'Think of all these bones and stays they endured! But there's yards of stuff to let out, isn't there?'—anxiously. 'Look at all this rucking and the little slots where the steels went in. It couldn't possibly have been comfortable, Jean, though it looked trim!'

'Different days, different ways!' Jean observed, viewing the effect critically. 'We'll take it to a good Princes Street house and they'll soon alter the waist. You can please yourself about the veil, Meg, but I think it would look prettiest the way it is.'

'I think you're right,' Margaret said, and then she laughed, because here she was accepting Jean's decisions again, but accepting them happily which made all the difference!

She went through the next few days in an ecstatic dream, scurrying busily between Collister and Princes Street and the Keep, deciding about the wedding gown and another dress which she would wear, first as Helen's bridesmaid, and then to go away in after her own wedding.

Grant Pemberton came back to the Keep two days before his wedding with the look of a man ready to set out on the conquest of the world.

'It's not so bad as it might have been,' he told Helen when she asked about his new job. 'It'll be up-country a lot, but my headquarters are at Taiping, so we won't be so far from the sea and we'll have Maxwell's Hill to fall back on in the heat. Helen, do you really think you'll go back happily?'

'It's a late hour to be asking me that!' Helen teased, her eyes full of tenderness. 'With everything arranged and the Keep in an upheaval of preparations for two weddings!'

He caught her to him, kissing her smiling mouth.

'Maybe it's the Keep and all this Border environment, but I feel as romantically inclined as Young Lochinvar and could carry you off this minute!' he told her.

'But Young Lochinvar only carried the bride off because she was going to marry someone else!'

His arms tightened about her.

'He has my sympathy,' he said. 'How well I know the feeling! When I thought you were going to marry Fergus—that you should marry him because it would be the best thing for you—I tried to feel resigned, but really I could have pulled down the Keep stone by stone and cast it all into the moat! It was something that stood between us in my mind, although it seemed your logical inheritance from Fate, who had treated you badly.'

She drew his hand through her arm, her fingers closing over his.

'I have all the compensation I'll ever want,' she said huskily. 'I have Tony—and you.'

THE END